Bella's Blade

Bella's Blade

GEORGIA ANGELIS

Black Lace novels are sexual fantasies.
In real life, make sure you practise safe sex.

First published in 1995 by
Black Lace
332 Ladbroke Grove
London
W10 5AH

Typeset by CentraCet Limited, Cambridge
Printed and bound by Cox & Wyman Ltd, Reading,
Berks

ISBN 0 352 32965 3

Chapter One

She looked a fetching creature, even in her plain black garb, with her head covered in the voluminous hood of her black wool-cloak, so that only a glimpse of chestnut ringlets could be caught against the scarlet lining.

She looked like a Puritan but she was a woman in mourning. She was solemn faced but she didn't cry; her regard for her deceased husband had not been that deep. If she looked distressed it was because the future frightened her.

The mourners who flanked her – and they were few – held handkerchiefs to their noses and sniffed vinaigrettes. None lingered once the first earth had been shovelled in atop the plain pine coffin.

Jeremy Flowers had been an admired costumier for the Drury Lane theatres, but, since the commencement of the present outbreak of plague some months before, public entertainments had suffered badly, and many theatres had closed until further notice. Flowers' business had suffered in consequence, and then he'd fallen to the ripe pestilence in the miserable, beleagured capital, and was dead within a week.

People spoke, stilted but sympathetic, then replaced their hats and hurried off. They were eager to be out of the over-full graveyard where the gravediggers couldn't work fast enough to clear the backlog of diseased corpses, and where death's stench filled the air.

Bella's brother-in-law, Oswald, took her firmly by the elbow, unbidden, and led her away towards the hired coach-and-two. 'We have business to discuss, Madam. The matter of your unfortunate indebtedness to my good self.'

Her violet eyes sparked with dislike. 'Brother, must we speak of it now? This does seem a moment most inappropriate.'

'The debt is a large one, and payment is long since due. It was agreed between Jeremy and myself that, should the unthinkable happen and he be unable to repay, I was to take possession of your house and relieve you of your property.'

She gasped in alarm. She had feared as much yet found it a shock even so. 'Would you see me out on the streets and destitute at such a fearful time?'

'I shouldn't like to, m'dear,' he said, blatantly false in his concern, 'but business is business, even between brothers. He knew the risks when he borrowed heavily from me. However . . .'

She didn't care for the way he spoke, letting the word hang heavy and full of meaning and smiling deviously. She had never cared for Oswald.

'However,' he repeated, 'I think perhaps we could come to a compromise that would suit us both and be of mutual benefit. You know I've always admired you.' His small eyes in his weasely face raked insolently over Bella, leaving her in no doubt as to what he proposed. But he elaborated anyhow. 'Be my mistress and you may keep the house.'

Her look was full of contempt. She paused on the churchyard path and pulled free of the arm that had locked upon hers so possessively. Her flesh crawled. He was odious indeed to broach such a subject at such a time. And never could she have brought herself to enter into so sordid an arrangement with such a man. She'd always found him distasteful in his familiarity with her but now she was just disgusted.

'I'd rather succumb to a thousand plagues, Sir. I'd rather die!' She spat the words out, her lip curling and her voice full of loathing.

His nostrils flared as his eyes riveted upon her with malevolence. 'And likely you shall, Madam, should you be foolish enough to turn me down. I could have you thrown in debtor's prison, y'know, sister-in-law or not,' he threatened.

'Somehow or other I shall get you the money owed, Oswald. But under my skirts you shall never come, ' vowed Bella. She sped on ahead and one of the mourners, Anthony de Vane, fell in beside her.

'Madam, is Master Flowers causing you some distress? Shall I see off the fellow?' he asked with his hand on the hilt of his dress rapier.

Bella's alarm only increased at the offer. 'Please, Sir, no, not on my behalf. I want no violence done in my name and my husband dead in the ground but yards away.'

'Then let me at least see you safely home in my own coach, Madam, so that you aren't obliged to share a conveyance with that loathsome knave.'

'That would be most kind.'

His coach was freshly painted and lacquered, and the four horses that stood in the traces, chomping at their bits, were splendidly matched chestnuts. A footman unfolded the step and Master de Vane handed Bella in solicitously.

Oswald pushed up to the window by which Bella sat. His sallow features were hard set and determined as he delivered his ultimatum with malicious relish. He had no doubt that the silly female would fare disastrously on her own. She would default on their arrangement and, sooner rather than later, would have to warm his bed as he'd long since intended. 'You have a month, Madam. I shall give you that much grace. On the last day of it I shall expect first repayment of sixteen guineas; in all you owe me three hundred and twenty.'

It might as well have been three million. Bella couldn't pay; she had but two florins and a crown to her name. Nevertheless she glared in defiance.

Master de Vane shoved Oswald away with angry impatience through the open window, hitting him about the head with the wide-brimmed black felt hat he'd removed upon entering his coach. So violently indignant was he on Bella's behalf that he broke a dyed plume. He cursed, 'A pox on you, man!' and ordered his driver, 'Home, Partridge.'

Oswald spun on his heels, raising his fist and shaking it. Bella worriedly watched him until the coach had carried her away.

She stared bleakly out of the window, looking over, but barely seeing, the deserted streets through which they passed. Very few people were venturing out unless they simply couldn't avoid it. They feared everything – the weather, their fellow man, their food. No-one knew from whence or how the plague descended and many saw it as punishment for the decadence that had transformed London since the Restoration of the Merry Monarch, Charles II in 1660. His was a country fit only for libertines, reprobates and whores.

Many houses bore the plague mark, warning passers-by to keep clear with huge, crudely-daubed crosses on bolted or barred front doors. As the coach turned a corner Bella and Anthony were confronted by a charnel cart piled high with the wasted corpses of victims being unceremoniously trundled away for mass burial. They buried their noses deeply into handkerchiefs liberally doused with rosewater and clutched the tighter at the lucky, protective unicorn's horn and slivers of wood from the True Cross that they carried at all times, having bought such articles from street vendors who swore their effectiveness in warding off the pestilence.

Bella's bleak look turned to one of worry as she noted the thoroughfare. Rosemary Lane was in the opposite direction. Her violet eyes fastened upon Anthony, questioning. 'Sir, this is not the way home.'

'You should not be alone, Madam. Come and dine with me.'

She shook her head, although calmed by the kindness of his voice which dispelled the feeling that she'd been saved from a weasel by a wily fox. 'I would be poor company, Sir.'

"I'd bear it no mind, Jeremy Flowers was a good friend. I do not like to think of you alone in your grief.'

'You are good to me, Sir.' She capitulated gracefully.

'Nonsense!'

He was a personable fellow, burly, handsome and the up-and-coming playwright in town. Her husband had liaised with Anthony personally over the finer details of the costumes for his Drury Lane productions. Anthony was exacting and knew precisely how he wanted each member of his troupe to look upon stage.

They dined plainly and simply in his rooms at the Reindeer Inn. His study was an untidy clutter of books, miniature stage sets and scattered vellum sheets of penned ideas for forthcoming entertainments. The walls were darkly wainscoted, and chairs placed around a dark oak gateleg table were high-backed, cane-seated, and daringly modern in design. Everywhere was a muddle; the place needed a woman's touch.

Through the diamond-leaded casement Bella could see clearly into the jutting upper-storey of the house opposite where Anthony's neighbours were taking their supper. Below, the street was quiet and the traffic light; London had never been so subdued. It added to Bella's sadness.

She ate little, sipping at her wine and raising no objection when Anthony refilled it for the fourth time. She desperately needed the artificial raising of spirits she knew the liquor would provide. Her mind wandered as Anthony talked. He was assembling the little wooden figures and explaining the running order of his next play within the tiny walls and backdrop of his tabletop theatre. He was talking to her just as he once talked endlessly to Jeremy, enthused and obsessive concerning his own projects and, inevitably, a bit of a bore. Then she'd been able to leave them to it, wandering off thankfully to make supper and replenish the wine jug. Now she kept up a wan smile, trying to hide the glaze in her eyes and found herself murmuring appreciation though she was barely paying attention.

Out of the window and across the street things were much more interesting. Supper was over. A servant was clearing away pewter and steel cutlery, while a gentleman took up the mandolin, his foot on a stool and the bowled instrument resting on his knee. He strummed and he sang, his not unpleasant voice reaching Bella faintly across the narrow, over-crowded thoroughfare. The lady whom he serenaded leant back replete in her heavily carved chair, smiling charmingly and obviously enjoying the entertainment. The man's romantic attentions evidently were appreciated.

She was a fetching creature. A moppet with bur-nished ringlets precisely coiffed around the sides of her head, the hair drawn smoothly from a centre parting and with little kiss curls running across her forehead. On her temple and at the corner of her mouth black patches in the shape of crescent moons and stars had been coquettishly applied, perhaps to cover smallpox scars. She leant towards her minstrel, her breasts pressing and swelling against the scooped neckline of a satin gown coloured the yellow of topaz and trimmed with ecru lace.

Her serenader's strumming broke off. He put down the instrument. Leaning across the table, he drew down her gown, and with a duck of his head he took the nipple and surrounding area of pale, globular breast into his mouth with a hard, greedy suck.

7

Bella's breath caught and, deep down in her long-neglected woman's place, an intense ache began.

Still chattering, Anthony never let his eyes stray from the figurines at his fingertips. He leant back and unknowingly shut out the unauthorised entertainment across the street. Bella's mouth fell open and a sigh of disappointment escaped her.

Anthony smiled. 'Yes, the end of another day. Though I doubt you'll be sad to see the last of this particular one,' said the playwright, softly sympathetic. 'More wine?'

She held out her silver cup, sighing and thinking that the curtailing of illicit pleasure was very much the way of things for her; it had ever been so.

She watched Anthony instead, noting his barrel chest and strong legs, his good, regular features and clean, wavy shoulder-length brown hair speckled with grey. He was a fine looking man, and a strong man, no doubt. She needed a man – needed arms around her and a man within her. Suddenly it was imperative. She all but threw herself at him.

'Sir, hold me. Stroke me. Warm my lips with yours, please,' she blurted out insistently.

He was amazed and almost speechless at the idea. 'Madam! Bella!'

'Please, Sir, do me this kindness. Give me some comfort.'

'But are you sure?' He was worried. Anxious on her behalf, he thought she proposed this familiarity for all the wrong reasons and that grief was affecting her judgement. He liked her and had always harboured a deep affection for her, but his emotions were kept in check in the past because of his esteem for her husband. What sort of a friend would he have been if he'd tried to steal the man's wife?

8

His delay was beginning to irritate her inordinately. What was wrong with her? She set down her cup and fell into his arms, crushing herself close and leaving him, she hoped, in no doubt as to her true wishes.

He looked down at her pert, miserable little face and at the fruit-like swell of her white breasts above the scooped neckline of her funeral garb and he began to thicken and harden, pushing into her belly. Immediately he tried to coax Bella to his bed but she shook her head.

'No. Here, on the Turkey carpet before the fire. I should like to feel the heat on my legs, and to see the embers cast their warm light over the two of us.' She pulled him that way, dropping to the rug and arranging her skirts most enticingly with her legs exposed to well above the knees. She showed pale limbs dressed in white cotton stockings, pink silk rosetted garters just above her knees and black, silver-buckled shoes with red painted wooden heels.

Anthony threw paisley cushions and bolsters down upon the cobalt and scarlet Turkey rug to give a softer support more to his liking. He thought Bella a strange baggage indeed to prefer the hardness of his floor to the softness of his bed.

Knowing he'd be a damned fool to look so enchanting a gift horse in the mouth, even if bedding Jeremy's widow with the husband barely cold in his grave sat ill with him, Anthony undressed. He stripped off his braided red and black frockcoat, his profusely buttoned long waistcoat and fiddly cravat, fumbling with the buttons of his ballooning white lawn shirt with its pin-tucked sleeves and frilled cuffs.

She smiled tipsily as she watched him. He was thick-set about the waist and his chest was smattered

9

with crinkly grey-peppered hair. When he removed the sash from his waist and unbuttoned his breeches, his erection was a sight to gladden the heart of any healthy young woman. Bella's look brightened. She held out her hands to him, beckoning and opening her legs.

Immediately he was between them and upon her, kissing her noisily, squeezing her breasts and fumbling beneath her numerous petticoats.

She was trying to find that marvellous thing of his. She wanted to get a grip on it and to toy with it unmercifully. But he was already prodding and pushing at her yielding entrance, slipping into her, filling her but all too soon. She wasn't ready. She'd wanted his hands on her but he didn't seem to have even given that a moment's thought. He was thrusting and thrusting, making delighted grunting noises and calling her 'lovely' and 'sweetheart', as he raced full pelt towards his crisis.

Beneath him, clutching at him in frustration, her skirts bunched up about her, legs spread slim and pale, accomodatingly wide, Bella felt tears pricking her eyes. She wanted to scream with frustration.

This couldn't be all there was to it, it just couldn't. That would be just too unfair. There was such a terrible yearning inside of her. She'd had years of this with Jeremy; a devoted husband but a hopeless lover. Anthony seemed to be much the same. He had an impressive shaft, yet didn't seem to have a clue what to do with it, save a basic type of animal joining. He seemed to be enjoying himself though Bella felt cheated.

She was a little stimulated, having instigated this development from a desirous frame of mind in the first place. As he moved inside her, filling, withdrawing, his cods slapping against her bottom mouth, Bella felt a pleasure of sorts and even a building of sensation, but she knew such strivings would get her nowhere ultimately. Anthony would be done all too soon, and long before her.

He was. He took his weight on his arms, wanting to hover over Bella, looking down at her as he filled her tight spot with its dark pelt, and was engulfed in her, lost. She was lovely – delightful. He still couldn't believe his luck as he stooped his head and kissed a plump breast.

She wore an encouraging smile but she wasn't happy. She just wanted him to be quick about things now that disappointment seemed inevitable.

He was red in the face with exertion, and began to look pained as his desire spiralled. He jerked, groaned, gasped and began to come, spasms of pleasure rippling through him and a sob choking in his throat.

Bella was touched by his undeniable delight. He clung to her, calling her name, his voice hoarse and sounding like someone drowning. She felt happy for him.

He took his handkerchief and thoughtfully wiped between her legs before pulling down her skirts and handing her a cup of wine. He downed his own in several thirsty gulps. 'My dearest Lady, I hardly know what to say. I never, not for one minute, expected anything like that to happen. You must think me a villain,' said Anthony, genuinely concerned that he had lost her regard.

She smiled as she stood up and straightened her bodice. 'Dear Anthony, you have nothing with which to reproach yourself. 'Twas I who asked for your attentions.'

His breeches were buttoned. He was pulling on his shirt. 'I have always admired you greatly, though I had never thought to make my feelings known. I respected you too much.'

She wanted a man who could give her love, not just respect! 'It is time I went home,' she said.

'Not now! Not after what has just happened. Please!' He begged her, wanting to talk and declare himself fully.

She guessed as much. But that was the last thing Bella wanted. If he said anything that put her in a corner, she would have to set him straight and that would hurt him. She didn't want to do that. 'No, really, I must go.'

He nodded, looking contrite. 'Yes. Of course. I understand. It is too soon. I am being indelicate. 'Tis wrong of me to press. My coach is at your disposal. And, because dear Jeremy and I were always such good friends, and because I cannot bear the thought of you being coerced into something odious and shameful by your brother-in-law, I want you to accept this purse.' Anthony handed Bella a laced up leather pouch.

She wasn't going to be a principled fool and turn it down. She held out her hand. 'You are a true friend.'

'In time I should like to think there is a chance I can be more?'

She smiled kindly, uncommitted. No, she didn't think so. He was too much of a friend. Not enough like a lover.

At home, not long after, she was alone. The tiny cottage on Rosemary Lane suddenly seemed much too big and empty as Bella lit the candle in the brass night-light and mounted the stairs, her skirts hoisted safely about her knees.

She donned her modest white cotton nightgown and brushed out her darkly burnished hair almost viciously. The stimulation roused her just a little from her state of apathetic lethargy. She was full of sadness and disappointment. She missed Jeremy, though he had been less than a model husband and had played her false with a string of pretty young actresses and strumpets throughout their six years of marriage. He'd been weak and had always given in to temptation. Her affection for him had waned accordingly. To begin with it had been no love match. Jeremy Flowers had spotted her and wanted her, for at twenty she had been deliciously fresh and pretty. The fact that her shopkeeper father was proud and generous enough to endow her with a healthy marriage portion had doubtless further whetted his appetite. Anyhow, she had agreed to his proposal, encouraged by her father who saw how the theatre business was now thriving after the drab, straitened years of Cromwell's Commonwealth.

Love hadn't lasted long, but there had always been deep affection. She could have done with his arms around her this night and the warmth of his body.

Propped up in bed, Bella drew open the strings of the purse Anthony de Vane had given her, dropping the coins onto the russet woollen counterpane that covered her crossed legs, and began to count.

Her spirits lifted and she smiled in the poor candlelight. What a kind man indeed – a pity she knew she could never love him. Twenty golden guineas. That would keep Oswald off her back – or, more accurately, Bella off hers and out of his bed – for the next

13

month as least. It would give her time to think of a way to make some money for herself.

Carefully she put the heavy pouch in the hidy-hole beneath the floorboards beside the water closet. Then she reclined, snuggling back against her soft pillows, and feeling better. She sneaked a hand beneath her pillow inside the feather stuffing, and felt for the stiff crackle of folded vellum. She drew the paper forth, unfolding it reverently in the candlelight, her heart tripping at the sight of the engraved visage revealed.

She was holding her husband's royal warrant as costumier to the Prince's Theatre and the Theatre Royal on Drury Lane. Jeremy had thrown it into a drawer and forgotten all about it, for such royal patronage meant little to him. He'd been of the opinion that it was a clever man indeed who could make royal patronage pay. Usually such prestige cost a pretty penny and there were few real benefits.

Anyhow, Bella had found the grand looking document with its illuminations and seal and secreted it away, bringing it out, as now, to stare, spellbound, at her king, Charles Stuart.

If the engraving was a true interpretation of the man then the Merry Monarch was as swarthy as a gipsy and more handsome by far than any dandified actor whom her husband had ever dressed.

Black hair flowed down over his shoulders, the thick, curling locks as intricately styled as any peri-wig, and a clipped line of moustache hedged his upper lip. The eyes were raisin black, the lips full, the nose prominent and strong, just like his jawline. The snowy cravat of Belgium lace that cascaded from his throat was in startling contrast to the foreign darkness of his skin. Bella had heard it said that he got his colouring from his French mother.

14

There was an ache in her belly and a yearning in her heart, as her hand strayed over her breasts, feeling the nipples harden beneath the matronly gown. She went lower, down to her knees, dragging up her nightgown, and coming up between her legs that were warm and slightly damp. She buried a finger amongst her own intimate folds, concentrating on the flourishing little bud and stroking herself leisurely as she stared at the swarthy royal. She thought about him doing what Jeremy, and today, Anthony, had done to her, imagining how much he'd weigh. Would he take that weight on his elbows or his hands? Or would he like to smother her really close, squashing her breasts against a dark, lean chest, touching her toe to toe, belly to belly, lips to lips? Would a king do it like a mere mortal? Would she call him Sire or, much more familiarly, Charles? Was she being wicked and was it sacrilegious to think of the man in that way at all?

She imagined his shaft of desirous flesh piercing her, fulsome as it moved in and out purposefully, and pleasuring her without end. He would wait for her, wait, as no man had thus far, for her breathing to shallow and turn to gasps, and her body spasm with delight. Oh! Lordy, yes! Charles would know, she saw it in his face.

The sensations fluttered through Bella delightfully and then died, leaving her hard-nippled and panting, her cheeks flushed. This was the only way she had ever known true pleasure.

Now, instead of hiding away the vellum portrait, Bella smoothed it out lovingly and laid it out on the snowy, empty pillow beside her own. There was no need for subterfuge now. The first day when it seemed safe to do so, when there appeared a lessening in the virulence of the plague, Bella silently vowed she would have the likeness framed and hung in a place of honour in her bedchamber.

With the coming of Winter 1665 the plague lost its ferocity and those who had fled to the safety of the countryside began slowly to return to the capital, to try to take up the threads of a normal life once more. Trade picked up, theatre audiences filled out and the usual meeting places in the city saw their takings go healthily into the black. People were going out and about and were beginning to enjoy themselves once more, believing perhaps that if the plague hadn't smote them after all these months it wasn't going to at all. Perhaps they were charmed.

Master Rosewood sipped his ale and then leant back into the high-backed settle, puffing absently on his pipe, his eyes intently watching the antics in the large pool of candlelight before him.

The Ryegate was a private club for gentlemen of a certain sexual persuasion. John Rosewood went there once a week as regular as clockwork, every Thursday. It was his only vice but, in those times, it was a serious one, indulged in behind closed and barred doors. The king was a great lover of women and frowned upon any habit that strayed from such 'normality'. His grandfather had been a blatant homosexual, filling Whitehall with his feuding, vying favourites. Charles disliked such behaviour around him and had been known to order certain lords home to their country estates when it had reached his ears that they indulged in 'shirt-lifting'.

Astride a wooden, model horse sat the most beautiful blond youth of perhaps eighteen or twenty. His long hair cascaded over his shoulders and his face was that of an angel. Leonardo da Vinci had painted lads such as he, and bedded them to, if rumour was true. The horse was an artist's prop, short in the leg for ease of mounting. In previous decades, before the Commonwealth, when Charles I was still in possession of his head, it had been fashionable to be painted on horseback, depicted as a soldier or hunter. Van Dyck had painted the old King upon such a beast in the guise of a Field Marshal, the lofty pose lending the monarch much needed inches.

The youth was naked, his skin looking Mediterranean or tanned under the bright yellow glow of candles. He caressed the beast's back with his belly and torso, insinuating himself down its length teasingly, so that every customer at The Ryegate twitched with longing to be mounted at that rear. It raised now, as pert as a mare's tail for a stud, and Rosewood laid his money down, adding to it whenever men at other tables matched his amount. He was determined. He wanted the Adonis with a single-mindedess that robbed him of his usual commonsense and miserliness.

The boy was beautiful, perfect, slim-limbed and delicately featured. An angel indeed. Master Rosewood paid the high but necessary price for the privilege and stumbled towards the stage, now solely ruled by the heavy shaft of longing that filled his breeches and made it difficult for him to walk.

It was a custom at The Ryegate that when a new boy came upon the scene and was displayed before the clientele, whoever bought his first favours had to perform for the delectation of the others. John Rosewood would have preferred to take his pleasure in private, but customs were for the upholding and,

17

anyhow, he was too far gone with desire to be much put off by the ogling, breath-bated, knee-trembling audience who dined and supped wine and ale at their individual tables. Besides, he'd be the first to admit that to watch two men at it thrilled him immensely. Who was he to deny his brothers?

He unbuttoned the flap of his breeches, bringing forth a meaty penis heavy and long with lust. He advanced, jerking it purposefully, until he was standing at the rear of the wooden horse, with the youth's arse hovering and wriggling enticingly just above. A pot of goose grease lay on a table alongside the candlelit stage and John drew his fingers through it to take up a generous dollop and work it between the youth's buttocks like a sculptor with clay, so lovingly.

This brought falsetto giggles from the lad. John's fingers worked around the tight orifice, teasing it, trying it, and finding it pleasingly tight. Then he put the bulbous red head of his member at that spot and worked it in.

The men in the shadows paused in their consumption of food and drink and watched the fleshy blade sheath itself, hearing the boy gasp appreciatively as he was filled, playing his part of happy recipient to the hilt.

'How's he feel?'

'Splendid!' cried John, withdrawing then thrusting forward deeply, again and again.

'Worth the money?'

'Every farthing!'

The boy squirmed, calling out encouragement and bringing John speedily to a noisy, red-faced climax with his practised movements and extraordinary muscle control.

John's place was quickly taken by the next man. All those who had put money down now took the youth in turn, until he looked limp from a surfeit of loving.

John left after midnight, the worse for drink and somewhat confused by the sight of Britannia upon stage, dressed with flowing robes, a trident and shield. But as he left someone pulled away the diaphanous robes to expose a hairy pair of legs and a rigid penis pointing upwards to the navel. Britannia was brought to her knees and buggered, to the raucous approval of all.

The cold night air hit him, a sweet change after the foul months of plague. He took a deep breath, chuckling all the while and staggered off homeward, his wooden heels clacking on the cobbles.

He turned a corner, singing as he went, and cannoned into a jostling, ugly band of ruffians who'd been thrown out of a nearby tavern. They shoved him around a bit, laughing at his feeble attempt to unsheath his sword and defend himself, and taunted him, menace growing with each moment that they tormented him.

'Hey now, I say, enough. Let me pass, there's good fellows,' said John, politely.

One of the ruffians snorted and guffawed in derision, mimicking the gentleman's limp-wristed mincing mannerisms. 'Well, lads, what have we here?'

'A nancy!'

'A practiser of the Italian vice!'

'A filthy bugger!'

'Let's show him what we think about men like that, men who do indulge in unnatural pleasures, who do shun the love of good women, preferring pretty boys. Wicked men with foreign ways.'

'Aye, let's show him. Let's loosen his teeth and beat blue the arse he do offer t'others of a like vile persuasion.'

John threw up his hands, trying to reason with them. But it was hopeless. They were much the worse for drink. They didn't want to hear anything he had to say, just to give him a good thumping.

He fended them off as best he could but he was no fighter. He pleaded all the while as the breath was knocked from him.

'Please – no! Why?What harm have I done?'

'Y'be scum.'

'Nasty. 'Tis because of the likes of you that the good Lord brings down pestilence upon us. 'Tis punishment,' snarled one of them as he punched John in the stomach.

John went down groaning.

And then a virago entered their midst, lashing out at all of them with a large and heavy bag of laundry, kicking, pulling hair, shrieking like a banshee.

'What the bugger!'

'Begone, bullies and lummuxes! Go before I scream for the watch and bring the King's men down upon your heads. A night in the Bridewell would do y'all good.' As if to make up their minds, the laundry bag did the rounds again, clouting them painfully about the heads.

Deciding it was beneath their masculine dignity to become embroiled in a fight with a washerwoman, they reeled off, belching and farting in truly loutish fashion and cursing Bella in gutter language.

'And the same to y'all,' she snarled, spitting after them as they faded into the darkness down the lane.

John clutched at her skirts and levered himself, bruised and bloodied, to his feet. 'Madam, I am indebted. They were about to rearrange my features permanently.'

'Think nothing of it, Sir,' assured Bella, cheerily, inspecting the blouse that had been ripped when one of them grabbed for her during the fracas. She frowned and tutted, picking up the scattered wash, for the bag had burst.

'Are you qute unharmed?' asked John.

'Quite. Honestly.'

'Then you must let me pay for the mending – nay, the replacing – of your garment. 'Tis the least I can do. Let us walk together, Madam, thus affording each other some modicum of protection, for there is safety in numbers. I live on Chancery Lane. Do you know it?'

'Aye, I've passed that way on occasion.'

'I have the money there. I have not a suitable sum upon my person after some costly entertainment this night.'

'Costly entertainment and pricey wine,' expanded Bella, smelling his breath.

He tittered. 'Yes, just so. I own a coffee and eating house and am in the habit of going abroad on Thursdays to indulge my own pleasures.'

They stepped out briskly together side by side, alert for anything else that might be lurking in the shadows ready to waylay them.

He laughed ironically. 'Saved by dirty washing.'

''Tis a living.'

Then he saw her for the first time. He shot her a surprised look as an overhead lantern lent some poor illumination. He knew a looker when he saw one, even if she stirred nothing within his own good self.

'I think we can do better for you than that. A strong wench of good character. Let's just see if we can't.'

21

Chapter Two

She had no trouble from her employer; customers, however, were a different matter. She was a challenge. To a man they wanted to bed her. Just as determinedly, Bella had decided to grant that privilege to none. Work and pleasure didn't mix.

John Rosewood was a good employer, generous and kindly too. Between them had grown a mutual fondness. Quickly enough Bella had deduced the reason for his total lack of interest in her sexually. It was a blessed relief. When she went to church at one of the humbler houses of worship in the shadow of ancient St Paul's, she prayed for his mortal soul. He was headed for Hell, she didn't doubt, but while he continued to provide a decent wage, Bella figured that that was his business and his alone.

At The Painted Parrot she was expected to put her hand to many tasks, from grinding the coffee beans to stowing away the customers' hats and swords. The gentlemen were not required to remove their flamboyant wide-brimmed, plumed hats, but usually did so because of the confines of the establishment. But remove their dress swords they must, to reclaim the weapons later, on leaving. Thus bloody arguments were pretty much a rarity, to the harmony and benefit of all. When disputes did flare they were settled with fists or the sharp side of someone's tongue.

She dressed modestly, favouring grey, brown, burgundy and black, the necklines and elbow-length sleeves trimmed with frothy lace. Such trimmings were the only frivolous touch to Bella's clothing. At that time she was a serious young woman and this was very much reflected in her garb. Her hair was brushed off her face and parted down the centre, soft curls framing her face and ringlets bouncing about her ears. She looked cool, demure and rather unapproachable. Such a demeanour didn't deter everyone, however.

Jasper Sweetly, the heir to a baronetcy, had made her seduction his personal crusade. So far he had made little or no progress. Undaunted, he kept trying. He would not take no for an answer.

He was attractive, wealthy, full of himself and, to Bella's mind, insufferably irritating. He was a regular at The Painted Parrot, his visits increasing as his determination to win Bella became all-consuming. There seemed to be no respite from his advances and lately she found herself groaning when he swaggered through the squat portal of the half-timbered Tudor building. Every night he seemed to appear; this night was to be no exception.

The door flew open and the cool night air swirled in; stirring the pipe smoke, bringing in welcome fresh air, cooling the hot room, and diluting the body smells.

From the counter and customer tables clientele and serving wenches looked up at the newcomer. Greetings were called, bodices pulled enticingly low and breasts thrust forward as the women smiled a welcome. 'Jasper!'

'Evening!' he replied generally, eyes already raking the public room for Bella. But she had slunk off to the kitchen the moment she caught sight of him to cut ham and cheese for a supper trencher.

He frowned, then sweeping off his rusty coloured felt hat he launched it, like a skimming stone, at the wench behind the hat counter. His aim was deadly accurate. She caught it gingerly, with a nervous yelp, mindful of the expensive plume that adorned it. If she accidentlly broke it there would be a complaint.

'Bella?'

'Preparing food,' said John Rosewood, from the quiet corner table where he sat most evenings keeping a watchful eye on events. 'Susie, see to the gentleman.'

The girl nodded and came quickly forward, knowing that John wanted her to keep Jasper happy and to keep him from making a nuisance of himself with Bella. 'What can I do for you, sir?' she purred, smiling seductively and sticking out her pert chest. She was young, blond and pretty. She knew that a man like Jasper Sweetly tipped well if pleased by the service he received.

He paid her scant attention as he took a chair by the fire, propping a foot against the beamed mantle and considering with much thoughtful wrinkling of his brows. 'Coffee, Turkish, and baccy, Virginian.'

'Right away, Sir.'

She was gone in a trice and Jasper's eyes fastened expectantly upon the kitchen door, watching the comings and goings, and waiting for Bella to appear. He drummed his fingers on the carved arm of his chair impatiently. If he didn't know better he'd think the chit was avoiding him. But that was absurd. He was Jasper Sweetly. She'd not get better than him and she was a fool if she couldn't appreciate the fact. He wanted to set her up in a modest cottage out in the countryside of Chelsea, where he could escape from his wife and his business worries to find joy in the arms of a fetching woman. A fetching woman indeed. He wasn't the only man after Bella Flowers, he knew, but he was prepared to become the most generous of her would-be suitors in order to achieve his aims.

Then he saw her, pushing through the door with a fully laden trencher. But her breasts, swelling above the scooped neckline of her dress, were more appetising by far than the fare she carried – bread, cherries, cheeses, cold cut meats and three pewter cups of coffee.

In a instant Jasper was up and out of his chair, intercepting Bella in the middle of the room. 'Madam.'

Bella frowned and tried unsuccessfully to push by. 'Sir.'

'Dear Madam.'

'I am busy, the tray heavy. Will you not return to your table?'

'Only if you promise to come and speak with me directly.'

She sighed heavily, making her reluctance plain. 'Very well.'

When Susie returned with his coffee and tobacco, she hovered with a smouldering spill from the fire to light Jasper's clay pipe but he barely registered her existence. It made her want to stamp her foot in temper.

Bella tried to avoid him but after ten minutes of watching her flit like some nervous bantam around the crowded, noisy room, with other men encircling her waist in their arms and other palms playfully patting her rump, Jasper Sweetly snatched out a hand when she passed near and captured her, fired by lust and jealousy. He'd wanted her for weeks and he knew that his scant patience had now all but evaporated.

'I am still busy, Sir.'

'Let someone else see to the gentlemen's needs. Mine are greater,' he breathed huskily, full of conceit. Pulling Bella onto his lap he squeezed her breast.

She drew in her breath indignantly and raised a hand to slap him. He caught it and laughed, kissing her exposed throat and her swelling, heavy globes of flesh. 'When will you agree to move to Chelsea? To be mine?'

'Never. I've no mind to be less than a wife to any man, Sir. And then only if I do love him.'

'But you've had marriage, Bella' he cajoled. 'Was it truly so wonderful? I can offer you everything but. Fine clothes. A coach-and-four. Suppers. Theatre. Devotion. Jewels.' He said the last so enticingly, as if she couldn't possibly resist them, that Bella had to laugh.

'How little you know me, Sir, if you think you can buy my regard. You talk of everything but love.'

'That I love you goes without saying,' said Jasper, smoothly.

'Of course, Sir. How could one doubt it?' she scoffed derisively.

26

He frowned in consternation. 'I love you as well as any man could.'

She shook her head, struggling ineffectually to excape from his arms and off his lap where she could feel his hard shaft of manhood through the russet satin breeches. 'You love me as well as you are capable of, sir. Yet that is still not enough.'

His expression turned fierce, his fingers digging into her arms and his amber eyes sparking. 'I could make you love me,' he threatened.

She shook her head. Fastening a hand tight about his balls as earlier he had grasped her breast, she squeezed until she knew he found it uncomfortable. 'I don't think so.'

He released her, furious but restrained, then watched her ominously as he smoked and drank coffee, engaging in political debate with one or other of his cronies. Sometimes they talked of her. Bella could tell, their eyes following her, appraising and lascivious. A thrill of apprehension and excitement ran through her.

'Be careful,' warned John Rosewood. 'The man is smitten and determined. Love makes men mad. I've never known him not get what he wants, and I cannot protect you every hour of the day.'

'I can handle him,' she insisted, spiritedly.

John said nothing, looked doubtful.

Coffee houses had a bad reputation, as notorious as the worst ale houses when it came to the misconduct of their patrons. Coffee houses were beds of vice, havens for gentrified felons, and meeting places for the politically discontent. Many a plot of national importance had been hatched in such an establishment. John Rosewood had had painted and framed a bold sign in scarlet and gold that ruled insistently:

27

No Papists. No Harlots.
Beggars will be Whipped.
Cutpurses given up to the Watch.
No Credit. No Spitting.

It was difficult to say whether such a notice had any notable effect upon the behaviour or morals of those who could read it.

The lantern clock on the oak mantle over the fire struck the hour of nine and simultaneously the door burst open and the establishment was invaded. There were so many bodies and so much noise that for a long time there was naught but confusion. Bella and the other girls were running to and fro to fill orders and to keep the newcomers happy.

They were gentry. More than that was difficult to deduce for they were masked and cloaked, and would give up neither their hats nor swords. Eventually, after patient persuasion from John, they capitulated. They sat down to take a rowdy supper, read the daily broadsheets and talk about the play they'd just attended on Drury Lane.

They recognised Jasper and called out to him to join them, but he declined with jovial politeness, saying that he would be leaving at any moment. In truth he didn't care for any company save Bella's and wanted to concentrate on nothing but her movements around the public room.

The new arrivals were dressed in the height of fashion – satin and lace, black masks, black beauty patches, their black, silver-buckled shoes with red painted heels, their stockings snowy white and embroidered, their coats and waistcoats profusely braided and buttoned. The five men wore black periwigs which were an affectionate caricature of the king's own curly, gipsy-hued locks. The three women wore gowns of cerise, aqua and cerulean satin over stiff brocade petticoats that showed down an open front panel. The whisper went around that two were actresses, the third a lady of the court.

'Castlemaine?' wondered Susie, filling Bella's tray of tankards with cider.

Bella shook her head. 'I heard tell that the Countess is a redhead.'

'Not her then.' said Susie, disappointed.

'There are many women at court.'

'And many in the King's bed, though not all at once, of course' she giggled, giving Bella a meaningful nudge with her elbow.

Barbara Palmer, newly created Countess of Castlemaine, was Charles Stuart's favourite and official mistress. She was a great beauty, red-headed and vividly blue-eyed. Bella very much doubted that such a personage would have frequented The Painted Parrot, unless, of course, she were very heavily disguised. Though it was said Barbara had a taste for the licentious and that she was no more faithful to the King than he was to her, or his neglected little wife, the Portugese princess, Catherine of Braganza, come to that.

Barbara's beauty had set the standard for the day. She was fleshy, pale and voluptuous, with remarkably limpid eyes. Lely, the official court painter, idolised her and, it had been noted of late, every other woman he was obliged to paint ended up looking more than a little like the Countess.

The new arrivals infected the regulars with their high spirits and very soon the party atmosphere was running out of control. The noise and laughter was deafening, and the screeching song from one of the women brought forth guffaws, lewd sniggering, and vulgar suggestions. The naughty song left nothing to the imagination. It was not the softly rendered tune accompanied by a delicate lute, mandolin or suchlike that one might more readily have expected from a woman in such obvious – though maybe too gaudy – finery.

'He dipped his wick, dipped his wick,' she sang, rubbing the crotch of the gentleman she was obviously partnering for the night. 'Give me a little prick, though, nay, not such a little prick!' There were roars of laughter.

John sidled up to Bella and Susie. It was getting near to closing time, but he perceived that this night he might have problems clearing the premises, that certain patrons might be reluctant to go home. 'Clear the tables and then be off. Methinks our betters are in the mood to party. 'Tis wisest to let them get on with it. Doubtless they'll pay well for the privilege.'

Bella looked worried as a roar of laughter diverted her attention momentarily. Over at the theatre-goers' table things were hotting up apace. The gentleman who'd been having his crotch toyed with so teasingly only moments before was now pulling the female astride his dining chair, her skirts pulled up and aside to expose pale legs in white, gartered stockings and a mound covered in silky, dark pelt.

Agog, Bella watched as the man released his member from his breeches and slipped it up through the woman's wide-open womanhood. The head disappeared and the man took the woman by the hips, pulled her down onto him and impaled her, to make a present of the remainder.

'Into the kitchens,' instructed John, blushing. He herded his serving wenches ahead of him, a self-appointed protector of their morals. 'I'll clear the tables. You help the scullions with the cleaning of the dishes and sanding of the pewter.'

Bella was anxious. 'Will you be safe?'

He nodded, smiling reassuringly. 'I can contend with their high jinks well enough. Do not fret. Now off with you,' he instructed, seeing how Susie was peering avidly over his shoulder, 'out of harm's way.'

When all in the kitchen had been scoured, cleared and set aright, the two young women crept back to the door, watching through the crack as John served ale, coffee, malmsey and sack, insisting that the party pay as they went. He was no fool. Many a landlord had played the perfect host to such types only to have them get out of control, wreck the establishment and abscond without producing payment for the bill, usually fending off the irate landlord at swordpoint. John was having none of that.

The lady who had earlier sat upon the gentleman's rampant manhood, taking his length to her very core, had passed out cold. Her head was down on the table, her masked face bedded in a plate of over-ripe figs. She was snoring but the comical noise was drowned out by all the other disturbance.

The female who had taken over the rendering of bawdy songs still did so, only now the words were slurred, their lewdness not always obvious. She was pacing the table, scattering the cups and tankards. John was glad he hadn't succumbed to temptation and bought the novel little china clay cups he'd seen the month previous on a visit to Bristol. Though her skirts were hoisted with her petticoats frothing about her knees her cerulean satin dress was quite ruined from stepping through the food. At a chant of, 'More, more, more!' from the men who crowded around,

31

she hitched the skirts higher, exposing her white thighs. She was growing as excited as they, a true exhibitionist. She squealed delightedly. Fired by the lusty admiration on their faces, she finally showed off her puss with its darkly furred mound as russet as a vixen's.

Susie and Bella exchanged a startled, knowing glance.

'Castlemaine?'

'Could be!'

'God's nightgown!'

They watched the more intently as the woman strutted the length of the oak table, hiding her treasure one moment only to expose it the next and thrust it forward into the eager face of some male onlooker. Hands reached for her, eager to part those lips, and tongues flickered.

Suddenly she fastened her eyes upon Jasper. Her look was smouldering, her eyes narrowed and bluer than blue, as she crooked her finger and parted her legs.

He laughed jovially but rather than advance as Bella would have expected, he swept the room with an encampassing flourish of the arm. 'Surely you have enough admirers here already this night, M'lady? My favour is pledged elsewhere.'

'Would you resist such an offer, Jasper?' she asked archly, in a tone that might have intimidated a lesser man.

'They do know each other,' observed Susie.

Bella muttered derisively. 'That is no surprise.'

'There are so many present apparently more eager than I. Honour one of them, why don't you?' he suggested graciously.

Even hidden behind her mask there was no disguising the irritation that consumed her at such an obvious rejection, no matter how politely phrased. She turned her back on Jasper, displaying herself to the men on the other side of the table as the Honourable Master Sweetly set down his pewter cup and went to collect his hat.

A young gentleman with flowing auburn hair and Van Dyck beard caught the lady about the upper thighs and forcibly drew her forward until her puss was a hair's breadth from his face. Then he took the lips and delicately parted them, snaking out his tongue to sink it into her folds as deeply as he could. She gurgled delightedly at the back of her throat. At the other end of the table the third woman now tumbled to the floor spreadeagled, sending dishes and cups, tankards and candlelabra crashing with her. Several pairs of hands helped to pull up her skirts, then a line of men waited their turn to climb between her fleshy white legs and sink their hot and heavy members into a seemingly insatiable honeypot of desire.

It was exhausting just to watch and eventually Bella and Susie, highly amused by it all, let themselves out of the back door to head for home.

'Night, Susie.'

'Night,' called her friend as they parted at a street corner.

The night was hot and the narrow streets stank, with the smell of smoke dominating. Her nose seemingly wearing a permanent wrinkle of distaste for such noxiousness, Bella hurried on, tired and footsore. It had been a busy but enjoyable night. On some nearby lane the watch called the hour. 'Twelve o'clock and all be well.' From the shadows a dark figure leapt, grabbing Bella and clamping a hand over her mouth. She gasped with fright and annoyance as she recognised Jasper's voice. Immediately she began to struggle.

'All's certainly well,' Jasper leered, his voice full of meaning and menace. From a side alley came a coach-and-two as he swept Bella up into his arms. Her face was held against the russet satin of his chest, smothering her cries as her struggling, kicking form was bundled aboard.

'Drive on!' he yelled up to his driver, then speedily he tied the fighting woman's hands behind her back and cut off her cries for help with a kerchief turned into a gag.

Jostled and jounced, Bella was spirited off to some unknown house. She couldn't see clearly in the dark but it looked Jacobean. It was four storeyed and sharply gabled, and there was a strong smell now of river, which led her to believe that either the Thames or Fleet ran nearby.

'Now, now,' he said, trying to placate but also amused as he carried her inside. A grand marble hall was lit by a solitary candelabra on the pier table beneath a vast Venetian mirror. 'There's no point in struggling. What Sweetly wants Sweetly gets. I'm going to make you want me also. And when you've come to realise that life with me really could be – shall we say – sweet, we're going to take a pleasant trip to Chelsea and look over a quaint little cottage I've got in mind.'

She objected into the gag, her eyes piercing and giving a withering look, her nostrils flaring.

He laughed delightedly. 'Such spirit and pluck. I love it.'

She groaned with exasperation and struggled the harder.

He wrestled with her happily, certain of his strength and finding that this was yet another aspect of her abduction and seduction to be enjoyed. It wouldn't have been half so much fun if she'd come quietly.

He strode across a chequered hallway, his heels clacking on the Italian marble, then up a bulbous rotund balustraded stair-case that ran, cantilevered, around the square vestibule.

Bella felt her heart beating in her throat, panic growing out of bounds as he ran up the stairs with her, laughing like a madman, her weight seeming not to trouble him at all.

Apparently there was no-one else in the house, neither family nor servant, or if they were they were keeping purposefully out of the way. She wanted to scream and bring help running but she had been effectively silenced and perhaps there was no-one to hear.

He threw a door open, carried Bella in, kicking it shut behind them with a red heel and threw her onto the bed. She bounced several times, then lay there writhing and kicking her legs about furiously. All that that succeeded in doing was sending her petti-coats and skirt flying up over her knees to show off her slim legs in their white cotton stockings and black, buckled shoes. His eyes lit up at the sight.

Jasper lit the candles, pulled the heavy brown and gold paisley drapes and divested himself of frock-coat and embroidered waistcoat. He cut an unde-niable dash in his russet satin breeches and billowing white shirt. He unbuckled his sword and removed his cravat, opening several buttons on the shirt, to

35

display a muscular chest adorned with burnished hair.

The bed was as old and heavily ornate as the staircase up which she'd been carried against her will; four posted, canopied and hung with umber and gold curtains. In no time Bella had her wrists and ankles secured to the posts with curtain cords, and her bodice laces were undone. She struggled and cursed, chocking on the gag, but there was nothing she could do. Her breasts were released from the white confines of her chemise and her skirts set up about her hips so that her sex was fully exposed. She felt the chill air of the bedchamber on it acutely.

Sweetly hovered very close, watching her with burning amber eyes – just watching and laughing.

'You'd like to kill me, wouldn't you, sweet puss? You'd like to take your sharp little nails and rake my face, to scar me for life for having taken such a liberty with your puritan body. Doubtless if you could speak you'd curse me to hell and back and mayhap be justifiably unladylike with your language. But, poor Bella, you can do nothing, can you? Nothing but lay there upon my bed in an empty house – because my wife is at our country residence and the servants have gone with her. You lie there and wonder, Bella, in fear and trepidation, just what I'm going to do to you. Perhaps I'm not going to do anything. Would that be a disappointment?'

Her disgusted response behind the gag was definitely in the negative.

He had long, elegant fingers, unused to any form of manual work. The only strenuous occupation Sweetly had ever engaged them in was the control of his horse's reins. He had sensitive hands.

He ran them over Bella's throat and breasts, which

grew hard-nippled despite her aggressive display of loathing. He bent his head to her breasts, his moustache tickling her, and sucked hard, drawing the peaks deeply into his mouth. She gritted her teeth, trying to deny the tingling in her belly and the sudden throb between her splayed legs. This wasn't fair!

'Do you know what I've always imagined doing to you, precious? Have thought of so many times?'

He slithered between Bella's legs, his face so close to her sex that with a flicker of his tongue he could have entered her. Then he did just that.

Her body went rigid with the shock of sublime sensation. Her eyes flew open, wide and startled. What was he doing? It wasn't right. Surely it wasn't natural? An abomination. She'd have to pray doubly hard for forgiveness of her sins at church on Sunday, she decided, even if this truly were none of her fault.

He withdrew chuckling. 'Ah, you are appreciative. I'm so glad. But also you look so shocked. Did your husband never do that to you, Bella? Nay, I daresay it would never have occurred to one such as he, unimaginative clod. How sad that he likely never saw the expression on your face, as I did then. Such things gladden a man's heart and heighten his own pleasure. Madam, you are beautiful. So sweet and so tight,' said Sweetly. His long fingers delicately eased back the folds to Bella's secret place and his tongue explored every cranny. 'There's naught so heady as the scent of a female. I grow alarmingly hard in my breeches. Look.'

He sat up and unlaced the finely tailored garment to let his engorged manhood spring forth.

Bella drew in her breath, alarmed. It was huge: a daunting beauty. Even to her novice's eyes she knew it to be the most impressive she'd ever seen. It was long, perhaps eight or nine inches, meaty, the head bulbous and red with the sheen of marble. The balls were taut beneath it amongst a veritable forest of burnished curls.

Her puss cried out for it in an agonised, pulsating rush of sensation, her bud standing proud. Sweetly took the little pink arrow between his lips, nipping and sucking, to drive her quickly to madness. She was twisting dementedly on the bed, her crisis rushing in to claim her, leaving her panting and sighing, with perspiration pricking her brow.

He smiled at his accomplishment, rubbed his turgid flesh caressingly against her inner thigh, then untied her, much to Bella's bewilderment, and pulled her across the Turkey carpet to the gateleg table in the window alcove.

There he bent her face down upon the oaken surface, lifting her skirts and exposing her white and rounded buttocks; she was as luminous as a moon in the near darkness. She was still trembling from his earlier administerings, and was compliant, even passive. She wanted him and that huge, meaty thing of his, wanted it deep in her, wanted the stretch, the fullness and the excess.

He spread her legs, found her wetness, and pushed the head in, making her pulse around the tantalising girth with delight. Then he pushed all the way, until his belly was against her rump and his balls were dancing against her. He withdrew, then went in deep again, feeling her quiver. He pulled the gag from her mouth so that he might see her lovely face in profile and kiss the full lips, certain now that she wouldn't scream for help.

His hands cupped her pendulous breasts and he

took her with deeply penetrating strokes, making Bella cry out time after time. He rammed hard when his climax neared, wanting to vanquish her and bind her to him, to enslave her as surely as he was.

Her senses were afire, her puss molten where he ravished her, tingling with pin pricks of ecstasy. She cried out, 'Fire! Fire!'

He came with some final half dozen, violent strokes, jerking and groaning, his hands kneading her flesh. 'Yes,' he agreed, 'fire.' His closed eyes flickered with bliss.

His pulsing member still deep within her, Bella lay atop the table, replete as if from some luxurious banquet. 'No, fire! look. Through the chink in the curtains,' she gasped out.

Still in her, reluctant to withdraw and to give her up, Jasper reached forward to pull aside the drape. 'By Old Knoll's balls! London's burning!'

He slipped from her then, soft and sated, sobered by the infernal red glow over St Paul's.

That night a fire started that was to consume the ancient cathedral and vast acres surrounding it. Some fifteen thousand people lost their homes before, on the sixth day of the fire, the wind that had fanned the flames mercifully dropped. Houses built too close together went up like the driest tinder. People fled in all directions; out into the countryside of Spital Fields and across the Thames to Southwark.

From Westminster came the King and his brother, James Duke of York. The conflagration had been clearly visible from his palace at Whitehall. He organised the bucket chains, encouraging those who passed the water on to the next man, bucket by bucket, from river to fire. It was widely reported that the King, attended by the diarist, Pepys, and several courtiers, rolled up his splendidly frilled shirt-sleeves and worked alongside his subjects. He'd always been popular; after that night he was a hero as well.

Bella's house perished. So did that of her vile brother-in-law, Oswald. Yet another made homeless – at least in the capital – was Jasper Sweetly. The house on the Thames (where he had abducted Bella for a night of passion designed to secure her affections) and all the beautiful furniture and objects d'art therein, were consumed. The gentleman – suddenly in straitened circumstances – had to forget all about a Chelsea love-nest and retire to his more modest property in the countryside, there to join his wife until his fortunes improved.

When Bella might have needed him most and might have succumbed to his persuasion, Jasper's proposition was withdrawn with no small amount of embarrassed apology. Fortunately, John Rosewood proved himself yet again to be a good friend and offered her an attic room under his own roof.

Chapter Three

Old Percy Rosewood cackled, laughing like a naughty schoolboy as Bella slapped away the shaky hand that had tried to reach out and fasten on her breast. She tut-tutted, but there was humour in her eyes. His breakfast tray retrieved, she straightened up, her cleavage disappearing from view, much to his obvious disappointment. Such a glimpse was his treat for the day.

Almost forlornly, he said, 'I shall be thinking of you for the rest of the day.'

She raised her eyebrows, unimpressed by such flattery.

'Surely you can think of something more worthwhile?'

'More worthwhile than those delicious fruits of yours?' he queried, incredulous, his open mouth toothless and his eyes squinting at her neckline. 'Better than your pretty, dimpled smile?'

'You old reprobate! I've no time for such nonsense! I am to go across town and collect supplies for John,' said Bella, her hips swaying and skirts swishing as she passed out through the door.

'Will you bring my supper tonight?' he asked, hopefully.

She smiled, but shrugged her shoulders non-committally. 'Who doth know.'

Percy Rosewood was the randiest old goat Bella had ever encountered. Sometimes it was difficult to keep one step ahead of him despite his decrepid and bedridden state. He was a likeable old rogue, though.

She had a list of daily tasks as long as her arm and so, feeling kindly disposed because she was taking on the chore for him, John had leant her his modest coach-and-two. It was a worn out conveyance, third-hand and shabby, its upholstery threadbare, its lacquer dull and scratched. But it was better than walking.

By midday half her purchases had been completed and Bella had skirted Lincoln's Inn Fields and the Temple district. Sacks of coffee, crates of cheeses and baskets of oysters were taking up the space around her ankles and filling the coach with the oddest combination of smells. Along Holborn she went, climbing out to purchase linen and spiced sausages, and to take the cutlery to the knife grinder.

In the year and more since the Fire, rebuilding had begun slowly and the premier architect of his age, Sir Christopher Wren, had put forward grand plans for a new City of London. It would be crossed by elegant avenues, peppered with piazzas and dominated by the rotunda of the new St Paul's Cathedral.

Progress along the Oxford Road was hampered by the swell of crowds heading for Tyburn Field and the periodic spectacle of a public hanging.

Tyburn was no ordinary gallows. Some called it Tyburn Tree, others the Three Legged Mare. It comprised of three sound upright beams topped by three horizontals. This allowed for greater productivity and less wasting of time, for three felons could be hanged at once.

Bella collected John's new cravat from the milliners and then climbed aboard once more. She was just about finished when there was a commotion all around her of a sudden. She popped her head out of the window and shouted up at her half dozing driver, 'What's happened?'

He shrugged. 'Search me. I was taking forty winks.'

She addressed the same question to those passing close by her window. The whole street was buzzing. 'What's happened?'

'He's escaped! The highwayman, Will Hardcastle. On his way from Newgate Prison he just jumped out of the tumbril, by all accounts, and legged it down an alley. Took his guards completely by surprise.'

'Good grief!'

'Best keep them coach doors secured.'

Militia men ran everywhere, brandishing unpredictable looking muskets, obviously more than a little annoyed to have lost their star performer of the afternoon.

It seemed to take for ever to turn the coach around and head for home because the crowd was so dense and undisciplined. Adding to the overall chaos was a swineherd and his dozen Saddlebacks on their way to market.

'Madam, I am for ever in your debt,' said a disembodied voice.

43

Bella sat bolt upright, her head swivelling. 'Who said that?'

'Tis I, Madam, hiding amongst your purchases,' said a sandy-haired fellow, emerging from beneath the cover that hid the coach's contents from prying eyes. London was full of thieves, so it was wise to take so simple a precaution. 'Don't be alarmed. Don't scream, I beg you.'

She gasped in fear and no small measure of indignance, not caring one little bit to be taken so unawares. 'Sir, whatever are you doing down there?'

'Like I did say, Madam, I'm hiding. I be the bad boy what's escaped on me way t'Tyburn.'

'Hardly a boy,' quibbled Bella, looking over the strapping fellow. He was broad, not too tall, bearded after several months without the luxury of a barber in prison, and he stank like a compost heap. 'You're the highwayman everyone was yammering on about?'

'The very same.' He stood up and bowed in the lurching coach, his balance impressive. 'Will Hardcastle at your service, Madam.'

'Tell me one good reason why I shouldn't scream for the watch?'

'I be too young t'die.'

She laughed at his woebegone expression but chided him, 'You're a rogue.'

'Can't deny it. Where be you heading?'

'Not Tyburn way, you'll be pleased to hear. I've come from an eating house on Chancery Lane.'

'Well, if you'd be so kind as to convey me some ways in that general direction, I'd be eternally grateful.'

She was being foolhardy. The man was a gallow's bird. He was desperate. He could do anything. Just

44

because he had a winning smile was no reason for Bella to lose her senses and forget caution. But she'd ever been a creature to gauge people by appearances. She liked what she saw and anyway she didn't have time to think. Ahead, the militia were stopping all the traffic, searching coaches, carts and drays.

'Quick! Hide!'

They ground to a halt. The door was opened and a musket-wielding soldier stuck his torso in intrusively. 'Sorry about this, madam, but a condemned felon has escaped his gaolers on the way to Tyburn. We have to search all vehicles. What's under there?'

'Supplies for my master's coffee house.'

He wasn't about to take her word for it, so he caught at the oilcloth and whipped it aside. There sat the cheeses, sausages, coffee and suchlike.

The man nodded all clear, retreated from the doorway and mumbled an apology of sorts somewhat mechanically as he slammed the door. 'Sorry for any inconvenience. Drive on.'

She collapsed back into her seat, sighing heavily with relief and trembling a little. Then she lifted the hem of her skirts and told the man curled in a tight foetal ball amongst her petticoat folds, ' You can come out now.'

'Must I, really? I was savouring it. You are the most ingenious of females, Madam. Without your quick thinking all would have been up for me and I'd've been off for a neck-stretching.'

'Come out.'

'Presently. First, please let me show my appreciation.'

'What d'you . . .' Her words dried and she gasped.

Concealed completely beneath her skirts as Bella perched on the edge of her seat, Will Hardcastle ran

45

his hands up the insides of her thighs. He eased them apart and went at her with his tongue, piercing through her fleshy pink folds and whipping around her bud. She arched in delight, presenting her puss the more fully to his ministerings, then felt for his head beneath her clothing and brought him the closer, capturing him there.

Busy London was right outside her coach window but Bella saw nothing, her blue eyes were glazed and her pretty mouth moved with unconscious expressions of delight as the thankful fellow beneath her skirts showed the depth of his gratitude. She was so wet, so hot, feeling his tongue slip in and out of her and shuddering with electrifying jolts of pleasure. Then her eyes widened as his hand groped about her on the floor, searching for something, and fastened on the huge spiced sausages. He grasped his fingers around one and his hand disappeared back beneath her skirts.

She laughed uproariously. 'Don't, for one moment, think you're going to – !'

He slid it into Bella, silencing her and leaving her open-mouthed with surprise.

Oh, it felt so good, so big, and it went in for ever. He moved it every which way: in and out, first deeply, then short, exquisite stabs; then gyrating it so that it stimulated every sensitive inch of her puss.

She started to gurgle and clutched at his head frantically. She came, throbbing, as the highwayman plunged the odd instrument of pleasure deep into her repeatedly and she fell back against the seat, limp but thoroughly satisfied.

They were at Holborn before Bella knew it and Will Hardcastle kissed her on both cheeks, then jumped out of the slow moving vehicle, blowing Bella a kiss before he turned and bolted off down an alley, heading for friends who would harbour him in Smithfields.

It was several moments later, still smiling with the afterglow and craziness of the adventure, that Bella looked about and realised that not only had he helped himself to her eagerly offered body, but to John's purse of coins also. How would she explain that away?

A rogue indeed! She should be mad, as mad as hell, but Bella could't stop laughing.

One man lay unconscious in a full water trough at which two tethered horses drank on, unperturbed. his mouth had lolled open and he was snoring. Another was bent over double, retching noisily from one end and farting from the other.

Nearby, in a dark doorway, a whore stood with her legs spread while a man took her most basically against the door for thruppence. Those that hadn't been able to find women as they spilled out of the tavern at closing time, now indulged in drunken, uncoordinated horseplay with their male friends, some even going so far as to bugger any companion whom alcohol had rendered semi-conscious and therefore a touch acquiescent.

These were the sons of the ruling classes; young, arrogant, and with too much money and too much empty time on their hands. They did, and got away with, anything, even murder. Their elevated positions put them far above the law. Aristocrats were a notoriously bad lot.

For instance, the exceedingly proud and charismatic Duke of Buckingham, a constant favourite of the King's, had killed the Earl of Shrewsbury in a duel which was fought over Shrewsbury's wife. The unfortunate earl had objected to Buckingham taking the wayward female as his mistress and had paid for the exception taken with his life. Buckingham had then had the audacity to take Lady S home with him. The Duchess of B, not surprisingly, took exception to having his whore installed under her own roof. The Duke was well prepared for such an indignant reaction and told her, so it was subsequently reported at court, 'Why, so I thought, Madam. And I have ordered your coach to take you to your mother.' Goodbye Duchess!

On another occasion Sir Charles Sedley, courtier and playwright, and that renowned gentleman of fashion, Lord Buckhurst, spent the night in gaol for being caught naked upon London's streets. Why they were so was never made clear.

And then there was the King's dashingly handsome, illegitimate son, James, Duke of Monmouth. he killed a beadle who took exception to his and his companion's riotous merrymaking. After a strict ticking off, the King pardoned him – of course.

Bella turned the corner into Chancery Lane and literally fell over two gentlemen who were on their knees playing at pigs in the farmyard. The one was mounted and pumping at the rear of the other who was even snorting! Black masks concealed their upper faces.

It was a foggy night in the Autumn of 1668. Percy had taken badly with a chill and John Rosewood had sent her out for medicine from the apothecary.

Bella pulled up abruptly, instantly alarmed, more so when one of the gentlemen by-standers spied her and came lumbering purposefully in her direction.

'Why, Bella. Good evening to you. Long time no see,' he said, his voice irksomely familiar.

'You have me at a disadvantage, Sir. To whom do I speak?' she parleyed, trying to cross the filthy road where a thousand chamber pots had been emptied and countless tons of refuse dumped to rot over the years. The man stepped into her path, barring her way.

She frowned, her heart thudding with alarm. They might, for the most part, be stupid drunk but once they smelled prey the old pack instinct invariably took over and things turned nasty.

'I'm disappointed that you don't recognise me.'

'If I recognised you, Sir,' she said, short of patience and growing steadily more dismayed, 'there wouldn't be any point in your wearing a mask, now would there?'

'How true. How logical you are, my sober little Puritan. Then I shall remove it forthwith,' said Jasper Sweetly, pulling the velvet mask free of his flowing locks.

She'd guessed it was him in the last moments before the mask came off and had hoped desperately that she was wrong. Now she groaned, recognising him well enough even in the dark.

He made much of looking wounded. 'I am hurt, Madam, by such a reaction. Haven't you missed me just a little?'

'Nay, I should say not!' she said, slapping him in exasperation as he stepped to one side and then the other, preventing her from getting by and making a run for it.

'I am ready to start up where we finished. My fortunes are on the up once more. Indeed this very night I visited the Painted Parrot in hope of seeing you and putting forward my proposition.'

'You are wasting your time, Sir. Now, I have urgent business elsewhere . . .'

'Nothing can be more urgent than our future happiness.'

'We have no future, Sir, happy or otherwise. Though with you it would undoubtedly be otherwise.'

He laughed dismissively at her blunt rejection then caught her and crushed her to him, kissing her all over her face and neck. 'All you need is a little persuasion. You'll change your mind.'

'I won't!'

Some of the others were looking on now, standing around drunkenly and enjoying the entertainment. Watching an unwilling woman tamed rated highly among the things they most enjoyed.

She began to struggle and Sweetly became more insistent. Roughly he pinned Bella against the wall of a pie shop, holding her head between his steely hands so that he could kiss her. She bit his lip.

'Why, you little bitch!' Sweetly raised his hand to slap her about the ears but an authoritative voice stalled him in mid-air.

'Violence against women is cowardly in the extreme, you knave. Let her go or face the consequences.'

Sweetly raised an eyebrow and turned, frowning at the unknown gentleman close behind him.

Bella was watching the stranger too, not that his features were easy to make out on the dark London street. She'd recognised Jasper by his manner rather than any physical characteristics for, surely, there could be no one quite as arrogant and obnoxious as

50

he? She did not know, or was almost certain she didn't, the newcomer. Certainly he wasn't one from the rowdy bunch already littering the corner of Chancery Lane.

'Mind your own business,' warned Jasper, his hand going to the hilt of his sword.

'A woman's honour and the guarding of it should always be a gentleman's business, sir,' said the newcomer, his voice suave and smooth as velvet.

Bella watched, mesmerised, as he too drew his sword and parried with Sweetly. God in Heaven, they were going to fight over her. A duel for her honour. She was aghast. 'Please, let us finish this now with no harm done.'

'Does this gentleman mean something special to you?' enquired the stranger.

She shook her head adamantly, 'Oh, nay!'

'Then let him be taught a lesson,' said her rescuer. He called out, 'En garde!.'

All fired up with drink and lust, Jasper was a willing opponent and they sparred most artistically, their movements graceful and athletic. It was strangely beautiful somehow. Those that weren't totally inebriated egged them on, a sword fight being yet another welcome diversion.

Steel clashed as grunts and cries of exertion and anger filled the air. Then, suddenly, out of nowhere, came a superb thrust with the rapier and Jasper was down, bleeding like a pig from the stomach and rolling in agony.

'Oh, I say! What dashed bad luck!' cried one of his companions in a polite though monumental understatement.

'Yes, bad luck. Silly mistake, old friend. Left yourself wide open to that one. Never drink and duel, that's what my father always used to say,' said another.

Bella was still standing with her back flat against the pie shop wall. She was in a state of shock. She'd detested Sweetly. But dead, no, she'd never wanted that.

The avenger of the night strode over to her, snaked an arm about her waist and pulled her hard against his lean, tall length, her feet leaving the floor. With his sword still in his right hand, he kissed her, deep and long, his tongue invading her mouth and sending shock waves right down to her toes. His moustache and flowing locks caressed and tickled upon her face and the swell of her breast. She clung to him – surely she was drowning, swooning, dying?

He set her on her feet again, and she felt rather than saw him smile in the dark, the moonlight catching a glint of teeth fleetingly. His tall frame bent at the waist in a deep bow, he removed his broad-brimmed hat and swept it in the dust with a flourish before Bella. He couldn't be for real.

'Off you go, my pretty. Run along home.'

Almost reluctantly, Bella did so. She didn't want to leave him. She wanted him to kiss her again and to feel his manhood pressed bruising hard against her belly, as her senses reeled. But the sound of Jasper moaning and groaning was upsetting and a little off-putting.

She ran, as he'd told her to, pausing a fair way down the lane, when she thought herself safe, to turn and look back as the tall, black, rakish silhouette vanished in the fog.

Jasper Sweetly died some days later. It was a particularly painful, lingering death. Bella even felt a little bit sorry for him. Just a bit. The unknown man

with whom he had fought the duel was never identi-
fied. He occupied Bella's thoughts the most;
intriguing and infuriatingly mysterious.

It had been a busy day at The Painted Parrot, the
serving wenches truly earning their tips. John said it
was the first true day of Spring 1669 and it was
bringing London's males out of the woodwork.

By early evening Bella was looking forward to
taking the rest of the night off, clearing her tables
and taking her final order of the day.

Smiling, she approached a rather secluded corner
table. 'And what can I do for you, sir?' she asked.

'Hello.' The voice was warm and expectant, full of
delight.

'Hello,' she echoed politely, giving the face a closer
look over with her eyebrows raised. He was familiar,
and yet she could not place him, 'Do I know thee?'

'Very well, on occasion,' laughed the man.

He was broad, ruddy of complexion and sandy
haired. Dressed in plain dark woolens and simple
linens, he cut no dash, but he was, nevertheless,
undeniably engaging. Bella looked him over from
head to toe, noting the far from new but well cobbled
knee-high boots with their deeply cuffed tops. Then
her eyes went back to the face and she uttered a gasp
of recognition.

'Ssh,' he cautioned, 'speak not my name.'

She did anyhow, very low and incredulous. 'Will
Hardcastle!'

'Aye. Cleaner and plumper these days after the
privations of His Majesty's Prison at Newgate.'

'You rotten little thief. After all I did for you. Going
off with my master's money and getting me into
trouble!'

He looked genuinely contrite, even while he continued to smile, 'I'm sorry for that, after your undoubted kindness, truly I am. It's been on my conscience. But I was desperate. I hope he did not beat you?'

She giggled. 'John? Oh, nay. He's too fond of me for that. He gave me the sharp side of his tongue for being so careless, for I told him that I'd lost the purse, but then forgot the matter soon enough.'

'I'm relieved to hear it. I have prospered in the interim and I shall pay you back, in full measure and then some, all that I took. And you must call me Adam Lyons, for that is my name now. A new name and a new identity.'

'And what be your profession these days?'

'I am a journeyman cabinetmaker working out of Saffron Walden.'

'A cabinetmaker? But how so? That be a highly skilled occupation. The sort that do require a lengthy apprenticeship.'

'My apprenticeship was done several years ago. 'Twas shortly thereafter that I gave in to the stupidity of youth and decided that robbing travellers on the King's highway was more to my liking. It took a scrape with the Grim Reaper to make me see the error of my ways and to end my foolishness. With the money I stole from you I bought basic tools and set to work. I was determined to make the most of the second chance that God had graced me with.'

'I am impressed and pleased. I feel instrumental in your salvation, Adam Lyons.'

'I be in London for two days.'

'Then we must sup together. Yes?'

'I was hoping you would oblige me,' he said, nodding.

Bella looked to the cast iron lantern clock on the public room mantle. 'I be finished in half an hour. Shall I bring you coffee to help pass the time?'

Rare were the men who had ever seen the interior of Bella Flowers' bedchamber. The two of them supped simply on cold meats and cheeses, fresh fruit and a bottle of sack. Adam made Bella laugh when he lamented that she hadn't served up spiced sausage for old time's sake.

The furniture in the room was scant: a trundle-bed, on which they sat to eat, a table beneath the dormer window on which stood a cracked earthenware bowl for washing, and a three-legged stool that had a leg loose.

By the door sat Adam Lyons' sacks of samples; miniature pieces of furniture, perfect in every detail. While they finished a second bottle of wine he showed them to Bella and let her open oak cupboards and drawers in tiny sideboards, commodes and wardrobes. She was greatly impressed.

'When I'm rich I shall commission you. I shall fill my house with your furniture.'

'You really like them?'

'Of course. Truly, they're lovely.'

'Certainly I have enough work to keep me out of mischief far into the future.'

'Amen to that,' said Bella with a giggle, falling back into the straw stuffed mattress of her bed.

Adam lay down beside her on his belly, studying her. 'Why don't you come back to Saffron Walden with me, to be my wife?'

She shook her head, smiling gently. 'No.'

'I'd be a good provider. A serious wooer. An ardent lover.'

She laughed, hugging the man close. 'I have no

55

doubt, but I've been wed. It was a disappointment. I'd not be content. I'm going to make my fortune, Adam. I shall be famous.'

He took it philosophically and shrugged. 'Should you change your mind 'tis not so very far to Essex.'

'I'll remember that.'

He kissed her sweetly and gently, lulling her into a dreamy state of well-being. His hands going to the laces of her black stomacher, he loosened it so he could coax down her cotton chemise and suck at her hardening nipples. She moaned and ran her fingers through the sandy locks that dangled about her flesh, tickling her.

He stood up, unbuckled his breeches and let them fall, doing a jig as he escaped from the clothing and boots and prancing around in naught but his voluminous linen shirt with its full, plain collar.

She smiled at his erection, eager and impressed. He was well endowed. It wagged, hard and silken, rising up rampant from his curl-clustered loins.

He pulled Bella gently around until her legs fell over the side of the bed, then he lifted her skirts and numerous petticoats and knelt between her legs. The sight of her white thighs and dark mound sent his senses reeling. He ran his fingers through the ribbon of her garters and kissed the quivering pale flesh, then stroked her hidden place with a finger, losing it in her then drawing it forth once more, glistening wet. He repeated the procedure once more, only this time with his tongue, making Bella tremble with delight and longing.

His body glided up over hers and he entered her in a fluid, masterful stroke of possession, taking her to the hilt and holding his body poised there. He watched the pleased expression on Bella's face chuckling, then rotated his girth within her.

She gave a long, moaning sigh of pleasure, her eyelids flickering.

His weight taken on his palms and toes, the reformed highwayman took Bella leisurely. In total control of things, he stroked for minutes on end his face tense with lust and exertion. He drove her to a noisy, intense climax that throbbed on and on for what seemed an eternity. Then he grew progressively more single-minded as he neared his own goal, his face reddening and every muscular fibre of his being taut with a sense of approaching climax. He reared and trembled, his buttocks clutching and his loins throbbing, then he released. 'Ah, heaven . . . heaven . . .' he croaked.

They drank more wine and lay dishevelled and sated atop the crumpled bed. Next door, Percy banged on the wall. He was thirsty and wanted a cup of beer (for no one willingly drank the city water). Minutes later Bella was back. She straddled the dozing body of Adam Lyons, running a hand between twitching thighs that seemed to open to her of their own volition, so that she could toy with his balls and smooth the length of his flaccid though, perceptibly, rousing shaft. It responded by degrees, quick and eager, soon rigid and long in her hands.

Adam murmured, grinning and only feigning sleep. His eyes still closed, he pulled a fresh sheep's bladder condom from the side pocket of his shirt and Bella chuckled as she fumbled inexpertly getting it on.

She spat on the tip and then, deliciously slowly, lowered herself onto it, taking him in inch by tortuous inch, sinking until they rubbed pubic bones and ground against each other.

Adam's grin broadened. He moved a leg from between Bella's, tightening the angle of penetration exquisitely and, instantaneously heady from the intense sensations this evoked, Bella started to arch and tense, riding him hard with her head thrown back and her breasts straining.

He reached for them, cupping and squeezing, caught up himself on an ever-growing wave of sublime pleasure. Her body dragged back and forth on his, his shaft buried, captured deep within her, until her precision brought them to crisis point together. They made a hell of a noise and Percy banged on the wall again.

Adam Lyon stayed another day and night. Bella spent every spare moment with him that she could. Indeed she was tempted by his marriage offer and gave it much thought as she served at The Painted Parrot. But no. She must be resolute. She had decided on her husband's death that she would be her own woman, and that, henceforth, she would please herself. Later on circumstances might alter her outlook or change her mind, but for now she knew quiet Essex was not for her and nor was one particular man. At least not until the right one came along.

He left her the money he owed, with interest, as promised and when Bella retired that night, lighting her candle and taking a brush to her hair, she saw, upon the table beneath the window, an exquisite cupboard in oak and walnut, its drawers and handles perfect in every detail. Inside the top centre drawer was a tiny love token in the form of a nosegay. Lavender, rosebuds and rosemary were tied up with lilac ribbon and on one trailing end of the ribbon had been written a message in black ink. 'Yours, always.' Bella was touched.

'Look at her!' mused Tom Havelock, with somewhat clinical admiration. 'She's a born actress.'

Bella was waiting tables, all sweet smiles and charm.

From the other side of the table John Rosewood smiled. 'There's no denying she knows how to handle the customers.'

'A fine figure on her also.'

You're not thinking of trying to poach her, now are you, my friend?'

'She'd make a creditable addition to my troupe at The Consort's, I'll not deny.' said Tom, honestly.

'But she's the best wench I've got.'

'Then surely you can see that she deserves better than serving coffee and oyster pie all day and every day?'

'I don't want to lose her,' said John, quite serious now.

Tom Havelock covered the other's hand atop the table, looking deeply and winningly into his eyes. 'Surely you'd do it for me, Johnny?'

John immediately felt his resolve faltering. He liked Bella a great deal. But when Tom Havelock looked at him in that particular way he invariably went all to mush. He just couldn't help himself.

'It's up to her.'

Tom smiled, triumphant.

'But I must insist, on her behalf, that you pay her a decent wage.'

It being Christmas and the season of goodwill to one's fellow man, Tom rose in his seat, caught John about the sides of the head and landed a noisy, smacking kiss on his forehead. 'I'm a generous employer. I shall be especially so, knowing how much she means to you.'

'She's been like a daughter. and my father will be up in arms when he knows what I've done,' said John, pink with pleasure from the kiss.

'Then you'll be glad to know she'll be bettering herself. This may be the start of great things for Bella Flowers.'

Bella was not so sure. Yes, certainly she could handle the gentlemen in the coffee house well enough. But that wasn't real acting, that was being diplomatic. Tom insisted there wasn't much difference. He'd teach her timing and suchlike and she'd be wonderful, he was certain. She thought he was mad and that his faith was truly misplaced. She declined but he told her how much money he was willing to pay and she said she'd give it a try.

On Christmas Eve she let her hair down, serving the roasts and puddings with wine-induced gaiety and a double dose of nostalgia. She would miss The Painted Parrot. She wore her best frock, a cobalt-blue velvet-trimmed woollen dress to keep out the chill, and her dark hair was brushed out of its usual ringlets and allowed to hang naturally over her shoulders and down her back. Many were the men who admired those dark tresses and the plunge of her neckline.

The Painted Parrot was gay and noisy. Few customers left for home without being either over-fed or over-watered from the establishment's fine selection of imported wines and sherries.

The last day of business before the holy day was

fast turning into a farewell party for Bella. She tried to keep to coffee, but many were those who insisted she must take a drink with them. From some there were even keepsakes: small pieces of jewellery in silver and semi-precious stones, or small, leather-bound volumes of poetry. More than once she had to dab at her eyes with her handkerchief.

By late afternoon, as it began to grow dark, the lute player arrived, treating them all to music in exchange for free coffee. By night he entertained in the big houses on the Thames. As Bella tried to serve her customers she was continually whisked away to do a step dance or a jig.

She found herself in the arms of a huge Scotsman who, far from forsaking his native dress for more stylish garb while in England's capital, was sporting the full plaid regalia, from his trews to his cockaded tammy. He was six foot six at least and as big as a bear, lifting Bella off the floor and twirling her effort-lessly as he danced making her squeal delightedly. His hair was carrot red and he sported a full set of whiskers.

Twirled one moment and hugged the next, Bella grew progressively more hot and bothered, her head spinning from the drink. The public room was too hot with all the bodies therein and the roaring fire in the hearth. When finally the music stopped, she clung to Angus McBride for dear life, hopelessly dizzy.

Never one to miss an opportunity, he hugged her closer, liking the feel of her breasts squashed against his burly torso. With shock she felt the shaft of him rising up, hidden from public view beneath his plaids. He was impossibly huge, very much in pro-portion with the rest of him. She pressed against him again, thinking that she must have been mistaken. But no, it really was him.

He grinned and winked. 'Och, but ye make me ol' todger hard as an iron bar, lassy.'

'So I noticed.' She winked right back, wanting that todger of his and wanting to make her feelings plain no matter how brazen that might make her seem. She wanted him and didn't care to waste time.

'He likes ye.'

'I like him.'

'Shame 'tis we're not alone.'

'There is a quiet passage beyond the scullery. I have to take dishes out there. Maybe you could give me a hand, it being Christmas and all?'

'Anything to oblige so fine a looking lassy as yourself,' he agreed readily, not slow on the uptake by any means. A canny Scot indeed.

Susie and a gentleman were just leaving the dark end of the passage as Bella and her Scotsman arrived. The women exchanged knowing giggles. Susie's gentleman actually blushed and stammered something to the effect that he'd just given her her Christmas present.

'Och, now that I can well believe,' said Angus McBride, roaring with laughter.

Alone with him Bella leant backwards against the wall and held out her arms welcomingly, snaking them around his neck when he walked into them. He kissed her. It was a rather uncouth procedure. She was disappointed but she felt better when he tickled her fancy, showed surprising gentleness for such a big man. She strained her excited mound against him, rubbing her palm up and down where his todger reared in mind-boggling proportions.

'You're ready, aren't you? Hungry. I like a lass

who's eager,' said Angus with his lovely burr, lifting Bella with his palms beneath her buttocks and sliding her down to meet his meatiness. He pushed and he wriggled but she shook her head. She couldn't manage him, he was just too enormous.

'Put your legs around me, lassy. Open yourself more.'

Bella obliged, so eager and then, yes, very carefully, she felt his huge thing force its way in, thick, uncomfortable, and seemingly without end.

The anticipation of such a coming together was better than the reality. In truth the discomfort hardly decreased even after things became more lubricated.

Angus enjoyed himself immensely and didn't seem to notice his partner's waning enthusiasm and gritted teeth. She'd never believed that a man could be too big but Angus definitely was. He was aptly named, especially being a native of Aberdeen!

When she re-entered the public room a short while later, Bella hoped it was only Susie who noticed that she walked gingerly, legs splayed, as if she'd just got off a horse and was saddle-sore.

Chapter Four

Acting was the greatest challenge of Bella's life. And, lo, how she enjoyed it. In front of a crowd she came fully alive, taken over by the posing, posturing, scene-stealing thespian she had within. She tingled through every fibre of her being, knowing she had found her vocation.

Havelock mostly steered her clear of Shakespeare, perceiving that her forte was the irreverent comedies of Sedley or the plays of sexual politics beloved by Dryden and Etheredge.

In *Macbeth*, playing one of the witches, she hammed unmercifully, but dress her in a man's surcoat and hose and put her in farce, and Bella was a winner. She seemed to grasp the deliciousness of comic asides with ease, her ad-libbing infuriating some of her fellow actors but delighting the audience. On stage she was merciless in her pursuit of the ultimate humourous performance. She went out of her way to make those who tripped the boards beside her corpse over their lines or succumb to uncontrollable giggles and these and all the other antics guaranteed to get the crowd roaring with laughter in the pit.

She was a great success supporting in *The Rival Ladies* and highly watchable as a South American native in Dryden's dramatic *The Indian Emperor*. But even Dryden was too serious for her talents. In Sedley's *The Mulberry Garden* she excelled, and Killigrew, owner of The Drury Lane Theatre, much patronised by his friend the King, made a point of turning up one night to watch her.

Tom Havelock was wary. He thought they had a poacher in their midst so he reminded Bella – needlessly, because she loved The Consort's and wouldn't have thought of moving – of the loyalty she owed. He even promised her an increase in wages. In any event Killigrew made no approach and showed no interest. He had many fine actresses already, including Moll Davies and Nelly Gwynne, who'd once sold oranges in the pit. He'd probably just been curious, Bella told Tom, brought along by the gossip.

After the performance he was indignant on her behalf, as if personally slighted that the man hadn't tried anything underhand to steal her away. 'Jumped up arse! Mediocre playwright! Who does he think he is? I never rated him. He wrote one rather second-rate play which was coarse, I always thought. And not particularly witty or funny either.'

Bella patted him on the arm, her make-up garish in the harsh light off-stage. 'It really doesn't matter, now does it? Calm yourself. Better still, go count the takings; that's guaranteed to cheer you.'

One day, during a rather serious play that shall remain nameless and in which Bella was conducting herself with her usual marked irreverence, the her-ione – a buxom, red-headed actress called Phillis Sharp – was making the most of her death scene, ekeing it out with a dagger clutched to her bosom.

She staggered and sagged against the furniture. 'I'm dying,' she moaned, her face a heavily painted, tragic mask. The audience watched intently.

Bella had been watching the same performance for days, and was tired of it. She was playing Phillis's dismayed chambermaid, running to aid her and lend the comfort of her arms in which to die as per the script. But Phillis wasn't ready. She fended Bella off with uncanny strength considering her supposed tenuous grasp on life. Bella looked immediately to the audience and pulled a face. There were sniggers.

'I'm dying,' Phillis repeated.

Bella trailed behind trying to anticipate her collapse and offer her her arms in which to expire.

'Dying . . .' came the murmur, much fainter now, but still elusive.

Enough was enough. Bella caught her by the hair and brought her up short. Her line was 'Madam, how shall I bear the pain of your leaving me? What will become of your poor Nancy?' But for some demonic reason it came out as 'Well, bloody well die then, you stupid bitch!'

Forced to the floor and held there with determination, a glowering, spluttering Phillis was forced to concede that she could do nothing else and, duly died most prettily. It was not, as already stated, a comedy, but the laughter went on for a very long time. In the wings Havelock rolled his eyes with mock horror, chuckling. When they came off stage he'd have to be prepared to separate them quickly and forestall the otherwise inevitable cat fight.

* * *

When finally Bella got the leading role in *Miss Hopkins' Marriage*, her usual devilment deserted her and nerves took over. An hour before she was due to go on she was violently sick. A quarter hour before and she was flying to Tom in a panic, convinced she'd forgotten her words completely.

With a canny knack of knowing just what she needed to snap her out of her terror, he gave her a look of commiseration, took her hand, patted it and said, with understanding, 'Never you mind, dear girl. I'll put on the understudy. Marian won't mind going on at short notice. She's been waiting for her chance.'

Bella's eyebrows lifted and she instantly pulled herself together. 'I feel much better now. And, yes, I think I can recall my opening line. I'll manage. I couldn't let you down.'

Tom was smiling. 'I knew you wouldn't.'

The curtain parted and Bella was on, dressed in the latest fashion and a picture of rustic prettiness. She was playing the part of Miss Hopkins, the vicar's daughter who meets her lover in the graveyard every Sunday after family service. The plot was daft and contrived, a series of accidental meetings, mishaps and misunderstandings that centred around Miss Hopkins' matchless skill at hoodwinking her strict and puritanical father.

On stage the wooden scenery had been painted to look like a flowery bower with a couple of tombstones backstage left and a swing centre stage, its ropes entwined with lilac and primrose. It looked a picture but it was the strangest graveyard and Heaven only knew what the swing was doing there. Tom wanted it; that seemed good enough.

Bella took her place upon the swing, setting it

gently into motion and allowing the audience to feast their eyes on her and to get their murmurs of approval over and done with. Then she spoke, swallowing down her terror. 'Will my dearest love come today? Will he dare? My father is a Godly man who approves not of any man for me, and thinks music the business of the devil. Alack and alas, my heart belongs to a penniless musician. If *only* he were rich mayhap 'twould be better for us . . .'

At this point the said penniless minstrel was supposed to enter stage right and creep up behind Miss Hopkins, putting his hands over her eyes and telling her to guess as to his identity. But suddenly there was so much noise in the gallery that he missed his cue. Several gentlemen and a couple of ladies were seating themselves and greeting each other noisily. Hands were shaken and hats removed. Bella frowned and got up off her swing.

Standing at the front of the stage she glared up at the dark silhouettes, dazzled by the torchlight at her feet. 'If you gentlemen have quite finished making yourselves comfortable?'

A voice called down apologetically. 'Pray proceed, Madam, and forgive our tardiness.'

'Thank you!' She stepped back and perched once more on the swing. 'As I was saying. Will my dearest love come today? Or will he be forever left waiting in the wings because certain loud sorts in the audience keep drowning out his cue?'

There was a tittering wave of laughter and on came her suitor. He was so nervous that he grabbed Bella about the head rather than covering her eyes and so unbalanced her that she whipped over backwards with her legs in the air and her petticoats flashing. She and her lover lay in an untidy heap on the floor, belly laughing, then she kissed him smackingly on the lips and got to her feet, dusting herself off and straightening her apparel as best she could. Her voice having to be raised considerably to be heard above the laughter of the audience, she said, 'Once again, sweetheart, you have swept me off my feet.'

There was a round of merry applause.

Thereafter things went as well as they ever could with Bella on stage. She was always going to be unpredictable. The curtain came down to warm applause and, after a curtain call, she walked off stage as if in a trance. Her legs were trembling as the delayed reaction hit her. She was so exhilarated she felt almost faint. This was helped very little by Tom Havelock taking her aside to offer his congratulations on her performance, but then adding with amusement, 'A word of caution, however, my sweet. No-one, but no-one, admonishes the King for being late. He can turn up any time the fancy takes him.'

Her eyes popped and her mouth dropped open. 'The King?' She gasped, but no noise came out.

He nodded. 'The King.'

On cue Charles Stuart, his retinue in his wake, came backstage. He shook Tom Havelock warmly by the hand whilst tendering his congratulations on the success of the new play, and briefly making the acquaintance of the principal players.

Face cleaned of make-up, but still in her charming costume, Bella stood in line, quaking at the knees and dry-mouthed.

He was wonderful – so awesome he turned every woman in his presence into a simpering, coquettish fool. All sensible thought simply fled, and if he smiled, showing his dazzling white teeth beneath a clipped black line of moustache, words failed as well.

Well over six foot with his swarthy, indolent good looks, he would have turned all heads even had he been lowly born. But he had presence. Beside him his brother, the fair, rather austere James, Duke of Monmouth, paled significantly. It was always Charles who commanded the attention and Charles who one remembered.

Bella dropped to the floor in a deep curtsey, looking at the silk rosettes that adorned his black, red-heeled shoes. He held out his hand and helped her to rise. When she looked at him Bella could see he was smiling with amusement and wasn't cross at all, thank Heavens. She didn't fancy the Tower.

She opened her mouth and began to stammer an apology. 'Sire, I had no idea. I am so sorry.'

'It is I who should apologise, Madam. I regret missing even a moment of your delightful performance.' His eyes roved over her face, her figure – he was a blatant connoisseur. 'And to make amends for my shabby behaviour I should be honoured if you would sup with me?'

She stabbed her own bosom with an index finger, looking stupified. 'Me?'

'Aye, definitely you, Mistress Flowers. Tell me, is Bella truly your given name?'

'Well, yes, in a manner of speaking. That is, I was baptised Arabella. 'Tis shortened is all.'

'Arabella I like,' said Charles firmly. He looked to his son and brother who hovered, looking Bella over speculatively and guessing well enough at the evening's likely outcome if their royal companion was true to form. They'd have tried to woo her themselves if he hadn't made his intentions so plain and chosen her first. One would be a fool indeed to steal a woman from the King. 'There's a change of plan, friends. I'm going back to Whitehall with this young lady, yes?'

Bella nodded agreement, mumbling dry-mouthed, 'I'm honoured.'

This couldn't be happening. It couldn't be true. This was Charles Stuart, the man of her dreams and the man of a thousand sexual fantasies. She feared she might blink and he'd vanish. But he didn't. He took her hand to lead her past a bowing, grinning Tom Havelock and the rest of the troupe and out into the cobbled lane before the theatre.

Postilions and footmen ran hither and thither, letting down the steps on the gleaming black coach-and-six and fetching a cloak for Bella to cover her charming yet flimsy costume so she didn't shiver in the night air.

She sat facing the King on soft seats of purple velvet and heard bystanders shout out, 'A health unto your Majesty!' and 'God bless the King!'

Beside the coach ran liveried lads with flaming torches. This couldn't be happening. She was staring, she knew, but couldn't seem to help it being too terrified to speak.

He smiled, a flash of white in a dark face with his black eyes twinkling. 'You are a peach, Arabella. A succulent peach. I hope you don't mind me telling you so?'

She shook her head quickly in reassurance. 'It thrills me to hear you speak thus, Sire.'

He laughed. 'Did you enjoy your first night?'

'Acting?'

'Aye. What else could I mean?'

71

She blushed. 'First night with a man did spring to mind, Sire.'

'Really? Now I'm intrigued. And did you? Or am I being too bold by asking? Yes, I am. I can see. I'm making you blush.'

'No,' she protested politely, though it was true. 'In all honesty the reality was disappointing.'

'Oh, for shame. Someone so lovely deserved better. Was the second night an improvement?' He laughed.

Bella chuckled, relaxing somewhat, but wouldn't be drawn.

'And how shall it be with us this night, dear lady? I have pursued women for months, years even when I have felt the prick of Cupid's arrow and they have been reluctant. Seldom do I not get what I want. You, dear Arabella, seem a woman of the world and appear to know what's what. We are well matched. I don't think I shall have to play games with you. I am heady with sudden desire. Must I be patient and woo you with trinkets and flowers? Will you make me wait in torment before the final surrender? Have I read you wrong? Could you love this hulking gipsy of a man?'

There was mirth in his voice and he made Bella smile. She wiped it away looking at him very seriously. 'I shall make you wait . . .'

'I knew it,' he cried in mock distress.

'. . . at least until after supper,' she finished.

'I am transported! I am in heaven!' Laughing Charles thrust his head out of the pushed down window and shouted at the team of greys that pulled them, rather than the driver. 'Hurry, horses, hurry.'

* * *

The King's secretary, master of the backstairs and sometime spy and confidante, Chiffinch, served them a light supper. An astute man, he could see that the King and the young woman had their minds on things other than food.

From Chiffinch's apartments a staircase ran down to the privy stairs on the palace's watery edge and there were moored two or three boats to take the king secretly upon his nocturnal pleasures. It was his means of escape from a crowded court where he seemed to be forever on show. Why, even his eating of meals in the banqueting hall was a public spectacle with hundreds milling through the gallery to observe him.

Chiffinch was the custodian of the King's pleasure, smoothing the way with practised ease and discretion for Charles's amorous escapades. He served his master as if mute and blind. There could be no more perfect a servant.

After they had supped on braised pheasant and syllabub, Charles took Bella by the hand and led her down those secret stairs, a candelabra held in his hand to light the way.

She was giggling and the infectious noise made him chuckle.

'Have you ever travelled the Thames by moonlight, Madam?'

'Nay, Sire.'

'Don't call me Sire.'

'Nay, your Majesty.'

'Don't call me Your Majesty.'

'Then what?'

'Call me Charlie.'

'Is that not a little informal?'

'I intend doing very informal things with and to you, Mistress Arabella Flowers.'

'Ooh,' she chuckled, thrilling with anticipation and loving every minute of this escapade.

The smell of the river rose to meet her, pungent, rotting even, as Charles handed her into the craft. It was a sizeable barge, with a curtained, canopied sitting area for the passengers and manned by a dozen deep-blue liveried oarsmen. Its prow was ornately carved and gilded in gold, as was the canopy. The sound of lapping water upon the palace steps seemed to blot out all else.

She made herself comfortable upon the couch beneath the canopy. Charles joined her, taking her into his arms immediately and sighing with what seemed content. 'Ah, I love the motion of a boat, whether it be barge or yacht. Had I not been a king I fancy I should have liked being a sailor.'

'Where do we go?'

'I thought along to the meadows of Richmond?'

'As your Majesty wishes.'

'Oh come now, Madam. Do you court my disapproval? I am Charlie. You are Arabella. When alone I would have it no other way. Is that clear?'

'It takes some getting used to – Charlie.'

He laughed. 'That's better,' he said, and kissed her.

She'd been expecting it. It was inevitable. Yet it still came as a shock. She was kissing the King of England for Heaven's sake!

Around her shoulders he pulled a sable-lined robe to ward off the night chill, insinuating his body down the length of hers.

The oarsman dipped and pulled rhythmically, the grunts of exertion almost sensual in their unison.

'Thus must the galley slaves have sounded as they pulled upon the oars that propelled the royal barge carrying Cleopatra and her love, Marcus Antoninus. It doth send a thrill through me.'

'How romantic, Charlie! What a picture you paint.'

He hugged her close then, fired by passion behind the purple velvet and damask draperies.

This Charles Stuart was all man. All sex. She could never have said, 'No,' to him. He was irresistible.

His hand strayed beneath the skirts of her silly costume, and found her warm and damp, trembling a little with expectancy. He was a king. Would it be different? Would she be forever changed by the experience?

He fondled her like an ordinary man – delicate, tentative, considerate, not rushing things. His kisses, to begin with, were exploratory and tender, then probing and demanding, his tongue invading in the French manner. Bella never quite got used to that approach, always finding such invasions of that particular orifice a shock, though not an unpleasant one. And a shock that was overcome, grant you, given enough delicate persuasion. When he French-kissed he used it to herald a new departure in the loving process. From kissing to fondling, from fondling to masturbation. He was a skilled seducer and knew exactly what he was doing.

When his finger found her and slipped into her, Bella couldn't believe what was happening. She fell into the same trap as every other female who had ever been loved by the King: she couldn't believe that he was a mere mortal; she was totally in awe.

She opened to him like a flower to a bee, sighing with delight as he buried himself deep within her and gyrated. His movements were faint yet deep, his shaft remaining hard and thickly swollen long after the first waves of passion had washed over them. He started to move again. He jerked and thrust, fucking her all over again. He lay claim to her and filled her, pushing into Bella to the hilt. She wrapped her legs about him to draw him in – absorbed and was absorbed. She forgot he was the King.

Just before dawn Bella had slipped unseen from the palace, a coach taking her back to her lodgings off Drury Lane. She was grinning from ear to ear. What a night! She'd never forget it. He'd kissed her tenderly goodbye and promised that they would meet again but she didn't believe it, she just thought him polite. She was glad to have had one night.

But he was true to his word. The coach came again to collect her after the play finished three days later, whisking her off to another intimate supper. The King turned up for further performances of *Miss Hopkins' Marriage*. Soon people in Court were whispering of nothing else, speculating with malicious delight that this new favourite might end Barbara Palmer's reign once and for all. Certainly Charles was tired of the Countess. He put up with her, it was said, out of a hard-to-break habit. She was demanding, imperious and he suspected that the last child she had produced and proclaimed his bastard hadn't been his at all. For old time's sake though he acknowledged it as such and created Castlemaine Duchess of Cleveland as a parting gift. Not that she left court; she stayed very much in evidence.

More and more Charles Stuart was seen with the actress Bella Flowers – at the Palace of Whitehall, in Vauxhall Gardens, at tennis matches, at private dinners in those grand houses that lined the Strand, their gardens backing onto the Thames and, in the Spring, at Newmarket.

The King adored Newmarket. He threw off kingship for the duration of his twice-yearly jaunts there and took on a jockey's persona. He had had Wren build him a little house facing the Maiden's Inn in the village. In the mornings he went hunting and hawking, in the afternoons he attended either horse or foot racing and in the evenings he dined simply and informally with his cronies. Sometimes, though, he dined alone with Bella and, if she was starring in one of Tom Havelock's new plays and couldn't be spared, he went whoring, frequenting the racing town's brothels. On one such escapade, disguised as a country squire out for a night's pleasure, he was set upon by a cutpurse and only escaped with his life after revealing his identity to the low-life and doubtless stunning him into foregoing his robbery.

Bella rode out with the King one morning on the most docile mare that could be procured from the many stables in the town, out onto the heath where the wind whipped across the arable land from Swaffham Prior and made her cheeks pink.

The King looked dashing and desirable in scarlet woollen breeches and jerkin with his shirt showing a froth of white lace at throat and cuffs. His feathered hat took some punishment in the breeze.

Bella, daringly, had donned boys clothing for comfort and convenience and rode astride, the sapphire wool ensemble suiting well her pale colouring and sable hair, and matching exactly her lustrous eyes.

The King's eyes had lit up appreciatively when he'd met her over breakfast and thereafter he couldn't seem to keep them off her.

They rode leisurely, the King not tearing off at his

usual gallop in deference to Bella's novice status. This was only the fourth time she'd ever been on a horse.

A sudden gust took the King's hat and carried it off and up, depositing it on that ancient rib of earthwork that ran through the heath, known as the Devil's Ditch.

Bella laughed. Holding on to her own headgear which was a fetching copy of the men's fashion, she turned her mount in the same direction as Charles' and dug in her heels.

They dismounted, climbing the steep bank of the old boundary fortification to retrieve the King's hat at the top and then they paused, close together, to take in the view. They were breathing heavily from the climb, wind-tossed, exhilarated, and smiling at nothing in particular.

They could see for miles – the rolling Suffolk hills in one direction, the flattening fens of Cambridge-shire in the other. It was a crisp, clear day and they could pick out the recently constructed smock mill on the hill at Swaffham Prior, its sails turning quickly.

Charles pulled Bella back against him and held her tightly to his length, growing hard at the contact. She could feel him against her buttocks, pressing entic-ingly. He chuckled.

'Madam, you're a wanton,' he said, as if she were incorrigible.

'No more so than yourself, Sir,' she pointed out, turning in his arms, grinning, and pulling him with her down into the long grass at the top of the dyke.

He kissed her long and deeply, his tongue probing, his moustache tickling and his fingers making short work of the jerkin and its row of tiny, cloth-covered buttons. He paused over the breeches, feeling compelled to tell her, 'In truth this shall be the first time in my life that I'll have removed a pair of breeches.'

'How novel! A new experience!' Bella tittered. 'Even the worldly wise King has not done everything.'

He laughed. 'How did I manage before you came along to cheer me?'

'Well enough, I suspect.'

Entwined, their breeches down and tangled with their boot tops, Charles wasted no time on preliminaries. He was hot for her and eager to be in her depths. Bella was used to his style, she found it flattering in one way if slightly frustrating. He was a man who enjoyed women, enjoyed them a great deal. And he was the King, a very handsome and personable man. There would never be a shortage of women who would take him any way they could get him. Bella knew that; she was one of them. She'd lusted after him since the first time she'd ever seen his likeness. Usually she was as hungry for physical love as he and needed very little stimulus to become aroused satisfactorily.

She cradled him between her thighs, enjoying immensely the long strokes he made and the way he took his weight on his hands so he could watch her face and gaze upon her breasts while they were joined, bone to bone, flesh to flesh, bodies damp despite the cool breeze, their body heat building. At his point of crisis Charles lowered himself, holding Bella almost suffocatingly tight. He lay there, sated after the crisis, until every last throb and quiver had passed through him and his penis slipped from her, small and soft. He was the only man she knew – and she really hadn't known that many – who tied on his sheep's bladder condoms with the most expensive blue silk ribbon. That thought always made her smile.

Back in the saddle they toured the King's stables, looking over his fine string of Arab horseflesh. Bella knew nothing about horses. She was just required to smile charmingly and look attentive as Charles eulogised. This he could do at considerable length. He explained the benefits of the teaser, a fine looking stallion who was paraded before the in-season mares to make them more receptive to the stud who was substituted when she made it clear she was ready to mate.

Bella's look was wry. 'So the mare fancies the teaser, this good-looking rogue on four legs and then, when she couldn't possibly bring herself to say, 'No,' he's whipped away and Laughing Boy, with all the qualities you wish the future foals to inherit, gets to have a cracking time without even trying? Seems just a bit mean to me. Does the teaser ever get his just reward?'

Charles was laughing. 'He's kept happy.'

They leant against the rails of the paddock, watching the lads leading the Arabs around as the King pointed out a neat fetlock or a bright eye. She nodded, but truthfully thought they all looked much the same apart from their different colouring.

The King's reputation as a sexual being was such that through the length and breadth of his kingdom he was known by his nickname, Old Rowley. Old Rowley was, in fact, the most successful stallion in the King's Newmarket stud.

Sex, animal sex at that, breeding, leather, manure, straw and hay – the smells were all around, intoxicating. Bella felt charged, tingling and alive, a feeling that stayed with her all afternoon as, now changed into her finery, she attended the races on the Mile with her royal lover.

They were cheered by the crowd and Bella presented one of the cups to the winner of the Town Race, a steeplechase from far off Six Mile Bottom.

Charles was in high spirits, and looking splendid in darkest green velvet frock-coat, waistcoat and breeches, with a feathered hat wide-brimmed and black as the jet of his hair.

People bowed and pressed close in the hope that he would notice them, mayhap even recognise them and speak. His entourage moved in his wake, as splendid as he, lords, ladies, earls, countesses, duchesses and the two royal Dukes. And amongst them, to the fore even, strode the delightful Bella, Charles's current lady love. She still found that hard to believe. Rubbing shoulders with princes and the like and calling them by their first names! She didn't think she'd ever get used to it.

A cheer went up from the crowd. 'A health unto His Majesty!' 'God save the King! God bless Old Rowley!'

Disciplined fellow that he was, he gave no hint that he had heard them but just kept on smiling and inclining his head to left and right with his customary gallantry, though doubtless glowing inwardly at the adulation. He'd never been so popular. A far cry from his father who'd sunk so low in the esteem of the populace that he'd lost his head on the block outside his own banqueting hall at Whitehall.

Come six of the clock, with the last race won and Bella having lost the ten shillings which Charles had presented to her for the purpose of betting, the King and his companion climbed into their coach and moved off through the cheering, dispersing throng, while the army of pickpockets had their usual field day.

Bella breathed luxuriously her breasts rising above the deeply scooped neckline of her lace-trimmed sapphire gown. Her eyes rolled with the pleasure of it all. 'A lovely day.'

He watched her, smiling mildly, charmed. She looked a treat. Her skin was pale and flawless, her body full and curving in all the right places. He wanted her again as he always wanted her.

She noted the lascivious grin, the licking of his full, dark lips and the burning look. She saw how he grasped tighter at the long, silver-topped ebony walking stick which he held point down and embedded in the carpet between his wide spread knees. He was swelling in his breeches, causing a straining mass at his groin.

She smiled. 'Something trying to escape?'

Charles laid his walking stick on the velvet upholstered seat beside him. 'Let's see what it is.'

He made short work of his buttons, the breech flap falling aside to expose his hard and lengthy shaft. It curved upwards from a forest of dark hair, rigid, thick and as swarthy as the rest of him. A handsome, juice inducing member.

Bella cooed with theatrical delight and took the hem of her skirt in her dainty, beringed fingers, hoisting it slowly, inch by inch, up over her calves and knees, thighs and so on, all stockinged in white silk and gartered with silver ribbons studded with diamonds – a present from Charles.

His eyes fastened upon the creamy flesh above the stocking tops and the dark triangle that Bella began to expose, tantalisingly slowly, her legs gradually opening.

He ran his hand up the length of his shaft, teasing and engorging it still further, though hardly daring to touch the sensitive head that had reared proud of its protective skin folds. He never took his eyes off Bella.

She cupped her puss and ran one finger down through the cranny, stroking with such delicacy that her splayed knees trembled, enjoying herself and very much aware of the effect it was having on her lover.

He came onto his knees, crawled to her and, gliding up over the edge of the seat where Bella perched, sunk sweetly into her. His strokes were intense and made them both cry out and gasp. In moments they were clutching at each other; he at Bella's buttocks to sink deeper into her, she at his, lacerating the royal arse with her nails. They jerked, gasped, stabbed and devoured, ·making so much noise as their crisis came upon them thàt driver and footmen undoubtedly heard them, even above the noise of the horses. Panting and nearly spent they clung together, but his shaft remained hard and sensitive, eager, it seemed, for more.

Certainly Charles made no attempt to withdraw. He caught Bella more firmly about the hips and staggered with her, still impaled upon his shaft, back to his own side of the coach, she laughing uproariously and clinging to him for dear life.

Leisurely, he took her all over again. Her skirts discreetly hiding the evidence as she sat in his lap, facing him, his member slipped and thrust so sweetly up into her. The royal house was in sight before, once again, they reached a pleasant, toe-curling climax.

Chapter Five

She was feted and admired, plotted and bitched against. She was the undisputed King's favourite. Upon her had been bestowed the title Countess of Hawksley, a house facing Parliament Square and a generous yearly allowance. Bella lived in luxury and had long since given up acting. She was presented to the Queen and, when a vacancy arose, had been promised a position as Lady of the Bedchamber. There was no more prestigious a post for a woman at court.

The Queen accepted Bella with practised nonchalance. She had long since overcome her aversion to her husband's women, and had been told plainly soon after her arrival as a naive princess from Portugal, that her tantrums over the matter would not be tolerated. Either everyone got along together like one big happy family or Queen Catherine of Braganza could keep to her own company. Wretched at the thought of being ostracised in a foreign land, she had backed down, thereafter enjoying her husband's devoted attention. Charles was genuinely fond of his funny little Queen and even loved her after a fashion. Besides, Catherine had seen the constant turn-over of female companions who hopped in and out of his bed. Few had real staying power. And only Castlemaine still hung on doggedly to the illusion of past glory, her presence tolerated by Charles for old time's sake.

When the King was in love he'd go to any lengths to get the woman he wanted and win her favour, but once attained, the wild passion was quickly gone. The true joy was always in the chase, the pursuit and then the capture.

For instance, for years he had lusted after the demure and distant Frances Stewart. He was totally besotted. She had rejected him, wanting a husband and bedsports sanctioned by the Church, neither of which Charles could give her. He adored her, made a fool of himself over her and didn't care, bestowing his favours and following her around like a devoted dog. He even went so far as to have her sit as the model for Britannia, her regal figure in robed profile, holding a trident and shield and destined to be struck onto the coinage of the realm in perpetuity. But not even that honour could sway the cool Frances. Then the poor girl, married by this time, had contracted smallpox and her beauty was marred forever. It was she then who had done the pursuing, desperately needing the reassurance that she was still beautiful and desirable, and that she still held the King's heart. Charles, ever the gentleman, took her to bed and pandered to her need for flattery and affection. It was the briefest of affairs and in no time Frances, whom he had wanted with such a passion, was all but forgotten.

Queen Catherine knew, and so did Bella, that the King's favour was sweet and brief. One had to make the most of it.

Before leaving for the theatre one night Charles produced a large, shallow box covered in scarlet Spanish leather and lined with ivory silk satin. It contained a matching necklace, brooch, bracelet and earrings in heavy link gold studded with bloody cabochon rubies.

Bella's eyes widened and she sucked in her breath in a gasp.

He secured the necklace about her pale throat but couldn't resist letting his dark hand slip down the front of her gown where it found a nipple that hardened immediately at his touch.

'So beautiful! Oh, Charlie, you are an angel.'

'An angel? I thought I was the very devil,' breathed Charles, his mind not on the jewellery.

Her gown that night was midnight blue, the lace at neckline and cuffs silver, the ribbons on skirt flounces and elbows, violet and amethyst to compliment Bella's eyes.

The gems glowed warm and dark against her skin. They were worth a fortune, such a dazzling gift scrambled her brains. He was so demonstrative, so generous. Never again would Bella have to work. She was wealthy, titled and happy. For a fleeting moment the very world seemed to be at her fingertips.

That night at the Theatre Royal, Drury Lane, the actress Nelly Gwynne was in fine form. Pert, vulgar, unforgettable, she strutted the stage, enflaming male passions and making Charles chuckle. He sent word to Killigrew that he should like to meet the actress after the performance.

Bella raised an eyebrow but said nothing. One did not question the King, no matter the degree of dismay his request might have ignited in one's breast.

Beside her, that dashing soldier of fortune, Prince Rupert of the Rhine, squeezed Bella's hand and said in a whisper, 'Would the dear Countess sup with her humble servant tonight?'

She knew the signs. She felt hurt and not a little humiliated. She felt like a commodity rather than a person, a thing bedecked splendidly solely to please her lover, the King. And this wasn't the first time she had felt thus and questioned the worth of her own existence. The world might well appear to be at her fingertips but, in truth, what did she really have?

Fickle, woman-loving Charles was already looking elsewhere, captivated by yet another pretty turn of ankle, and had completely forgotten about Bella seated close by, trying to remain unaffected and keep her smile from faltering. She wanted to slap him, to say something truly vile, but one had always to remember that he was the King. He could damned well do as he pleased and there was no-one who could censure him. Well, very few.

'If His Majesty is otherwise occupied then, yes, Your Highness, I should be happy to sup with you. Charles?'

'Uh?' He turned, most obviously preoccupied. 'Yes, m'dear?'

'Prince Rupert has asked me to share his supper.'

The King raised an eyebrow, first at Bella then at his cousin, the older, heroic Rupert. 'I think not, m'dear, I have other plans,' said Charles, possessively.

Rupert bowed gracefully and backed off. Bella

sensed a reprieve. Mistress Gwynne should not have him tonight then, but inevitably there would come a time. Bella must make new plans for her future, and she consoled herself with the knowledge that, thankfully, she had fallen in lust with the Merry Monarch and not in love. She had never been so naive as to think their liaison of an enduring quality. She had lasted longer than many and had always looked upon it as a great adventure to be savoured while it lasted.

Prince Rupert was smitten and ardent. He kept turning up in the darndest places, ready to step into the breach left by a deserting Charles. But desert the King didn't, not straight away. Rather he had Nelly Gwynne and her fellow actress, Moll Davies, invited to party events, to swell the numbers of those who made up his intimate circle. Bella saw her with greater frequency but couldn't say for certain that Charles was bedding the wench. But then there came a time when Nelly, lewd and witty, was heard to tell a friend jokingly that when the King did become her lover he'd be Charles the Third because she'd already had two lovers called Charles before him!

At supper, seated next to her after some contrivance, Rupert covered her hand with his own as it reached for a fruit paring knife. 'Why wait to be deposed? I adore you, Countess., I can buy you jewels as dazzling as those around your slender neck, a bigger house, a coach-and-six, all matching greys. Leave him before he hurts you badly.'

She looked down the table at the King. He was laughing uproariously at something Mistress Gwynne had whispered. He leant close, his words meant only for her, his eyes ogling her considerable cleavage above the froth of lace at her low neckline.

Bella shook her head vaguely. 'When my time with the King is done, Your Highness, I think perhaps I shall be no man's mistress. Rather I feel inclined to be my own woman.'

He looked at her sadly, not put off, indeed more determined. 'A woman needs a man.'

'Much as a man needs a woman, or women,' said Bella. 'Mayhap I shall take a man as my lover, dear Rupert.'

'Then let me offer myself most humbly as your willing slave, lovely Arabella,' he begged playfully.

She considered thoughtfully and smiled. 'I shall keep you in mind.'

The supper progressed well, the wine flowing freely and the food plentiful and wholesome. At some point the King slipped away with Mistress Nelly Gwenne and Prince Rupert took Bella by the arm, leading her out to her coach for the journey to Parliament Square.

'Your house will seem big and empty tonight. Please, let me keep you company.'

She sighed heavily. Wearily she gave in. She'd eaten and drunk well, and really wanted to do nothing now save sleep, but she felt too drowsy to argue. And Rupert really was dashing and hard, a man of the world. And, too, she must not forget that Charles had now, apparently, strayed. She was free to do as she pleased. She'd always thought the seasoned soldier the most exciting, romantic fellow.

'Very well,' she said and allowed him to hand her into her coach and climb in beside her.

He made love as if it were some military campaign, a set play of strategies designed to sweep Bella off her feet and vanquish her most thoroughly and pleasantly. She was in the mood to be wooed and won so she let him have free rein.

Rupert was handsome indeed. Tall, slim, a Bohemian, his dark good looks were very foreign. He was not, and did not look, Anglo-Saxon. Also he liked making love with his boots on.

Bella had been coaxed to the dark oak, reed-seated day-bed in her drawing room. The curtains were drawn, the heavy velvet blotting out the moonlight, and candles burned in silver candelabra and wall sconces. In the hearth a modest fire glowed red and gave the occasional crackle.

The Prince had poured wine for her but took none himself, concentrating fully on the conquest of his lovely prey. She knew what he was about and his ardent endeavours made her smile.

He knelt at her side, kissing her hands a finger at a time, leisurely and methodical in his adoration. Turning them he kissed the palms, his dark moustache tickling deliciously.

Their eyes met and Bella's sparked with amused delight. His smouldered. The kisses travelled up over her wrist to the soft pale flesh of Bella's inner arm, and then his head changed course and he descended at her breast, nuzzling there.

He made noises of grateful pleasure, moaning. She found them endearing and relaxed back onto the grand day-bed – a present from Charles who'd liked impromptu love-making in the afternoons without actually having to go to bed.

'Oh Arabella. Lovely Arabella,' cooed Rupert, transported, as he slipped the gown off her shoulders and uncovered her full, pale breasts, the rosy nipples all hard with arousal.

He kissed them, nuzzling them with his nose and

taking them deeply into his mouth to suck like a babe. She ached deeply in her belly and felt her loins begin to tingle. Her legs, beneath the yards of silk taffeta petticoats, fell open accomodatingly. Her foot slipped from the day-bed and caressed the kneeling, attentive Prince's outer thigh, very lightly but heavy with meaningful invitation.

He all but gasped with pleasure, and catching her trim ankle, began kissing that, throwing petticoats out of the way impatiently, the silk rustling. Up went his full, dark lips, past embroidered shamrocks on stockinged calves, up over pretty knees and costly garters, to the marble thighs and dark, hidden place.

Breasts exposed amongst silk and lace, and skirts thrown up to balloon prettily about her, Bella laughed and struggled playfully as the Prince caught up her legs and hoisted them over his shoulders, exposing every fold and secret of her sex to his full frontal assault. Down came his silk breeches and out came a penis hard and angry-red with pent up longing.

Bella was damp and ready. She squeezed his shaft head mischieviously as Rupert tried to push it home. The contractions about his flesh were like torture and his eyelids flickered ecstatically, then he was past resistance and sank in deeply, pushing until he couldn't possibly go further. His eyes rolled then, showing mostly white and he mumbled, 'Sweet beauty . . .'

He pumped hard, Bella having to brace herself against such deep penetration. Oh, but he was good; as distinguished in bed as in battle! Temporarily she forgot all about duplicitous Charles Stuart.

* * *

91

Rupert wanted Bella to become his official mistress and wished to take her away from the King. But Bella told him kindly that she was of a mind to be her own woman and wouldn't be swayed. He'd heard all that before so he didn't altogether believe it. Every woman needed a man. She couldn't manage without one and she would come to her senses in time. Rupert was prepared to wait and prepared, too, for any unpleasantness with the King over this business; she was worth it.

Bella felt free, liberated. She was not the King's and not Rupert's. She could do as she damned well pleased, within reason, like Castlemaine, the Duchess of Cleveland. Her glory days with the King were seemingly over, but, in retrospect, they had been a great deal of hard work. Rewarding but wearying. Now she had the wealth and position that he had bestowed without the hectic schedule and the need always to be bright, accomodating and a constant bolster to a monarch's gigantic ego.

She took up with the fast set, Castlemaine, her cousin, George Villiers, Duke of Buckingham, and John Wilmot, Earl of Rochester, who had penned the wickedly accurate ditty about the king:

> *Here lies our Sovereign Lord the King,*
> *Whose word no man relies on,*
> *Who never said a foolish thing,*
> *And never did a wise one.*

They and many others of similar ilk treated life as one long social whirl, a never-ending party. They were lawless, licentious and downright bad beneath a veneer of aristocratic properness. Bella found them novel, courting the possibility of corruption she was open to new thrills and experiences.

The house was one of the great houses on the Strand. It had been built two hundred years before as a ducal palace. Its rooms were small, wood-panelled and marble-floored, its grounds walled and fortified and a barbican gate gave watery access to the Thames.

On party nights the pleasure craft and barges that moored there were too numerous to count. And at the main gates, crowding the cobbled forecourt, were dozens of coaches.

The food was light and fussy in the fashionable French style so beloved of the King's younger sister, Minette, who was married to Philippe d'Orleans, Louis XIV's homosexual brother.

The wine was plentiful and of the very best and yet by midnight the guests drank and spilled it like the most cheaply obtained beer or water, too drunk to care.

At one of the clock the servants were sent packing and the candles extinguished. The great house's curtains were dragged back and moonlight poured in through high, stained-glass oriel windows. The doors were flung open too, so that the frolicking could overspill into the garden.

The guests donned their masks and doffed their clothing. That was the only rule of night. What they did thereafter was pretty much up to them.

A certain duchess had brought her favourite servant, a virile blackamoor called Joshua. Also, from the court of Alexei of Russia, came his ambassador and entourage, for the most part seemingly bear-like boyars who were as hairy undressed as with their clothes on.

There was a delicious wickedness about being naked and anonymous. Bella mingled, quickly deserting those with whom she had arrived and dined, feeling her way around in the uncertain darkness. One could make out shapes but for the most part everybody and everything was featureless. Groping in the dark caused much merriment. She fondled a buttock here, a thigh there, not even certain whether it was masculine, and then bumped into a settee, staggering and falling into two bodies there entwined. She giggled and felt their contours, making a mind picture of the clutching legs and manflesh that pumped relentlessly into some drawing woman's puss.

'Oh, don't touch me! Don't, whoever you are, or I shall come. Shall . . . aah, I'm coming!' cried out the ecstatically dismayed female, sent over the edge into the pleasure realm by Bella's inquisitive fumblings.

Bella passed on, feeling for bodies on the floor and climbing over them. As she raised her leg on one occasion to straddle an obstacle, a hand reached up and cupped her, fingers invading back and front, leaving Bella a-tremble and wet. She would have come down upon the hand's owner but sensing that he already had a partner she extricated herself and moved on.

There was the faintest variance in the light through a doorway and Bella passed through it but was brought up short almost immediately by strong, entwining hands. Her breast was cupped and a head stooped with lips sucking on her nipple. Then the head came up and the man – she knew it was so because the chin was bristly – was kissing her demandingly and pressing her against the door jamb. He spread her legs with his own, cupped her splayed buttocks and hoisted her aloft, letting her slide down the oak panelled wall and onto his hard, piercing shaft. He was slim and juicy; she took him easily, enjoying the instant penetration and the race towards fulfillment. He teased her, stretching her a little and making the way easier for any who followed after. She loved the animal quality of this coupling, the way she took him to the core and felt him hard against her, bone to bone. He moved her upon his shaft, forcing her tight little puss up and down upon the length of his considerable desire. Very quickly he was thrusting like a maniac, finally crumpling in bliss, his body shuddering. His groans amused Bella. He sounded as if in pain, so vulnerable somehow in his moment of pleasure.

Her feet touched the ground again and she wandered off, her sex a-tingle now and in need of someone to soothe it.

A hand caressed her buttocks then came around the front and squeezed her breasts. She caught the balustrade of the staircase in what was undoubtedly the hallway and steadied herself, bending over accomodatingly. The unknown man slipped into her from behind, thick and nicely long, holding her hips as he pumped noiselessly. Rhythmically he squeezed her breasts, almost as if he were milking a cow, filling and pressing against her. Bella started to build quickly towards a pleasure crisis. She pushed her arse the harder against him, encouraging him to even greater boldness, until she was crying out. Feeling battered at her core she came in a long series of moans, her belly and arse trembling.

She lay back on the stairs. Her ravisher had gone to find wine. She relaxed, her legs open in the concealing darkness to cool her puss. Gradually her breathing returned to normal. She felt good, pleasantly drowsy and she closed her eyes.

Something warm and wet invaded her, slipping into her juiciness. Her knees came together involuntarily. Her senses were alive as her legs hit upon a body and once again the tongue which had roused her sank into her wetness. She grinned delightedly, let her legs drop open and then gave the mouth full access. The nose nudged her clitoris, the teeth nipped at her folds, while a wonderful tongue slipped into her and wiggled.

Bella shrieked and begged, 'Don't stop!'

The mouth apparently had no intention of doing anything of the sort. It loved her and caressed her, licking like a cat and pretty soon Bella was arching against it and holding at the full head of curls, wanting to keep it there, playing upon her pleasure button for ever. She came, then she came again, sated and licked clean all in one go. Panting, her hands fell from the silken locks and Bella collapsed.

The mouth, and the body attached to it, pulled away and the softest, gentlest of female voices said, 'I've always wanted to do that to you, Countess.'

Shocked, Bella sat up, peering hard into the darkness, incredulous. But the lovely mouth was already gone. She had slipped happily away. A woman! Bella was stunned. For several moments she just lay there, trying to digest the fact, then she shrugged, smiled and moved on.

There was an old, disused chapel within the house, its arched gothic windows spilling scarlet and indigo tinted moonlight into the vaulted stone room. Altar silver gleamed dully in the broken darkness. Bella was moving slowly, a little drunkenly, against her partner's swaying body, barely in time with the lilting virginals being played elsewhere in the house. It could hardly be called dancing. The man held a goblet which he passed between them, both sipping until it was emptied, then he dropped it carelessly, the silver doubtless dented.

Their bodies rubbed together and he came closer, holding tighter and squashing Bella's breasts against his lean chest. He felt for her pelt and fumbled, trying to join with her while they danced but he was too drunk. He sank to the floor and Bella went down on him. She took him easily into her wetness, rising and falling with sensual slowness. He clutched at her buttocks and stuck a finger up her arse, feeling the tightness as both passages were filled. She trilled delightedly and rubbed her mound the surer against him, going down on him to the core and grinding on him. He cried out loudly, his fingers plucking at Bella's softly fleshed buttocks, and came with much bucking and rearing.

She barely had time to catch her breath. Strong arms were catching her beneath the arms and pulling her purposefully off. There were several shapes crowding around her – dark, anonymous men, all naked and masked.

She brushed against one or two of them and feeling the hairy chests and thighs she guessed they were the Russians, though, diplomatically, Bella never said anything that might have made them reveal their identities. That would have been bad form.

She was guided to her knees onto the luxurious velvet of a cassock which caressed her belly and breasts as she obediently bent with arse presented, her body prone and her face lying comfortably sideways. Almost immediately an engorged penis nudged at her lips and Bella, thinking about it, decided, yes, she'd try it. She let it in, keeping her lips tight and sucking experimentally.

A finger traced the crease of her, from arse to pubic mound, then back again, slipping into her, then out again then coming up around the back and inching into her tightly clenched, unyielding arse. She wagged her backside teasingly. The big Russian laughed. He kept one finger in her and with his other hand he guided his penis to her woman's place and then caressed her bud. This was sublime over-stimulation. She groaned and pushed against the head of his penis which was only just in her and driving her crazy with the promise of things to come. He laughed louder and sank into Bella in one full, violent motion. She cried out. He stroked her bud, pumped fully into her woman's place and teased her arse. It was too much. Bella came almost immediately, trembling and quivering, her whole lower body seeming to throb. The Russian kept going for a long time, his staying power was impressive and his ministerings so thorough that Bella began to throb and contract about him again. He withdrew, slapping her rump which, she assumed, was his way of saying thank you.

Then the penis in her mouth was pulled free and the coolness at her rear was replaced by more warm flesh. She was tired now, almost too tired to care what they did as long as she wasn't called upon to strenuously participate. He used the last man's wet-ness to lubricate her arse and pushed himself home, laughing uproariously as Bella tightened and struggled in shock. He went in deep, so deep she could feel his balls dancing against her rear, while a hand came artfully to finger her folds and keep her happy. He shouldn't be doing that, she knew. It was wrong and a terrible sin, yet it was an unbelievable experience. With his fingers playing on her bud so skillfully she soon came again. He wasn't long behind her. She was exhausted now and wanted only to sleep. Almost immediately she began to snore so that she didn't hear the Russian call for a bottle of sparkling wine. He took a swig or two and then, finger over the opening, shook the bottle. In her dream she felt wonderful, her sated body cleansed sparkling fresh by a jet of chill liquid that burst, pressurised into her most intimate regions. When Bella awoke she couldn't understand why she was soaking wet, apparently doused with champagne.

James, Duke of Monmouth, was Charles's well beloved son. The handsome boy – born of the King's dalliance with one Lucy Walter whilst exiled at the Hague as a prince before his 1660 Restoration – was by no means an angel, but in his father's eyes he could do little wrong. James was given to political intrigue and meddling. There were those who said he'd be trouble one day for he acted like his father's heir apparent rather than his bastard. James looked much as his mother had done – brown hair and eyes, Celtic in looks, Welsh in origin. The King doted on him.

Just like his uncle Rupert he was smitten by the beautiful Countess of Hawksley and was determined to get beneath her skirts at least once. It had become an all-consuming challenge and was the first thing he found himself thinking of in the late hours of the morning when he awoke, and the thing that tormented him in bed at night so that he couldn't sleep.

He was beginning to get on Bella's nerves. She liked him well enough. He was prettily handsome and charming when he wanted to be, but she didn't want to try him out in bed. He just seemed too callow somehow, barely yet a man. Certainly he had none of the worldly-wise jaded dash of his father or, say, Buckingham and none of the admirable steeliness of Rupert of the Rhine.

She traipsed along a corridor through the palace, inclining her head here to courtiers who bade her good morning, smiling there when someone complimented her on the matchless splendour of her gown. Then, when she absently looked behind her, there he was, twenty yards behind, following her again. She growled and quickened her pace, speeding through the doors which liveried footmen hurried to open for her. She all but dived into the Queen's private apartments and came to a halt, sighing with relief. He wouldn't dare follow her there.

For two hours she, and a dozen other Ladies of the Bedchamber, kept the Queen's company, reading, sewing and gossiping about Nelly Gwynne. Then when the luncheon hour approached and the Queen left to dine with the King in the banqueting hall, Bella drifted off, wanting to return to her house on Parliament Square and change for the afternoon's outing to promenade at Vauxhall Gardens.

She almost screamed in frustration when she turned a corner and saw Monmouth coming towards her. Had he seen her? She thought – or hoped – not. She turned quickly and headed back the way she'd come, ducking behind the full length drapes that dressed a grand oriel window overlooking the Thames. She stood there motionless, barely breathing and expecting any moment to hear him pass. Instead she turned a fraction away from the view and found him standing there beside her in the bay, smirking at her. Her lips compressed and her eyebrows knitted. She did not curtsey but mumbled, 'Your Grace.'

'Enjoying the view?'

'I was.'

'So many little craft. So many little, insignificant people.'

'So are we all, Sir, surely, in the grander scheme of things?'

He laughed. 'You've been listening to my father expounding on the workings of the universe, M'lady. That scientific society of his is filling his head with all manner of confusion and nonsense.'

'Knowledge is never nonsense, Your Grace. Or at least not in the head of he who can digest it,' said Bella, scathingly.

'Come, M'lady. Would you have me believe you share my father's interest in the experiments of Newton, Halley and the rest of that eccentric bunch at Greenwich?'

'And why not, pray, Sir?'

'I should have thought a woman could find prettier ways to occupy her time.'

'Oh yes?' She sounded bored and tried to push past the Duke.

'On her back and in my bed for instance,' said Monmouth, grabbing Bella and pulling her close. He kissed her hard on the lips, then ravaged her breasts, roughly and without finesse, bruising her.

She gave him a stinging slap, and employing an old coffee house tactic, took a firm, threatening hold upon his wedding tackle. 'Let me pass or I'll wring them clear off!'

Showing sensible discretion, he shuffled sideways, his breath held fearfully until Bella let go and stormed off, her skirts billowing out behind her.

That was it, definitely it. She'd had enough. He'd made her feel cheap, like a whore and she wanted no more of it. Her lifestyle had become such that she feared she'd land up despising herself. She felt debauched and jaded and had lost her pride in herself. She wanted escape. She'd go and see the King.

Getting Charles alone was no longer as easy as it once had been. Mistress Gwynne was his all consuming passion now and she tended to monopolise him. Still Bella managed to get a message to him through Chiffinch, and that night was invited to sup with him. Bella was cheered by the promptness of his response. Evidently he wasn't as completely cold to her as she had feared.

The table was laid for two, the lace-edged napery spotless, and the silver candelabra setting a soft yellow glow over proceedings. Charles came forward warmly, took her hand and kissed it.

'Dearest Arabella. It is lovely to see you. You have been neglecting me,' he lamented.

That was an arguable point but she thought it would be foolish to do so. 'Your Majesty was most kind to see me at such short notice.'

'I was intrigued by the urgency I detected in your note. Come, sit down. We shall eat and talk. Duck or venison?'

'A little breast of duck, I think, thank you.'

He carved. He was wearing heeled shoes, stockings and breeches, his torso covered by a voluminous white linen shirt that was profusely ruffled and laced at the wrists and front, and unbuttoned to the waist. The darkness of his hair and skin were startling in contrast, as usual. 'Speak.'

She took a deep breath. 'Sire, I feel my time at your court done and have the urge to venture farther afield.'

'Abroad, do you mean? Surely not to my cousin Louis in France? Oh, Madam, I should be bereft. I would hate to think of you adorning his palaces at Versailles or St Cloud instead of my St James'.'

She shook her head in denial. 'Going to France was the last thing on my mind, Sire. Rather I have my eye on your islands in the Caribbean. My sister is married to a plantation owner in Jamaica. I thought I might join her there, who knows, maybe even find myself a colonial husband,' said Bella, lightly. Charles nodded, smiling.

'Your Majesty does not need yet another former love cluttering up your court and indulging in gossip and intrigue.'

He considered that and nodded unconsciously in agreement. 'Some of them love nothing better than making trouble and causing disharmony. You have family to go to, you say?' he probed.

It was a lie. Bella had no-one. But she sensed that to make the Caribbean more welcoming would alleviate any of Charles's worries, for he was a chivalrous man, a man of principles and, most times, a man with a strong sense of duty. His women could never merely be used and discarded. They were his family and he was always concerned for their welfare. That's why his court was full of them.

But, by crikey, thought Charles, they were a nuisance and a drain. If only they'd all show a little independence of spirit like the Countess of Hawksley! His life would be so much less complicated and his household so much more harmonious.

'Yes, Sire. My sister has written often begging me to go visit.'

'Then if that is what you truly want, Madam, you have my permission and my blessing. I like your show of initiative, Arabella. It's so like you. Would that my other ladies were of your ilk. Now, we must be practical. You will want to be rid of your little house on Parliament Square. I shall buy it back off you.'

Bella blinked. 'But, Sire, it is yours.'

'Not once I'd given it to you, sweetheart. Yes, I'll buy back the house,' he said, thinking aloud. 'You have your title, your jewellery, the money to come from the house. Then all you'll need is a pension. Yes. Two, no three thousand pounds a year for life.'

'Your Majesty is generous to a fault,' said Bella, delighted. It was far more than she could have hoped for. She was to escape from the corrupting influence of the court, and the King was actually going to finance her disappearance. She'd gone there that night solely to ask him, as was customary, for permission to retire.

''Tis a trifle, Arabella. Tell me, do you think I could talk Castlemaine into taking a like sea voyage?'

Bella chuckled. 'Somehow I do doubt it, Sire.'

His look was wry. He took her hand and kissed it on the knuckles and then the palm. 'I shall miss you.'

She met Chiffinch coming out of the King's private apartments. She'd always admired his uncensorious discretion. He'd always admired her capacity to treat her brief time as the King's favourite as a merry escapade.

Briefly, he laid his hand on her upper arm, cautioning in a low voice, 'Take care on the privy stairs, Countess,' before bowing Bella politely on her way.

She looked at him oddly but it was obvious that he wasn't about to be drawn and was already closing the door behind her.

Wall sconces lit the panelled walls along the way, but the shadows between were deep and the large bay windows concealing. Bella found herself moving cautiously, alarmed by Chiffinch's cryptic warning. Or maybe it had been no warning at all, just a general, masculine show of concern. The stairs were indeed well worn from centuries of use and slippery in places. Maybe she'd imagined the look he'd given her.

She was still thinking about it when she heard voices. They were coming from the stair-well. If she hadn't been walking slowly and thinking, she'd have met the pair of them there – Castlemaine and Monmouth. It was they the King's manservant had been warning her against.

Bella was caught in a pool of light. She was about to dash behind the curtains of the nearest window and hide again, but it was too late. They were up the last stairs and through the opening.

Their eyes widened brightly and they smiled – crocodile smiles. Chiffinch must have passed them on the stairs and heard them talking, or scheming, knowing these two, about Bella.

'Countess,' gushed the lady, 'as divine as always. You simply must give me the name of your hairdresser. Dear Jamie here is quite besotted. I'm quite jealous. One must feel sorry for the young man, especially when, it appears, you're being quite horrid to him in return.'

Bella was abreast of them but couldn't get by. The

105

Countess of Castlemaine was laughing unpleasantly and blocking much of the sparsely lit corridor with her windmilling arms and yards of skirt. Monmouth had drawn his sword. He seemed to have progressed far beyond the bounds of gentlemanly persuasion in pursuit of his goal.

Bella frowned disdainfully. 'Surely, Sir, that is unnecessary?'

'But with someone as rigid as yourself, Madam, it is,' said Barbara, shaking her head in admonishment. 'And for the life of me I cannot understand it. I told dear Jamie so. Bella Flowers is anybody's for the taking at those naughty parties organised by cousin George, but still she has the nerve to act like an ice maiden and rejects the King's own son. Such airs and graces, Madam. Tut-tut.'

Bella took a step back, another and then spun on her heel and ran for it. The long-legged James caught her within ten yards, yanking her to a halt with his arm roughly around her throat.

Barbara Palmer sauntered up, extinguishing the candles as she came, so that they were in darkness, with moonlight from the nearby oriel window affording the only light.

She slapped the struggling Bella for the fun of it as she had wanted to for a long time and, unstoppering a tiny glass vial, she held it under the Countess's nose. Bella's senses reeled and instantly she was spiralling crazily out of control. Everything distorted before her eyes and her assailants seemed to talk in slow motion, their faces twisted and grotesque.

Monmouth dropped his sword and levered the now limp Bella down to the floor beginning to unfasten his breeches. Barbara held Bella's hands above her head so that she couldn't fight or struggle, no matter how feebly. Monmouth was jerking at his penis, making it rigid enough to make an entry and fumbling with the voluminous layers of Bella's petticoats.

He was like a man possessed. Before him was the beauty he'd been lusting after ever since he'd laid eyes upon her. He was overwhelmed and went off in his own hand before he could take possession. He groaned in mortification and Barbara shrieked in derision. Angered that her plans to witness Bella Flowers' humiliation had been thwarted she slapped him about the head.

'Useless specimen! Imbecile! Is that it? The best you can do? God's nightgown! What a waste of time. Get out of my way. Next time you want revenge enlist someone else's help.'

She dropped Bella's limp arms and gained her feet, aiming a slippered foot at his bare arse. 'Perhaps she was right to reject you,' she sneered.

When Bella regained her senses she was alone on the corridor floor in the dark. She felt woozy and, when she tried to focus on the lights further along the corridor, there were two of everything. Her skirts had been hoisted up around her midriff and she felt for signs of violation. There were none. She was neither wet nor sore. How very odd!

Feeling silly and suddenly panicking lest someone should happen along and find her there thus, Bella got gingerly to her feet and started off, groping her way in the dark to the stair-well where wall sconces lit the way down safely. Her legs seemed to belong to someone else and she had the devil of a headache. Apart from that, however, nothing seemed amiss. She couldn't understand it at all.

Chapter Six

*T*he coach-and-four pulled up before The Mermaid Inn, the matched quartet of dappled-greys striking sparks off the cobbles with their iron shoes.

The lady within, who leaned slightly forward to peer out of the window and assess the suitability of the hostelry she was to patronise that night, was cloaked in black velvet and masked in scarlet satin, her nocturnal movements most definitely incognito.

She was expected. The dapper landlord of the half-timbered establishment instantly bowed and scraped before the black-lacquered coach door which her footman had opened with a practised flourish. He babbled a greeting, nervous and tongue-tied, and showed her in through the private entrance; she couldn't be expected to mix with the everyday customers.

'My wife, Meg, is at your disposal, Countess, if you need the services of a lady's maid.'

'Thank you, but I have brought my own servants. I left them sleeping in the coach. My maid, Hannah, and my blackamoor, Solomon. They shall see to my comforts for this solitary night beneath your roof. Also, good landlord, I should be obliged if my presence here was kept a secret until my sailing on the morrow. In London the King's mistresses attract the curious in droves wherever they go. Doubtless Bristol would be no different were word to get out. I covet my privacy. Is that clear?'

'Yes, certainly. Would M'lady like supper served in the private dining room? A fire has been lit in readiness,' coaxed Master Pudney, desperate that she shouldn't retire to her alloted bedchamber just yet and deprive him of her presence. He wanted to serve her, study her and have plenty to tell his neighbours on the morrow once she had sailed. It would be one in the eye for The Coach and Horses down the quay a ways. That establishment's landlord never ceased to boast about the two days Prince Rupert had billoted himself and his staff there after the fall of Bristol City during the Civil War.

'We dined at Marlborough,' said Bella, making his heart sink, 'but, yes, I should like just a little supper, I think. Some meat and fresh bread perhaps? And fruit?'

'I shall see to it immediately,' said the landlord, full of gleeful enthusiasm. 'And Meg will show you to your room.'

Bella descended to the dining room a short while later, refreshed with rosewater and her travelling cloak discarded.

Master Pudney's eyes grew as round as saucers as she entered the modest room where dark wainscotting glowed mellowly in the scattered pools of light from candles in pewter candelabra and wall sconces.

There was a royal blue and scarlet carpet on the dark boards and a crackling fire in the large hearth. He rushed to pull out a high backed chair for her. She smiled graciously. He felt the palpitations of adoration and blushed pink with pleasure, looking more than a little, Bella thought with secret amusement, like a perky suckling pig. She was the most divinely handsome creature he had ever laid eyes upon.

Her hair, falling in curls and ringlets to her shoulders, was glinting sable and her complexion was startlingly pale. And there was a great deal of flesh on show, Pudney noted with relish. He could see her neck, her swelling breasts with the nipples occasionally visible when she exhaled deeply, and her forearms extending from a dripping wealth of cream Honiton lace at her elbows. He tried not to ogle but it was difficult.

The eyes looking out from the mask were china blue, he guessed, not entirely sure in the false light from the candles.

She raised her eyebrows at his continued staring and he blushed, blurting an apology. 'I beg your pardon, M'lady. 'Tis just that I can't recall ever setting eyes upon a creature so lovesome before.'

She laughed and he thought it the sweetest sound in the world, tinkling, alluring and so bewitchingly feminine. No wonder the King had taken her for his mistress.

'Why, thank you, my host. That is most kind. But alas,' she said with cynical amusement, 'apparently there is. I am surpassed, my shoes and Charlie's bed already filled by another.'

Pudney shook his head. 'Surely not, M'lady?'

'Quite so. Her name is Nelly Gwynne and the King is smitten.'

110

'Oh, for shame,' commiserated the landlord.

'All good things must come to an end, my good man. I am not too distressed by events. He gave me a title and wealth, and many hours of pleasure,' she said with an amused wink. 'I am richer for the experience in more ways than one and, most sensibly, never made the mistake of actually falling in love with the man.'

He nodded, thinking her astute and brave in the face of adversity, as well as pretty. He was mightily impressed. Indeed he thought he might be falling in love!

'Now for supper,' she said, casting an eye over the fare set upon the dark oak gate-legged table before her.

'I recommend the pottage of eels. My Meg does them most tastily.'

She bypassed the eels with a grimace, chewing instead on slivers of roasted beef and fragments of golden-crusted bread, liberally buttered.

Bella enjoyed the relaxing solitude and stared dreamily into the red heart of the log fire. Her servants, she knew, were down below in the inn's kitchen, eating and drinking their fill. She needn't worry about them.

Master Pudney knocked and entered. 'M'lady,' he began with humble hesitancy, 'a delicate situation has arisen. A certain sea captain who oft uses this establishment between voyages has returned earlier than expected from a jaunt to visit his family in Gloucester.

'Yes?'

'Well, thing is, M'lady, he wishes to dine and he usually does so in this very room. The situation is awkward, I know, as you have asked for privacy. But he is a regular and valued customer. I'll quite understand if you – '

'Fret not, my good man,' she interrupted, 'Your captain may share my table.'

'Oh, M'lady, I am so grateful.' He bowed several times, smiling once again with relief as he stepped back out of the room and hurried down the stairs.

She watched him go, smiling with amusement.

Less than a minute passed before the door opened and Master Pudney stood aside with a flourishing bow to allow the gentleman entry.

Curious, Bella automatically looked up, impressed by the height and erect bearing of the man. He towered over her, as tall as Charles Stuart any day, sweeping the ground with the feathered, wide-brimmed hat in his right hand.

'M'lady,' he said, his voice deep velvet and full of seduction, 'my host has appraised me of your wish for anonimity and so, as you see,' he laughed, pointing at the black mask that covered the upper half of his face, 'I have entered into the spirit of the occasion.'

Bella laughed. 'Thank you, Sir, for your co-operation.'

'I am happy to play your game.' He threw his hat onto the caned seat of a vacant chair and seated himself with his long legs stretching out towards the fire. The black leather boots he sported were fashionably baggy and cuffed about the knees. His knee breeches were plain scarlet wool, cinched by a large belt buckled at his waist.

He cut a slice of meat and a hunk of bread to fill his pewter plate and considered Bella between mouthfuls. She made a point of staring into the fire so that he might enjoy what he could of her profile.

Master Pudney brought more wine then withdrew, wishing them both good appetite.

'More wine, M'lady?'

'Thank you, Captain, yes.'

They smiled across the table, her blue eyes locking with his. His eyes were silver grey. His abundance of shoulder length wavy hair was white-blond. His lacy shirt cuffs and cravat gleamed snowy in stark contrast to his black leather, metal studded jerkin. And his smile was as white as his shirt. It was a devilish smile, set beneath a neatly clipped line of moustache.

'Your health!' he toasted, raising his pewter goblet.

'Thine also,' said Bella, setting her drinking vessel clashing against his.

He drank deeply and she matched him, his presence igniting an instant spark of excitement that wouldn't be extinguished. There was a flutter in her belly and a moistening between her thighs. For a moment she'd even had the oddest feeling that she knew him from somewhere. But no. She would have remembered, surely?

They drank and they ate. He talked as he chewed, totally at ease. The Captain was definitely not a man who lacked self-confidence or social grace. 'As we wish to maintain a state of subterfuge concerning our identities, what shall we talk about?'

She shrugged her shoulders indolently, popping another grape into her mouth. 'You? Life at sea?'

'Nay,' he laughed, spearing a morsel of beef on the point of his knife,' I'm a very dull, uninteresting fellow.'

Her eyes gleamed. 'Somehow I cannot believe that.'

'Shall I talk about you, a bewitching creature set before me in silks and lace? Such glowing flesh, lustrous hair, come-to-bed eyes, lips like the ripest strawberries and, he reached out a finger to catch a droplet of grape juice at the corner of her mouth 'oh, so kissable.'

She was smiling and holding her breath, tantalised by his seductive behaviour. Obviously the man was a rake but she couldn't make up her mind whether she wanted to be seduced or not. The fact she was incognito made the prospect all the more tempting.

'But I talk too much.' He chided himself, 'I am, perhaps, too forward?'

She shook her head, watching him peel an orange and lustily devour a juice-dripping segment. 'Nay, Sir, I do not find you so. Pray, continue, if you've a mind.'

'But who can say such earthy thoughts put into words would not offend a delicate lady's ears?'

'If 't'were so, Sir, I should upbraid you and bid you talk instead of the inclemency of the weather this Springtime,' bargained Bella.

'I am forewarned,' he said smoothly, reaching across with a segment of orange and watching with an appreciative catch of breath as her pretty red mouth opened, forming an O, and she sucked the offered fruit in-between puckered lips. She chewed, giggling, with juice running down her chin. 'Such a tight little opening. Such a hard suck.'

He leant over, rising out of his seat with his blond hair trailing the darkly polished tabletop, to feed Bella grapes. Then he offered a peach after first taking several bites himself.

The peach juice ran down her chin and neck and then trickled between her breasts. He cupped her breasts and drew her up and out of her seat the easier to reach her, then he ran his tongue in the deep cleft between her perfumed mounds of flesh and up over them, to tease the nipples.

He pulled her gently onto the table and trickled wine from his goblet onto her breasts, which rose and fell rapidly now as her pulse raced and her sex tingled. Then he licked up the red flow, nuzzling down the neckline of her gown and sucking upon her hard points.

Her breath caught and she groaned.

He was poised over her with an orange segment between his teeth, so she laughed, loving such play, and raised her head to take the other half into her mouth. Their lips met in a hard, electrifying kiss and her hips strained up against him with sudden yearning, teasing the hardened length of his shaft.

He kissed her deeply. Crushed against her lips he could taste oranges. With his right hand he felt for the hem of her gown, dragging it and her several petticoats up past her knees, to expose her shapely legs in white stockings, gartered at the knees, and her pink kid slippers.

He smoothed the white thighs, cupping her dark mound and sighing at the feel of soft, springy curls, then he trailed a finger delicately down through her warm, damp sex. She opened to him with a shudder of longing and reached out a hand to caress his impressive girth of shaft through the fine wool of his breeches. She released the awakening serpent from its confines and encircled it, squeezing eloquently as he explored her pink softness with a gentle finger.

He kissed her breasts, her neck, her mouth, allowing her to tease the head of his shaft to the threshold of delight, then he plunged into her, deep and full, taking her to the hilt. She gave a little cry of pleasure as she cupped his neat buttocks.

He rode her deliciously hard, his pace leisurely, and she sighed with a broad and dreamy smile playing on her expressively animated mouth. He loved that mouth and fell upon it again with his lips, crushing it with a groan of masculine ardour. Suddenly he withdrew.

She cried out in alarm, reluctantly coming back to her senses. 'Don't stop!'

'Only for a moment,' he reassured her. He turned Bella over onto her belly and dragged her towards his engorged member, only her torso remaining upon the dining table. Standing at the end of the table, the captain caressed her tight buttocks and pushed into her once more, watching lasciviously as his considerable manhood disappeared into her softly accomodating haven little by little.

She reared against him, loving the feel of him and wanting more. She was presenting him with a delightful rump to study as he pumped away purposefully.

Bella hearing footsteps on the stairs, gasped, 'Someone comes!'

'Not I. Not yet.'

She laughed shrilly. Like a naughty child she was excited and afraid simultaneously at the possibility of being found out in mischief. 'No, Captain, I mean someone is on the stairs and will discover us.'

He paused and listened. He was deep inside her and she could hear him breathing in her ear. 'You're right.' He caught her about the waist and drew her up against him, with his flesh very much a part of her still, and then seated himself back in his dining chair to face the door. Bella's skirts hid all. There was not a second to spare.

Master Pudney entered with a knock, tactfully showing no surprise at finding the Countess sitting in the Captain's lap. 'I wondered whether you'd be a-wanting more wine, M'lady? Sir?' he enquired, bowing to each.

In unison they shook their heads, saying no, they'd had their fill. The Captain gave a playful thrust of his pelvis and Bella tightened her muscles about him. The captain drew in his breath sharply. When Master Pudney withdrew they both chuckled wickedly. The captain was holding Bella about the waist with one arm as he thrust up into her, while the other hand darted beneath her voluminous skirts to stroke her bud and bring her to a shuddering, groaning moment of the purest delight that matched the intensity of his own crisis.

Breathing heavily and still contracting about him as her rear quivered, Bella took several moments to recover and then disentangle herself from the sated mystery lover. She smoothed her skirts and neckline back into something resembling order. He buckled up his breeches and gave her a devilish smile. He bowed, she curtsied.

'Sir, I bid you goodnight, for I must admit to being pleasantly fatigued now.'

'Then goodnight, M'lady, and thank you profusely for having generously shared so delicious a supper with your humble servant.'

Captain Tremayne was up and away before first light, to take command of his ship and guide her out of the Avon and into the Bristol Channel with the first turn of the tide. The river pilot would already be a-waiting.

Before departing The Mermaid Inn, however, he took up quill and paper and scratched a hurried note for the lady of last night. He had to admit he was smitten and didn't like to think that she might only be his for a solitary night. He wanted to find out who she was, where she'd come from, where she was going to – indeed everything about her.

My Lady,
I cannot put you from my mind. I would know
more of you. Alas, there is no time for today I put to
sea and cannot tarry to approach you in person. Yet
if you be as curious about your Captain as I be about
your Ladyship, mayhap you will leave with Master
Pudney the means of my finding you so that when I
return we may be blissfully reunited.
Your devoted servant,
Captain Tremayne.

He shoved the letter, with its red wax seal, into Meg Pudney's hand as she dashed busily about her kitchen seeing to breakfast.

'See that the lady guest receives this,' he requested and gave her a shilling for her trouble.

'Course I shall, Cap'n. God speed. Take care.'

'So long' he shouted back, waving his wide-brimmed felt hat with the jaunty feather and then setting it firmly atop his head of white gold hair. He strode off down the cobbled quayside to his brigantine.

She rode at anchor amongst a muddle of other vessels, her masts skeletal as yet with no sail unfurled. Bristol's floating harbour teemed with life.

There were sailors, cargoes being unloaded by wooden, gallows-like cranes at the water edge, and sledges dragging away barrels and crates over cobbled streets too undermined by merchant's cellars to take the weight of waggons. There was shouting and whistling. Someone barked orders in a loud, autocratic voice that was pure, rounded Bristolian, and gulls screeched overhead.

'God's nightgown, Hannah! I should beat you for letting me oversleep this morning. I distinctly remember ordering you to wake me at five of the clock, so's we'd have plenty of time to breakfast and get aboard ship. Now we've not a moment to spare. We will have to rush, rush, rush,' Bella scolded. She pushed the yawning maid aside and shoved her overnight things into the oaken chest herself. 'There. Done. Now go find some porters and don't dawdle, or I shall be tempted to leave you behind to fend for yourself and be corrupted in this licentious, wicked port.'

Hannah made a face behind her mistress's back, not in the least bit scared by such a threat. She was way beyond corrupting.

Bella kept an eye out for the captain but he did not appear and ten minutes later they were negotiating the crude plank walk that bridged brigantine and quayside. Bella headed the odd column. She lifted her skirts a half dozen inches for safety's sake, well aware that every crew member on deck was stopping work to ogle her, but chose to ignore the fact. She heaved a sigh of relief when she felt the comparative safety of the deck listing beneath her.

Behind came Solomon, her blackamoor. Aged sixteen, he was dressed in peppermint satin livery

119

resplendent with military braiding, and carried naught but a black, leather-bound casket that contained Bella's cosmetics and patches. He was her pet; some people had King Charles spaniels, some blackamoors decked out in expensive satins and lace. It was the fashion. Some ladies, Bella knew, took these adolescents into their beds, enjoying the youthful attentions when their husbands had lost interest. But such licentiousness was fraught with danger, especially if they became pregnant, for how could they explain away a babe with dusky skin?

Behind Solomon came Hannah grumbling under the weight of Bella's sewing box and all the accoutrements pertaining to it. The porters brought up the rear, hefting the chests between them.

Back at The Mermaid Inn Jacob Pudney's wife ran from the kitchen into the taproom, exclaiming loudly and looking a trifle distressed, 'God Almighty! Help me for being an empty-headed lummux, husband, but I plum forgot t'give the lady the Captain's note. I just found it in me apron pocket when I searched there for me kerchief t'wipe me brow, meself becoming overly hot before the cooking range, you understand.'

'What be you yammering on about, wife?'

'I took the Cap'n's shilling, but I didn't do the deed.'

'Well 'tis no use concerning yourself 'bout it now. They be long gone and you have a head like a leaky bucket,' opined her husband.

Bella was leaning over a groaning, grey-faced Solomon in his cramped bunk in the cabin next to her own. She whipped a basin beneath his head just in time to catch the latest fountain of vomit that gushed from him.

She looked up to instruct her maid, who sat on the other bunk swinging her legs lazily. Hannah's face was vacant and a yawn contorted her comely features. 'Hannah, go to the ship's galley and ask the cook if he knows of any remedy for mal de mer. Preferably now, Hannah,' she snapped, as the slovenly girl seemed to find difficulty in removing her backside from its comfortable perch.

'There ain't no cure for seasickness,' she stated, smiling wickedly at the groaning boy. She felt malicious delight to see her mistress's pet in such distress. She was heartily sick of him being treated as something special, decked out in finery while she had to make do with cottons and homespuns. He was useless and did nothing to earn his keep. 'Nope. No cure at all. You either get it or y'don't. And if y'do then y'has t'put up with it.'

Solomon groaned the louder.

'Hannah!' Bella shouted then, causing the shiftless chit to scurry like a frightened rabbit out into the companion-way.

Hannah sauntered up onto the lurching deck of the ship, as sure-footed as the rats down in the bilge hole. She hummed a rude ditty she'd learnt on the London streets as she'd gone about her mistress's business, and she swung her hips beneath their plum coloured homespun skirts like the most brazen of the dockland whores.

She was a plump girl, all curves and roundness, her full, handsomely proportioned breasts causing a deep cleft above the straining white cambric of her off-the-shoulder blouse.

Her stomacher of black-dyed leather was laced tightly, the better to accentuate the ripe fullness of those breasts and hips.

She affected an air of maidenly innocence which was wholly misleading; the artful spark in her eyes gave her away on closer inspection. Her eyes of blue-green sparked with challenge and her wayward auburn hair hinted at the dangers of underestimating her.

She knew what she wanted: much the same as her mistress. To give the chosen men in her life what they wanted, but only if the price was right. In her lowly way Hannah wasn't much different from her mistress, or so she liked to think. It went a long way to explaining why she served the lady with barely concealed insolence, and why Bella continued to put up with it. Bella couldn't be doing with some vapid lady's maid who professed herself too fragile to undertake all the tasks that Bella had in mind. Hannah was rough, tough, discreet and loyal. She had no qualms about lying for her mistress or stealing. Only murder was out.

Beneath the railed fo'c'sle deck Hannah leant into the doorway of the galley, the heat from the cooking fire hitting her. Fire at sea was a terrifying prospect and so the cooking fire was contained within a recess encased by fire-bricks and metal. A bucket of water was forever at the ready in case of accidents.

The ship's cabin-boy-cum-scullion was hard at work peeling turnips and carrots. He blushed profusely at the sight of Hannah. He was bare-footed and wore no stockings, and his breeches and shirt were much mended. The younger members of the crew had been talking about Hannah and her mistress speculatively ever since they'd made their way gingerly up the gangplank. The Countess was definitely untouchable, but they felt they had reason for hope with her maid.

The cabin-boy was frightened and fascinated all at the same time.

'Cat got your tongue?' asked Hannah, arching an eyebrow provocatively.

'No; he stuttered,' ''Tis just that passengers don't usually come into the galley.'

'I ain't in, but I might be if y'ask me to,' she purred, draping herself all the more seductively about the doorway.

Her many curves assaulted Dan's senses and he moaned, wondering whether it was possible to die of embarrassment and whether she could see him swelling hard in his breeches. 'Come in, by all means.'

She did and suddenly he wondered whether that had been a mistake. The galley was tiny and somehow she seemed to fill it or, to be more honest, her lovely big breasts did. Dan backed off, getting as close to the fire as he could manage without actually beginning to scorch himself.

'What can I do for you?'

'Me mistress wishes t'know whether there be some remedy for her blackamoor's seasickness.'

Dan tried to look thoughtfully intelligent but couldn't quite manage it. 'Well now, cook he do swear by some remedies but they'm so foul, in truth, that your blackamoor'ld likely be better off not taking nowt at all. The sickness'll probably go in a day or two. Usually it do.'

'And where be the cook, pray?'

'He's down below in the ship's stores.'

'Will he be long, d'you know?'

Dan's eyebrows knit. 'Some time yet, I'm a thinking, aye. Why d'you ask?'

'No particular reason. 'Tis just that a body could get sorely bored without some diversion on a lengthy voyage such as we be on. How old be you?'

'Sixteen last month.'

'Ever done IT?'

He blushed scarlet and thought about lying, but she'd know, he just knew it. He cast down his gaze in mortification. 'No.'

'Well you're in luck then, laddy, for I do always let virgins dip their wick for free. D'you fancy it?'

Dan looked excited yet apprehensive. 'Yes, but . . .'

'Frightened you'll get caught?'

'Cook's got a terrible temper.'

'Danger makes it all the more exciting,' said Hannah, temptingly. She raised her skirts inch by inch, showing off her stockinged legs, gartered above the knees, and her white thighs and then, making Dan catch his breath, her mound with its pelt of foxy hair.

'Come on, m'lad, get them breeches undone and give me every inch you've got t'offer,' she coaxed. 'Ooh, look at that! What a beautiful whopper! Lovely! Just lovely!'

Dan came at her uncertainly, holding his hot, swollen member clumsily and not knowing quite how to go about things.

Hannah opened her legs. She held the boy tightly to her with an arm about his waist and took his generous shaft into her knowing hand.

He felt the sensitive head slide down through her wetness and then enter the most deliciously tight orifice imaginable. He slid fully into her with a surprised cry of joy.

'Now take your pleasure as fast or slow as you like.'

He jerked away hell for leather, dazed with delight and frightened witless in case the cook were to come upon them. If such did happen he doubted very much whether he'd be able to stop. In moments Dan was clenching his buttocks and stabbing dementedly through the final throes of bliss, his little yelps of pleasure punctuating each wave of crisis.

When he was done a smiling Hannah buttoned up his breeches as if he were a small child incapable of doing so himself and smoothed down her skirts. Cooly and calmly, she retreated to the doorway. 'Next time, if you've a mind, it'll cost.' Then she sauntered away, those oh-so curvy hips swaying, pausing only once to smile over her shoulder in his direction.

Solomon stayed abed, eating little, which was probably just as well because it didn't stay down for long. The cabin smelled of vomit and as frequently as possible Bella escaped above to cling to the rail of the quarter-deck and watch the horizon. She felt fine.

Day by day the weather warmed and the beautiful Countess gradually removed her petticoats until, eventually, she wore none at all. She was naked beneath her finely quilted muslin underskirt and lawn cotton gown. Upon her head she continuously wore a wide brimmed hat, or at least whenever on deck, being careful of her pale complexion. If not, Hannah warned, quite unnecessarily, she was going to end up as dark as the blackamoor moaning and a-groaning down below.

Captain Heathstone was a rather dour, uninteresting man. He sailed his ship, kept his log and generally steered clear of the dozen passengers on board. He didn't care to fraternise and left them in the care of the purser, one Samuel Stockbridge. He wasn't much interested in the well-being of his passengers either, but was obliged to make some effort. This he did to a minimum.

Bella, after the ceaseless social whirl of the English court, found life aboard ship very dull indeed. To pass the time she spent long evenings going through her trunks of belongings or else unwrapping and looking at her life-size likeness as painted by Peter Lely. She wondered what lay ahead in Jamaica and thought wistfully of all that had gone before. Her identity was known but Bella had requested that she be treated exactly like the rest of her fellow passengers so that her travels would be kept as low key as possible. Once in Jamaica she hoped for a simple, comfortable existence and perhaps, hopefully, a little romance.

To think of romance was to conjure up a mind picture of the mysterious gentleman at The Mermaid Inn. Then her thoughts became truly wistful. She'd probably never see him again but she knew she'd never forget him. So tall, lean and blond. Full of himself, and swaggering, yet, paradoxically, somehow self-deprecating. Certainly he hadn't seemed a man who took himself seriously, even when he did strut and posture. If she could find herself a planter like him in Jamaica she'd like as not be a happy woman. But, well, she was realistic. Life did you no favours; indeed, oft-times it had a nasty habit of kicking you when you were already down.

So she occupied herself with the trivia of her life. Her greatest decision each day was the choosing of a gown, her mind otherwise forever daydreaming, and her greatest concern was the watching of her maid's morals.

Not that watching did much good. Hannah was devious enough to know how to hoodwink her mistress when need be. The girl had a plan: she was going to work her way through the crew until such time as they reached their first port of call at Bermuda. By then, she reckoned, she'd have amassed enough in the way of valuables and money to strike out on her own. Perhaps she'd find a well-off husband on the island, or perhaps she'd open a little tavern somewhere on the waterfront. Her mind wasn't totally made up yet. The only thing she was certain about was of having grown bored of the life of a lady's maid. She was fed and clothed but it was no fun being – or pretending to be – a good girl. It took too much effort. Bad girls seemed to have all the fun.

One evening, after a particularly badly cooked meal that sent Solomon instantly head down into a bucket, Bella climbed the steep steps of the companionway and came out on deck, taking great lungs full of sharp fresh air. The boy was more trouble than he was worth. All he did was lay abed and groan, eat and vomit. He was supposed to be her servant, and yet it was she who was doing all the running around and serving. She had two minds to sell him, and thought that when they reached Bermuda she might do just that.

She stared at the horizon, scanning the birdless sky and noting how the descending darkness added menace to the deep, endless ocean. Their ship was good and sound, yet so far out in the Atlantic it felt about as substantial as a coopered barrel held together by naught but steel hoops. Bella longed for land.

She heard giggling and recognised it immediately. Frowning, she looked down the deck to the jolly boat. Hannah! Bella was about to storm over to the modest landing vessel and demand to know, in her most intimidating and imperious manner, just what the strumpet was up to when she should be down below looking after Solomon, when the giggles changed to raucous cackles of laughter and Hannah could be heard to say; 'Ooh, you bad man. You can't do that. It's just not possible.'

Bella's eyebrows lifted, her curiosity piqued. What wasn't? Just what were they doing in the bottom of that rowboat?

'But . . .' said a man's voice.

'But me no buts. You've had your shilling's worth. You want me to do more than suck you, it'll cost.'

The mercenary little trollop, thought Bella.

'How much?' said he.

Bella tried to place the voice but couldn't.

'Two more.'

'Two!' The man sounded incredulous, but he bit down his anger. 'You'd better be worth it. For that I want it on hands and knees, whatever I like.'

'Agreed,' said Hannah, as cool as you please. 'But no kissing. I don't like men with beards.'

Bella wracked her brains. Who had a beard? There were several candidates. However, she couldn't imagine more than two actually wanting to do it with Hannah in the jolly boat.

There was rummaging, the noise of exertion and then a great deal of heavy, belaboured breathing as the two of them got down to business once more.

Bella crept up. She just couldn't stop herself peeping over the high side of the ship-to-shore conveyance. She was presented with the full, hairy backside of the man who was rogering her maid. His movements were pneumatic, unvarying and forceful. He was deep in Hannah, between her parted legs and pressing hard against her buttocks. His shaft was withdrawing only to stroke in again the deeper, to stretch and fill her, and push at her core. Then he switched to her arse and Hannah stiffened momentarily, not caring for the impatient way he tried to shove it in. 'Oi, careful, you clumsy lout!'

Bella rolled her eyes but couldn't help smiling. That was likely the closest any man was going to come to an endearment from her maid.

Again they went at it with a passion, their groans in unison, and the very boat beginning to squeak and shudder around them. The man caught at Hannah's fleshy thighs. He thrust himself between them wildly, the thrusts shallow and hurried now as his crisis approached. His penis was so sensitive and his mounting passion so acute that he could think of nothing else. He was sinking deeply, repeatedly into his partner's warm, juicy depths. He cried out, 'God! Oh, God! Oh! Oh! Oh! Oh!' His voice was ecstatic.

Hannah was very business-like. 'Righty-o, Cap'n, now let's have your money.'

The Captain! With silent mirth Bella crept away again, knowing that if she encountered Captain Heathstone on the morrow she was going to find it difficult to keep a straight face.

Sex was a funny thing. You could go for weeks without thinking about it at all. Then something happened (in Bella's case the witnessing of Hannah's far from free but certainly very easy approach to men and the use thereof) and you couldn't think about anything else.

Every time Bella encountered Captain Heathstone, for instance, not only did she feel secret amusement, but she also recalled what he'd been doing with her maid that night in the jolly boat. Bella found herself hungry for a man. Though definitely not Heathstone. No, Hannah was welcome to him.

She kept an eye open but there really was very little on offer. The passengers were dull and uninspiring. There wasn't a handsome or personable one amongst them. She tried to make a selection from the crew, but they, on the other hand, were too numerous to catalogue. Some never seemed to leave the lower decks and others seemed to be forever in the rigging, furling this and unfurling that. Only the purser and those serving at table were frequently in her company and, frankly, she didn't fancy any of them.

She took to pleasuring herself but didn't have much success with that either. She was embarrassed by the thought of being caught and couldn't think of anything stimulating enough to focus her mind upon. Once upon a time she'd stared at Charles Stuart's likeness and imagined what a man like that might do to, and with, her. Now she knew and all the mystery and promise was gone. She could find no relief and was only adding to her own frustration.

She then took to long periods on deck to gulp down the brisk sea air and try to quash her, as she saw it of late, unnatural appetite. There was something wrong with her. She was sex mad.

At the stern of the ship on the quarter-deck, watching the foaming wake stretching out far behind the vessel and the sails full and crammed upon the three masts, Bella willed the ship on with all speed, wanting nothing now but to reach land.

She wanted terra firma and fresh, good tasting water, freshly laundered clothes and decent food. She wanted a better selection of men.

The wind whipped at her hair and skirts, flapping the material around her legs and messing her curls. She knotted on her hat all the surer under her chin. A gust came out of nowhere, taking the hat clear away anyhow and lifting her skirts to send them flapping up around her shoulders.

Bella gasped as she felt cool air on her naked buttocks and struggled ineffectually to pull the skirt down. But no, perhaps she wouldn't, not yet. No-one could see. From the front she looked perfectly respectable and, besides, there were only a handful of men on deck. One was scrubbing the bleached boards with Holystone, another taking a compass reading, someone else standing, his legs braced, with two hands on the great wheel that steered the ship, and so on. There was no-one nearby.

Bella gloried in the stinging coolness of the wind smiting her buttocks. She had a pleasant smile upon her face for the first time in many days. Ooh, that felt good! And then, startling her so that she nearly screamed with fright, a man slid effortlessly down from the rigging by means of a stout rope and dropped with a gentle thud on the deck directly behind her. So close did he land that Bella felt the whisper of his cotton breeches skimming over her buttocks.

Quickly he said, 'Don't be alarmed. I've got your hat.'

'My hat?'

'It was caught up in the rigging of the lateen sail, M'lady.'

Desperately she tried to pull some material over her naked backside and come up with a plausible excuse. 'That was . . . most kind. Fearsomely breezy, isn't it? I can't seem to keep hold of my skirts!'

'Bear me no mind, M'lady. Your arse is a glorious sight. Nay, don't feel obliged to cover yourself. You've gladdened this sea-dog's heart.'

She turned, smiling, curious to see what he looked like. He was a pleasant surprise. Strong and burly, he looked like a Viking. His naked torso was tanned darkest brown and his shoulder-length hair, his beard and the hair on his arms and chest were like sun-ripened corn.

She said, 'I haven't seen you before, have I?' If she had, she would have remembered.

'Probably not, M'lady. But I've been admiring you for days,' he said huskily, close by her ear.

It sent a thrill through her. And that was quickly followed by further pleasant shocks as his hands fastened upon her, one caressing a curve of hip, the other gliding, calloused but gentle, down between Bella's buttocks.

Immediately her legs began to tremble with reaction. She needed a man. Oh! How she needed a man! She corrected her stance and stood then with her legs apart to allow the blond giant access.

He wasted no time.

To any who might be watching them it looked as though Bella had asked him some nautical question and he, standing behind her in deference to her rank, was explaining patiently, occasionally pointing to the sky or the sea for good effect.

In reality he had released his lengthy member from his breeches and was drawing it back and forth

132

through Bella's wetness before finally taking mercy on her and pushing it all gently home.

She tightened about the considerable shaft and braced herself, loving the crafty way he held her hard against him, all unseen, with his hands on her hips beneath her all-concealing skirts. Now and again his hand slid to the front, to possessively close over her mound and run an exquisitely teasing finger in between her lips. She came quickly, then a little later, as the blond man plunged on without flagging and with unhurried delight, she came again. Only then did he allow himself to lose control. He thrust hard and quick, kneading her flesh with his big, rough hands and found release, stifling his cries in the hair at Bella's nape.

His name was Erikson, Runyan Erikson. His father had been a Norwegian sailor and his mother a jet collector from the beaches around Whitby. She sold the coal-like stone by the basketful to trinket makers. And that was just about the sum total of their intimate conversation, for when they met talking was a very low priority.

The next day Bella dragged a grey-faced, protesting Solomon out of bed, helped him to dress and then sent him up on deck with Hannah. Fresh air would do him good, she told him, and they were to stay up there until she personally came up to collect them. Bella had an assignation.

She went through the double, connected cabins like a whirlwind, changing the bedlinens and tidying herself just in time for Erikson's arrival at the end of his stint on deck as an able seaman. They'd have themselves a little loving before he took himself off

133

to his hammock on the lower deck and some much needed rest.

His eyes and teeth shone out of his tanned face and his large frame, in naught but faded cotton breeches, shimmered darkly with the sweat of his labours. He wasted no time, being as hungry as Bella and as unconcerned with false niceties. As he closed the door and turned the key, he inclined his already bent head and politely acknowledged her. 'M'lady.'

'Master Erikson.'

Instantly they were in each other arms. As if attracted by magnetism they were inseparable. The fair Viking carried her to the narrow confines of her bunk and lay her there, on her back. He threw up her skirts and parted her legs, lifting them up at the knees then pressing them out so that Bella was exposed with her mysteries unveiled. He knelt between her legs, took her buttocks into his big calloused hands and raised Bella's sex to his hungry mouth. He nipped and licked, leaving no fold unattended and no cranny unexplored. He teased her bud unmercifully and then delved deeply into her secret place as far as he was able, his tongue a hard, insistent dart that left her weak and wet, panting and writhing.

She clung to his curls, making small noises and gurgling, then throbbing uncontrollably as she came. She lay quietly then, relaxed and replete, with her legs flopped open with abandon. Erikson stripped off his threadbare breeches and came at Bella again, this time with his beautifully engorged manhood battering at her puss and sinking into her, deeper and deeper. She gasped with delight. Wrapping her legs up around his back she could feel his cods

134

smacking at her arse and his silken length thrusting in and drawing out, deliciously huge.

They groaned and clutched at each other. Her arms and legs imprisoned him in welcome bondage, keeping him close, keeping him in her, thrilling her, until they both reached crisis point. They came with little cries of anguish, as if in pain.

A pattern was established. The next day her servants were shooed out and, on the cabin's tiny table, she set down two glasses and a bottle of fine wine from her travelling chests. She perfumed herself and waited, though not for long. It seemed that she barely had time to pause and catch her breath before Erikson was tapping discreetly upon her door and Bella was bidding his stooping form to enter.

She handed him a glass and took one herself, downing the wine hurriedly. She hardly tasted it. He followed suit. Then they set down the glasses and fell upon each other, kissing and fondling, with everything done in fervent noisiness.

He kissed her eyes, her ears, her throat. His lips trailed around to her nape as his arms moulded Bella to his will.

She found herself down on her hands and knees on the bare boards of the cabin, bending over her bunk. She felt him at her rear, still kissing her nape sweetly but his hands snaking beneath and lifting her skirts. He unfastened his breeches and dropped them as he knelt behind her. Then he caressed her round, white rear, gazing on it delightedly for several moments as his fingers touched, explored, and played.

She wriggled it, enticing and excited – a wanton. She wanted him and wished he'd get on with it, so she rubbed her buttocks against his rearing, silken member. He was hard. Hard and long and warm as he guided the meaty length between her cheeks, down through her excited silkiness and into her woman's place.

He slid it in beautifully, to the hilt, with Bella contracting about him and crying out as he pushed home the surer to fill her completely.

He pumped as his hands delved within the confines of her bodice, to grasp at her full breasts and squeeze them rhythmically as he moved in and out. He thrust deep, impatient and of a mind to find quick satisfaction this time. He carried Bella right along with him, her passion matching his own.

Erikson couldn't get over her. She amazed him. She seemed to be insatiable and totally without inhibitions, though, with a body as flawless as hers, the latter was hardly surprising.

Selfishly now, Bella didn't want them to reach land. No matter that it would only be a short stopover to let off passengers and take on new. She wanted Erikson and wanted him all the time, so she cursed every day that brought Bermuda the nearer. With all the chaotic goings-on in port they mightn't be able to find time for each other. Bella didn't think that she could bear it.

And then, on the very day that land was sighted, Erikson had an accident and put an end to their amorous escapades once and for all anyhow. He didn't fall from the rigging or anything awful like that; he tripped over a wooden pail whilst, someone observed, he was mooning around on deck with his head in the clouds, and fell heavily, fracturing his collarbone. When they docked Erikson went ashore, there to stay until he'd recuperated and mended, and that was the last Bella saw of him.

Chapter Seven

*T*he ship docked at night and, early the following morning, while Bella was helping her incapacitated lover to pack his scant belongings into a canvas bag prior to going ashore, Hannah and Solomon scarpered down the gangplank, disappearing into Bermuda's sleepy dawn.

There were cockerels a-plenty on the island, crowing in the dawn, but they seemed to be the only living things showing an enthusiastic spark of life. The island slept on until the sun was well up.

Bella waved Runyan Erikson a wistful goodbye then went below, spotting the missing belongings immediately. That Solomon had run off didn't surprise her at all. Ever since he'd been thrown out of his sick-bed and made to go on deck and take the air (air which, incidentally, did him the world of good and cured his seasickness), he had been surly in the extreme. Bella had finally lost patience with him and, a day or so ago, she had boxed his ears.

She was surprised that Hannah had absconded,

but she shrugged philosophically and decided that it wasn't worth worrying about. The girl was an opportunist; she would make out wherever she was.

Actually, Hannah was, at that precise moment, wishing she'd slept in that morning and forgotten her ambitious plans for going solo.

Two hundred yards from the ship she'd gotten rid of Solomon, stopping and turning, to tell him plainly. 'You're on your own now, laddy. Scram. I don't want you along with me. I've got plans and they've no place in them for a useless, lazy lummux like you. Go on, get lost!'

Solomon frowned. 'But . . . but aren't you going to look after me? I thought – '

'You thought wrong, laddy. I've no time for the likes of you. All you know is how to eat and wear expensive satins. You're no good t'me.'

'But?'

'Shoo!' She shoved and sent him sprawling in the dusty street. Then she walked on and rounded a corner without looking back. Fending for himself would do him good. He should have stayed on board. She'd told him so. Some people didn't know when they were well off.

The men came out of nowhere. There were three of them and they jumped Hannah and wrestled her to the floor. She only had time to scream once, then a hand clamped over her mouth, cutting off further noise.

They rifled her clothes, finding her cache of money and valuables in the pouch beneath her skirts. The one who snatched it, shook it and beamed a bright smile as it made a pleasant jingling sound. They shared a congratulatory yell. Then they started to tear at Hannah's clothes, her bodice ripping as they struggled to free the skirts snarled tightly about her legs. Above the gagging hand her eyes darted from one unkept face to the next, panic rising. It was obvious what they had in mind.

Hannah was scared witless. She, the great manipulator of men, was at their mercy now. She doubted they'd be gentle. She struggled and resisted, but she knew it was useless. They were the scum of the earth. Slavers by the looks and smell of them. And they had all her money – her future. That broke her heart.

Two of them held her while the third unbuttoned his breeches. Hannah tensed, terrified, and willed her legs to offer iron resistance and to stay clamped shut no matter what. Then a strange thing happened.

The man poised to violate her, let out a startled howl of pain and slapped a hand to his stinging backside. 'By Barbarosa's balls! What was that?' he roared, looking at his hand, perhaps expecting to see it bloodied. It was clean.

He was hit again, this time on the head, and went out cold, keeling over atop Hannah. She shuddered and struggled under his loathsome weight.

The other two men looked at each other, at Hannah and at their felled cohort, then around the empty, dusty back-street off Bermuda's harbour. Nothing. Just white-washed houses with red tile roofs. One of them scratched his head, looking bemused.

'Let's get out of here. We've got her money. We can have ourselves a woman, any woman, another time.'

'Yeh. I'm with you,' said his companion, suddenly very jumpy as he clamboured to his feet and made off.

They got maybe ten yards, by which time Hannah

139

was coming up onto her knees and shouting,' 'Stop, thieves! Help somebody!' Then they too went down, still running, it seemed, as they hit the floor. First one fell, then the other.

Hannah could only stare open-mouthed. Her eyebrows knit. Just what the hell was going on? She appreciated the assistance but this was weird. Was God sending down invisible thunderbolts or something? And, anyhow, what would he be doing helping a sinner like her?

'You not hurt, Hannah?'

'Course not,' she answered automatically, then did a double-take at the sight of little, dandified Solomon stepping out of the deep shadow beneath a courtyard arch. 'Where did you come from? Was it you who?' She looked from him to the groaning or unconscious bodies littering the street. 'How?'

'I heard you scream. I had to think quick but I didn't have much on me, just a lacy handkerchief. "Solomon" thinks me, "make a slingshot; you know how." When I am small, before the big boat take me to your land, I see my father kill antelope with such a weapon. I play with one as boy. Not plenty good though.'

'Good enough,' Hannah said, not knowing whether to laugh or cry. She retrieved her worldly wealth and then hugged the boy tightly, kissing him feverishly on the forehead. He grimaced, acting as though he didn't appreciate such attention.

'What we do now?'

'Get out of here,' she said, taking him by the arm and hurrying off.

'I don't like Bermuda.'

'Me neither, laddy.'

* * *

Bella raised an eyebrow as her servants came back aboard at breakfast time. Solomon carried a large basket of bananas, Hannah mangoes. She asked no questions and they volunteered no information as to their whereabouts for the past few hours.

Solomon said simply, 'We went ashore for fresh fruit.'

What tosh. She let the matter drop. They were back and, she discovered with no small amount of amusement, they both seemed wholly subdued and far more obedient than usual.

By midday Bella's mind was on other things. The new passengers were coming on board and one in particular caught the Countess's eye.

He was an Italian gentleman, a mysterious man dressed entirely in black leather and silver lace. His colouring was dark with hair of jet but his eyes were deepest blue. He made Bella's heart pitter-patter and her belly quake.

Named Julius Pelegrini, he was on his way home to Jamaica where, apparently, he owned a vast amount of the island and was a notable planter. He'd been spending the Summer in Charlestown looking for a wife, without success.

Bella had never seen so handsome a man. He was perfect. His eyelashes were longer than any woman's she'd ever seen and his mouth was a sensually tight red line. She introduced herself before he'd even crossed the deck to the companionway.

It was silly, she knew, but he was so delicious that she couldn't help but think that here might be her future husband, a planter on the island of Jamaica. He was just what she'd been hoping for, handsome, wealthy and single. He was ideal prey, just perfect.

His manners were immaculately formal. He'd

bowed over Bella's hand as Captain Heathstone introduced them, his touch warm and his blue gaze piercing. 'Countess, I am honoured.'

She smiled winningly and warmly, wanting him to be much more than that. She wanted him to be charmed, captivated, and desirous to get her into the cramped but adequate bed in his cabin. She grasped his fingers and held on to them longer than was required, applying subtle pressure.

It wasn't the done thing but Bella couldn't abear to wait for him to make the first move; he seemed too rigidly formal and mightn't know how to. Why waste time? 'Perhaps we might share each others company when you are settled in, Sir? I am on my way to Jamaica and I would love to hear of the island from a resident.'

He nodded his head sharply, his look gauging her but willing however. 'It would be my pleasure. Tonight? My cabin?'

Bella nodded eagerly. 'I look forward to it.'

First steps taken, she had watched him stride elegantly to the companionway and disappear below. Behind him went his servants, two young men of like Latin origins, by the looks of them, hefting his travelling chests. They looked neither right nor left, as if they had no interest in aught about them, exhibiting quite superior hauteur for mere servants. Like their master they were dressed in black – black satin and silver threaded lace.

Bella bathed and perfumed herself liberally, dressing with great care that evening in cloth of silver and aqua. The quilted aqua underskirt showed down the front in an open panel where the overskirts were held away with swags of ribbons and waxed rosebuds. The neckline was very low, barely covering her

142

nipples, and quite off the shoulder. It was decorated with silver and lace and soft pink ribbons. She'd picked the colour with Master Pelegrini's liking for silver very much in mind and expected him to be impressed.

Hannah arranged her hair, fixing a diamond studded comb in the topknot. 'Beautiful!' she exclaimed when finished.

'I'm counting on it.'

'I hope he appreciates it.'

'I'm counting on that also. Though you don't sound so certain?'

Hannah shrugged. 'Just a feeling. Don't pay me no mind.'

'How can I not? Explain.'

'I thought he were a might cold.'

'He's Italian.'

'That don't account for it, I've met Eyties before. They're usually – '

'Animated?'

'Good word. Yeh. He ain't. There didn't seem to be naught going on behind his eyes, not for you. Kind of dead, like. He didn't look at your tits, not once, even though you had plenty on show! Not natural.'

Bella gave a scoffing laugh even while she felt a shiver of apprehension course her backbone. 'You're imagining things.'

'Maybe,' said Hannah. 'But be careful. I'll keep an ear trained. Call me if you need me.'

'He's wife hunting. That's a healthy sign, surely?'

'Ain't found one though, has he?'

'He's just not found the right one.'

'Or maybe no-one'll have him,' said Hannah prophetically.

* * *

One of his servants opened the cabin door, bowed and stood aside for Bella to enter. She swept in, her hand extended to the Italian planter. He was standing at a small table upon which had been set a salver of fresh fruit, a candelabra and two gem encrusted silver goblets.

Julius Pelegrini swept swiftly over Bella with his eyes, nodding with satisfaction. He smiled mechanically. 'You look wonderful, Countess.'

'Thank you.' She took a goblet of wine, studying him leisurely. Life at court had made her bold and being a king's mistress had instilled confidence; now she felt no need to carry out her own perusal surreptitiously. Her ogling was brazen.

He was delicious – in black leather again, his white cravat embroidered with silver thread. There were diamonds in the pin at his throat and on his fingers. She presumed the display of wealth was to impress her.

The evening was strange indeed. Try as she might Bella could solicit little information from him about his plantation in Jamaica. He was stilted and awkward, his behaviour developing an atmosphere in which it was impossible to carry on the openings of a flirtation.

Eventually the wine ran out and Bella was not invited to partake of more. Julius rose and took her hand to kiss, before seeing Bella the few feet to the door.

'Good night, Countess. I have enjoyed getting acquainted. Perhaps tomorrow we might take up where we left off?'

Feeling disappointed, her spirits lifted at that. All was not lost. He was interested. He was just slower than other men. Perhaps Italians were naturally reticent. She gave him a smile of encouragement.

'That would be nice.'

One of the servants opened the door. He was in his twenties, personable, handsome even and very well dressed for a servant. At any other time Bella might well have found him interesting, but . . . who wants beer when one can have the finest wine? Julius was the most devastatingly handsome man she had ever seen.

As if, almost, he had read her mind, the gentleman quizzed, 'Guido – you find him attractive?'

Bella was nonplussed. What a strange question. How did one answer? 'Well, yes.'

'Good,' said Julius, simply and flatly. And then the door was shutting and a bemused Bella was letting herself into her own cabin, totally confused. She had no idea what she was supposed to make of that.

The next night there was more fresh fruit in silver, new candles, trimmed and burning brightly, and a dish of bonbons to tempt her.

Bella drank, nibbled and sat prettily, devouring the man visually. He was so handsome but so reticent. He exasperated and intrigued all at the same time. Why didn't he make a move? She liked a man with will power but this was ridiculous! Was there something wrong with her?

They sat, he on the bed, she on the best chair in the sparse cabin, talking of the silliest inconsequential things: the weather, his tailor, the colour of his eyes which, he informed her, were the very same density of blue as the sitters in Titian's Portrait of a Gentleman. Really? She blinked, finding such a statement difficult as a conversation opener. She spoke in praise

145

of Lely and the portrait he had executed of her whilst she had been at the English court.

Julius, politely attentive, said, 'I should like to see it some time.' But Bella got the distinct impression that he was only being polite.

He studied her and, finding himself caught doing so, smiled, saying matter-of-factly, 'You are a beautiful woman, Lady Arabella. You say you were married once. Did you have children?'

She shook her head.

'Was there a problem?'

She gave a little laugh. 'None that I know of. It just didn't happen. And then, with some of my lovers, precautions were taken.'

'Precautions?'

She actually blushed. One minute they were talking about the weather, the next her ability or otherwise to produce children. 'Sheaths. Sheep's bladders or soft kid leather usually. There was a woman in Shoreditch who would stitch them most beautifully.'

'I see.' His mood seemed to lighten somewhat. 'You are a beautiful woman,' he told her again. 'I am looking for a wife. Might you consider?'

They'd progressed no further than him briefly holding her hand and now here he was proposing. It wasn't the way Bella had hoped or imagined at all.

She stared at him, unable or maybe unwilling to speak.

He pressed his suit. 'I can offer you luxury, servants to do your every bidding, wealth! Look!'

He opened a coffer before her. It was filled to the metal-banded rim with delights; bolts of silk damask, cloth of gold and silver, yards of lace. And resting upon so luxurious a bed were trinkets from the great goldsmiths of the Western world, ruby encrusted bracelets, emerald necklaces and hair combs, diamond studded shoe buckles. Bella couldn't see the bottom of the pile.

Neither could she help thinking about the other prospective brides in Charlestown who had been shown the hoard in the hope of tempting them into matrimony. They'd all turned him down.

If he wanted to marry her why didn't he talk of love or try to kiss her? She'd always thought that Italians were a romantic, passionate people.

'What do you say?'

'At the moment words escape me.'

'I am hasty, I know. But why waste time? You suit my needs very well and would be an ideal mistress for my domain. You'd want for nothing. Anything you wanted, it would be yours. A wing of the plantation would be at your entire disposal, to furnish in whatever style you desired. You could travel, once an heir was produced, go to Europe, the American seaboard colonies – anywhere you liked.'

She raised an eyebrow. 'But what about romance, dearest Julius? We seem to have left out the wooing and winning stage of our marriage entirely. I do not know you. I couldn't say yes, not yet.'

He rose and drew Bella up out of her chair, smiling warmly with his formality forgotten momentarily. Her heart leapt expectantly. She thought at last that he was going to kiss her. But no. He brought her hand to his red slash of a mouth and kissed the back of it, his blue eyes unfathomable.

'Until tomorrow,' he said, infuriatingly, and she was shown the door.

Forget it and leave well alone, warned Hannah. But Bella could not. She was uneasy, yes. But, well, he was the most divinely handsome man and she wanted a husband almost as much as he seemed to want a wife. He wasn't perfect. Who was? A few problems had to be ironed out. Bella convinced herself that she was up to the task.

The next evening she went to his cabin with high hopes, half prepared to give a tentative yes once she'd found out what made him tick. That was her objective for the night.

But he wasn't alone and his appearance, when she entered the candlelit cabin, quite startled her. She was wearing a gown of scarlet silk, and earrings, necklace and bracelets of rubies. He wore his black leather breeches, black, cuffed boots and naught else. Correction. There was a crimson cummerbund around his waist.

Bella's mouth dropped open.

His two servants stood stiff and formal just inside the door. One of them, Guido, closed it behind her. For the first time – whilst she avoided staring at Julius, thus giving herself time for composure – she realised how alike they were. She wouldn't have been surprised to learn that they were brothers.

They were slim and dark, with smouldering eyes, their jet hair curled and the front lock worked into a miniature braid that was secured with red cord. It was very rakish. They were dressed almost identically, in black satin and white linen, the lace of their cravats and cuffs stitched with silver thread.

'My dear.' Julius took Bella's hand and drew her to the familiar chair, putting a glass in her hand.

She raised a quizzical eyebrow. 'Are you going for a swim, sir?'

He laughed and sipped his wine. 'A sample of the English sense of humour? No, of course not – too many sharks. No, Marcus was giving me a massage. I have a little stiffness in the shoulder, a legacy from my days as a fencing master in Milano.'

A pity he didn't have a little stiffness somewhere else! The Countess raised her eyebrows with interest. 'I had no idea.'

'It was a long time ago, in my misspent youth.'

She sipped her wine and waited but he didn't elaborate.

'Would you mind if he continued?'

She shook her head. 'No. Carry on by all means. I am curious as to the technique. Your young man, Marcus, he is skilled?'

'I daresay there are some with more finesse, but he'll do for me,' said Julius, putting his arm around the youth's shoulders and drawing him into the light more. 'A fine young man, don't you think? More handsome a pair of brothers it would be impossible to find.'

Ah-ha, so she was correct. Bella mused over them politely. But, frankly, their presence was irksome. She wanted to be alone with the delicious Julius. His torso unveiled, he truly was delightful. A fencing master. Yes, she could well believe it. He was lithe, muscled and honed to perfection.

He lay belly down on the bed and Marcus knelt over him, dripping a headily fragrant oil upon his palms, and rubbed it in skimming his palms over his master's back and shoulders. Around and down and up and around pressed the palms and kneaded the fingers, leaving Julius's flesh pink and enlivened. He had his head turned sideways towards Bella so that he could smile and talk, not that he did much of the latter.

'Bella, dearest, have you thought over our meeting

149

of yesterday? Have you perchance come to a decision?'

'How could I not think of it? It came quite out of the blue and took me by surprise. But, no, I've come to no decision. And, anyhow, Julius, I don't feel this is something I care to discuss in front of your servants.'

His brow wrinkled. 'Servants?'

Guido laughed.

She was perturbed. What was funny about that? 'Why, yes . . .'

Julius spoke most condescendingly. 'Guido and Marcus are not my servants. I don't know what could have put that idea in your head.'

'Well . . . I just assumed . . .'

He laughed so patronisingly that Bella bristled.

'No, no, no. They are my companions and my dearest friends. They are like family and I love them.'

So at last he was talking of love but for the wrong people though.

'Guido, more wine for the lovely Arabella, Bella, Bella,' he said lyrically and sounding very Italian.

Once the young man had poured the wine he hovered at her shoulder, disconcerting Bella. She could feel the heat off his body in the confined, rather airless cabin.

Atop the bed Julius sighed beneath Marcus's clever hands. Bella felt jealous. Why couldn't the two of them just go away or disappear. Surely they knew where they weren't wanted? Alone with Julius she could work her magic and enslave him. It wouldn't take much, for she sensed that he was already aroused by the sensual touch of the masseur. She breathed heavily seeing those hands play over the lovely Julius. His dark, well toned body gleamed, making her long to be sandwiched between it and the bed.

Guido's hand coming to rest upon her bare shoulder made Bella jump. She shot him a startled look and shrugged beneath the touch but he didn't remove his hand. She frowned. Then she looked to Julius, expecting him to take the insolent young man to task, but he only laughed at her indignance.

'Divine creature, don't take exception. We are Italian, don't forget, and not so formal as you English. Guido means you nothing but respect and devotion. He wishes only to serve your needs, much as Marcus serves mine. Can you not relax a little and let him try?'

'I . . .'

'He is loving and very gentle. Let him ease away your tension. Go on. You'll like it, I promise,' he cajoled.

'Well . . . oh, very well,' she muttered quietly but unconvinced.

Guido oiled his hands, started on her nape and worked down to the shoulders. She'd felt perfectly all right beforehand but she had to admit that she felt wonderful after he'd been at work for a while. He had magic fingers just like his brother. What a strange pair – so accomodating and so silent.

'Nice?' asked Julius, his smile superior. She murmured a reply. 'Close your eyes; its even better then.'

He was right. She was thoroughly lulled. They were clever, for she never realised it. She hung in a sensual, tranquil kind of limbo, dreamily pleasant; she could have easily fallen off to sleep.

Julius was moaning softly, very obviously happy, his little cries becoming more audible and fierce. 'Ah! Oh, yes. So good my love – so good.'

Her eyes opened, curious and confused, then widened with shock.

Julius still lay on his belly. Only now his breeches had been eased down over his tight backside and clung about his knees, exposing his buttocks. Marcus was oiling them, touching between them with his fingers invading. Bella knew an instant horror and then jealousy erupted when the young man bent over the prostrate man and kissed first his cheek and then his mouth.

She gasped. 'What hell is this? Get off him!'

She tried to leap from her chair and set about the insolent lad, but Guido held her firm shaking his head beseechingly. 'No, no, lovely Bella. It is meant to be thus. They love.'

'Don't be daft. He can't love him; he loves me. We're to be married. Tell these young men, Julius. Send them away,' Bella insisted, angry and distressed.

'But I cannot. Don't you see? Marcus is my lover. It is he that I love.'

'No!'

'Yes, my dear. Listen on. Stay calm,' pleaded the sympathetic, persuasive Master Pelegrini.

But how could she listen and try to be rational and objective when Marcus had his hands all over the rear of the man she'd contemplated binding herself to for life? Even then the youth was divesting himself of his clothing and insinuating himself down the length of his companion's back. His manhood, dark, slim and hard, slipped amidst the oiled globes of Julius's arse and disappeared.

She gasped again and struggled. But Guido held her firm, insistent but never brutal, whispering in her ear, 'Listen to Julius. We could all have a wonderful life together.'

The handsome youth kissed her nape then her ear, setting off a shiver that coursed down her arm. He let his right hand glide down the front of her gown and close gently over a hardened nipple. 'Listen.' His voice really was quite hypnotic.

This was terrible torture. She could have loved Julius. Now she understood and was devastated and humiliated. She was furious that she had been led on and had been so gullible. What a fool! How they must have been laughing behind her back. No wonder they seemed permanently to be wearing those smug smiles!

The youth's penis stayed buried deep within Julius but he did not move his pelvis, rather keeping his loins quite still, his hands smoothed the man's back and shoulders like before.

Julius was able to speak quite calmly, though it was obvious he was in a permanent state of bliss, his thick, luscious black lashes fluttering eloquently over his intense blue eyes. Bizarre!

'I am a man of property, of vast wealth, and I was rich long before I settled on the island of Jamaica. I am also a man of a certain sexual persuasion – I love manflesh. I am devoted to Marcus and love him like no other. Certainly I could never love a woman the way I love him. I like women, however, especially you, beautiful Bella, so aptly named. You are a woman of the world. This may all have come as a surprise, but – I don't think – a great shock. You are not likely to become hysterical. Such did happen with certain young ladies in Charlestown when I put forward my proposal in detail. I even had to fight a duel with one irate papa and wound him just enough to render him harmless. You are too sensible though.'

Guido squeezed her nipple, making Bella draw in her breath. He was standing so close behind her she could feel his engorged manhood pressing between her shoulder-blades. It made it difficult to concentrate. Her emotions were in turmoil.

'You see,' continued Julius, his back arching with pleasure so that the arse rose to entice Marcus to begin thrusting, 'I have everything and yet I shall have nobody to leave it all to when I die. I do have a sister in Florence but, frankly, I wouldn't give her a penny if I could help it. She used to bully me terribly when I was a boy. I want a wife and the impression of normality. I would not be able to love her physically, but in all other respects she would be most cherished.'

'Then how?'

'How would I get an heir?'

Bella nodded, though she thought she could already guess at the answer.

'Guido.'

The hand at her breast squeezed possessively.

'I see. I would be married to you, but you would have Marcus and I would have Guido?'

'Just so.'

'Simple but clever,' Bella complimented. She was beginning to quake inside, with her bud tingling and her sex moistening. It was Guido's hand and the sight of all that bare flesh. She was hot.

'I am a clever man, yes, possessed of a high level of intelligence. That is what got me where I am today. Amassing wealth is not a matter of luck. It takes hard work and brains. Either that or you are

154

born with it. I was not. Neither were you. We are two of a kind.'

'And that makes us compatible?'

'It's a starting point. Well, what say you?'

She shook her head. 'Nothing yet. I am dazed and I must have time to think. And at present I cannot,' she said wrily, indicating the befuddling attentions of Guido.

'Do you wish to withdraw and be alone to think?'

Quickly she shook her head. She didn't want to leave, but she wasn't sure exactly what she wanted. For days she'd been teased by the imagined prospect of bedding Julius. Now that was presented as a complete impossibility. But what about Guido? Could she imagine herself living with him on a plantation, sharing his bed, making babies to carry on the name of Pelegrini? Certainly he was personable, attentive, and even loving. She couldn't think, couldn't decide. She gave an almost imperceptible shake of her head, completely confused.

Guido came around from behind her chair and knelt before her, showing commendable initiative. His hands crept tentatively beneath her skirts and stroked her calves, her knees, then her inner thighs. His dark head dropped to her breasts, nuzzling and working the heavy mounds free of their turquoise silk and cream lace confines, then kissing, suckling and smoothing them with a shaven cheek.

He was so gentle, quite lovely. Her knees fell open and Bella inched to the edge of the chair to let his fingers find her, gently inquisitive. He stroked, and sank one deeply into her, then two, working until she was very wet and quite abandoned. Then he lifted her skirts and pressed between her widespread

155

knees, unbuttoning his breeches and freeing his manhood.

He was slim, long, dark and veined, and he felt heavy in her hand as Bella clasped hold of him, savouring the touch of warm silk. She worked upon him only a moment or so. He needed no more. Guido put the polished head to her secret wetness and pushed it home. She was so aroused that it plunged in with ease and made them both cry out with the intensity of sensation.

He went in hard, clutching her about the waist and hips beneath her froth of laced petticoats, and thrust with measured pace and depth, determined to impress. He wanted her, madly, and had been in a permanent state of hope and desperation since that day he'd first spied her on deck. She'd only had eyes for Julius, of course – that was always the way – but Guido was sure that in time he could win her and make her forget all about the impossibly handsome Pelegrini.

She smelled wonderful and her breasts against his face were squishy – soft and pointy-tipped, so that he'd have loved to have died, smothered there.

She was crying out with each stab that he made, her toes curling and her fingers clutching at the satin of his jacket. He began to lose control, fired by her glazed look of consuming passion. She was completely at his mercy. He jerked and ground, he bit her earlobe and nipped her exposed shoulder then kissed it, he sucked upon a breast, then hugged her close, but always pumping mindlessly and mumbling words of adoration at her ear.

She looked almost pained, crazy with sensation as Guido filled her and thrust home again and again. He held her tight – tighter, crying out against her mouth. Their breaths mingled, their bodies fused, their very essence flowing. She throbbed, throb upon throb, each more intense than the last.

The two men on the bed watched, smiling and sated, their bodies entwined and their arms around each other. They exchanged a look of satisfaction, convinced that they had found their wife.

She tried and tried but she couldn't think straight and didn't know what to do. It was an absurd proposition and yet she couldn't deny that she was tempted by certain aspects of it.

The wind whipped at her skirts and hat as Bella stood at the bow on the fo'c'sle deck, the ship cutting swiftly through the water, its nose dipping and rising.

The day was sharp and bright, the wind cool, the sky and sea azure. Sails flapped then filled as the brigantine changed tack and went about slightly to capitalise on the wind. Orders were called up and voices shouted down the standard reply from the rigging. 'Aye, Cap'n.'

Below the scrubbed boards at her feet in some not-so-private corner of the fo'c'sle, where the crew lived and slept, Hannah was making the most of the final days on board. Captain Heathstone said they'd sight Jamaica in approximately two days if the winds stayed favourable. Idle men found the always available and willing – at a price – Hannah difficult to resist. She was uncomplicated and down-to-earth. She didn't want any pretence at romance from them; she just wanted their money and they knew it. Some of them might have wanted to be more to her, but she'd have none of it. Some time in her past one particular man had hurt her dreadfully and now she didn't care for them at all. The sex was agreeable, but the money even more so, it was the most important thing in her life. 'Twas, to Hannah's mind, all they were good for.

She was braced against a bulkhead, legs wide, making all the right noises of encouragement as one of the tars took her standing up. Another man passed behind him, just come off duty. He winked and Hannah gave him the faintest of nods, a tacit agreement to join him directly. The man between her legs, his breeches down around his hairy ankles, humped and pumped on, oblivious to her less than engrossed participation.

Oh, what should she do? Bella's head ached from thinking about it. She didn't need to marry anyone. She was wealthy already and pensioned handsomely. She'd never be poor again and she didn't need anyone. No – but then again she didn't like being alone, not all the time. She'd always imagined someone beside her in the future, even if she had no idea who. If she agreed, though, she wouldn't be taking on one man, but three!

'Ship ahoy!'

'Position?' Captain Heathstone called up to the crow's-nest.

'Four points off the larboard bow.'

The Captain extended his spyglass and put it to his eye.

Bella peered in the same direction, straining her eyes. She saw only a speck on the horizon.

Heathstone frowned, adjusted the lens and frowned more deeply.

The first mate hovered near. 'Cap'n?'

'Don't like the look of her, Walsh,' said the vessel's

master. 'She's still far off but I'm almost certan she's flying a jolly roger.'

'Might I take a look, cap'n?' His eyesight was better.

'Be my guest.'

Walsh studied her long and hard, his mouth thinning. 'I think you're right, Sir. It's a jolly roger all right. Red background, white cutlass and forearm, black initials set beneath – AK. Mean anything to you?'

Heathstone nodded instantly and went a shade paler. 'Aye. Abraham Keyho.'

Walsh, too, knew the name. 'But he's an out and out pirate! Not even a privateer. At least they stick mostly to preying on French and Spanish ships. Anyone's game as far as Keyho is concerned.'

'Aye. So let's be praying their lookout's sight ain't so hot today and we sail on undetected,' said Heathstone, gravely.

Bella heard none of the conversation and had no idea anything was amiss until the Captain approached her.

'Countess, I must request that you return below. We have been spotted and are being pursued by a pirate vessel. If we cannot outrun it, you will be safer down there.'

'Pirates!' Bella felt the chill of terror. And her fear seemed multiplied tenfold because of the confinement aboard ship upon a bottomless ocean.

'Do not be alarmed. We will do all in our power to evade them.'

'Can you not fight?'

He smiled patiently, as if Bella was a simpleton. 'This is a merchantman, Countess. Our space is taken

159

with cargo and passengers rather than cannon. Still, we have a swift ship and a well disciplined crew. We may yet escape them. Pray for us, Countess.'

She nodded. Her heart thumping and feeling ill, she headed obediently below. 'For all of us, Captain.'

The arduous game of cat and mouse seemed to go on for hours upon the sparkling blue ocean. Hannah and Solomon clung together sitting atop Bella's bed. Their eyes were wide and frightened. When the pirate vessel started firing at the brigantine, they began screaming and whimpering.

'Try to stay calm,' soothed Bella, who stood in the open doorway to her cabin, talking with Julius, Guido, Marcus and the other passengers.

Everyone was frightened and pale. It was plain to all that they would not be able to see off the piratical horde that now bore down upon them, gaining all the time and getting terrifyingly near. The crew were regular seamen from Bristol and Cardiff, Portsmouth and Falmouth. Only a handful possessed cutlasses. Doubtless the pirate crew would be armed to the teeth. The situation was hopeless.

'It's a hazard one takes for granted, sailing the Caribbean,' said Julius, sounding annoyingly blasé. 'Usually the odds of being safe aboard a British vessel are good.'

Bella nodded as if she understood. Though, in truth, she was hardly listening at all. Terror had temporarily numbed her brain.

'The British rule the waters here, their privateers preying on the Spanish and French. I've sailed many a time and never had any trouble.

'Until today,' said Bella, ironically.

'Quite,' allowed Julius, falling awkwardly silent.

160

'Will they sink us?'

He shook his head emphatically and smiled to reassure her. 'Oh no. Where would be the point? The thing is not to offer resistance and not to fight. I am no coward, yet I know how foolhardy such a course would be. Usually the passengers are of little interest to these sort of men – only their possessions. You must be prepared to lose your belongings, Bella.'

'I care nothing for any of that so long as they leave us unharmed.'

'Let us hope.'

When the pirate's cannons reduced two of the main masts to splintered kindling that littered the decks, Captain Heathstone knew they were vanquished and ceased trying to sail the crippled vessel out of trouble. He instructed his crew to prepare for boarding.

The enemy came nearer. They were visible on deck, swarming like an army of well-trained ants. They had boarding axes, cutlasses, crude pistols, muskets and daggers. They yelled and waved their arms about, intimidating those quaking in their boots aboard the merchant vessel. Nobody voiced it but everybody was thinking that they were done for.

The ships collided side-on, the bump sending the unprepared passengers below staggering and falling. Hannah and Solomon weren't the only ones screaming then.

'Oh, God,' moaned Bella, sick to her stomach. 'Oh, God help us.'

Guido put an arm around her. 'Courage.'

She didn't have any suddenly and was a quivering jelly.

From above they could hear the foot thuds of three score fighting on deck. Grappling hooks secured them to the other ship, while pistols were discharged and steel clashed. Men yelled and howled with pain. A while later things quietened somewhat and then Walsh came below, bloodied and shaken, requesting that they all come immediately up onto the upper deck.

Julius stiffened his spine and led the way.

The decks were a mess. Amidst splintered masts and torn sails lay the wounded, bleeding and moaning. Most of the casualties seemed to be amongst the able seamen. The pirates had won easily. The dead bodies were being thrown overboard. Relieved of their arms, the survivors of the skirmish stood in a dejected group, watched over by a ring of mean-looking musket-wielding men.

Standing, leaning on the rail of the quarter-deck was their leader, Captain Keyho. He looked almost reassuringly ordinary; quietly respectable in his dress like, say, the scientific Mister Newton or the diarist, Mister Pepys. When he opened his mouth, however, the illusion was shattered. He yelled at the top of his voice, making the assembled captives jump in alarm. Hannah yelped.

'Right, you voorking yellow scum, drop those weapons or my men with pistols'll shoot you where you stand. Now!'

The passengers complied like greased lightning. There was a clatter on the deck.

'You women are to remove your jewellery.'

Amongst the others Bella took off her necklace and earrings and put them into the hat of the pirate who came around.

'Where's yours, voorking bitch?' he yelled, pointing a black fingernail at Hannah.

She was so frightened she couldn't speak.

'She's my servant and has none,' said Bella, her head sunk down on her shoulders and trying to look meek. He seemed mad enough as it was; she didn't want to make things worse.

'Ain't she allowed t'speak for herself?'

Hannah opened her mouth. She could feel the money pouch heavy amongst her petticoats and was torn between the terror of being caught out in a lie and a determination to keep what she had worked so damned hard for. 'I . . .'

He rolled his eyes, exasperated. 'Voorking forget it! Put the jolly boats over the side. Captain,' he said disdainfully to Heathstone, 'see your voorking crew and passengers off this ship in orderly fashion. And be voorking quick about it.'

Out the side of her mouth Bella felt compelled to whisper inquisitively, 'What's "voorking"? Is he Dutch or something?'

'I did hear tell,' whispered Marcus, 'that he had a strict Presbyterian upbringing and cannot bring himself to curse properly, no matter what. Hence, he invented a substitute word.'

Bella sneered contemptuously. What an absurd little man – piratical acts were fine but swearing was not.

One by one the passengers and crew climbed down the rope-ladders to the jolly boats bobbing about on the starboard side. It was a lengthy process and at times the impatient Captain Keyho got tired of waiting and encouraged the odd crew member or belligerent passenger to jump overboard at cutlass point. Bella didn't care one bit for such unorthodox methods of speeding their unloading along and took care to draw no further attention to herself.

Eventually it was her turn and she lifted her skirts,

taking hold of the rigging fearfully tight, and pre-paring to go over the ship's side. Beneath were already seated Hannah and Solomon, and in the other boat, Julius and his young men were jostling for places in the unstable craft.

A crew member steadied her about the waist. 'Steady Countess.'

Keyho raised a bushy eyebrow. 'Wait. Back up here one voorking minute, thank you.'

Her heart flipped. She wanted to say, 'No,' or to jump but sheepishly, she came back on deck.

'What's your voorking name?'

'Arabella Flowers, Countess of Hawksley.'

His eyebrows knitted. 'Sounds familiar.' He lifted his cutlass and held the wide point to her breast. Below Guido protested loudly. 'Why should it sound voorking familiar, pray?'

'I have no idea, sir. 'Tis extremely unlikely that we've ever met before.'

The sarcasm wasn't lost upon him. He frowned and took it as a slight. 'Where's your voorking husband, the earl? Is that him, down there, shouting and voorking carrying on in the boat?'

She shook her head. 'No. I'm not married. There has never been an earl.'

One of his highly animated eyebrows now shot up on his forehead. 'Now that's a bit voorking odd, ain't it?'

'It's not common, I'll grant you, but it does happen.'

'Why'd it happen t'you?'

'My title was a special favour from the King of England.'

His eyes brightened and he grinned malevolently. 'Ah, I see. You were one of his whores.'

Bella shrugged. She wouldn't be baited as easily as

that. 'In some people's eyes, yes. Though I prefer to think of myself as his companion.'

'His whore,' insisted Keyho. 'His special whore, d'you reckon?'

'Doubtless all his women thought themselves special at the time. He held me in high regard, yes.'

Everyone else was in the boats now. Her servants, her friends and would-be husband and lover kept watching the rail anxiously, wondering what was happening. They could see nothing now that Bella stood on the deck with Keyho.

'Special enough that Good King Charlie might be prepared to pay a ransom?'

Bella gave a scoffing laugh. 'Sir, down below is all my worldly wealth. Also the coffers of Master Julius Pelegrini of Jamaica. Those two catches alone are equivalent to a king's ransom. Why be greedy?'

His eyes blazed and his stance became rigid.

Bella had known it was a mistake to make doubtful comment as to his character. It had just kind of slipped out.

He went to the rail. 'Cast off the boats!' he bellowed, then turned to Bella, smiling and bloody-minded. 'You voorking stay.'

She ran to the rail in desperation, but hands were quickly holding her and preventing her from doing anything so rash as throwing herself over.

Guido was standing up in his little boat, looking anguished and fearful, pleading pointlessly, 'Let her come. Take me instead.' He was rocking the boat; someone pulled him down and restrained him.

'Lock her in her cabin and put a guard on the door,' Keyho ordered the man who held her with her arms trapped behind her back and her breasts all but bursting from her bodice.

Chapter Eight

The brigantine, limping slowly under the wind power of its remaining sails, followed in the wake of Keyho's ship, the *Tortuga May*, manned by half the available crew. Orders were given and adhered to, Bella being fed twice a day but otherwise kept locked up and left alone.

At first she was frightened, then, as the days slipped by, she got fed up and angry. She felt the rise of her fighting spirit.

Three days later the two ships dropped anchor off Nassau in the Bahamas and Bella was rowed ashore for a meeting with Keyho. Nassau was one of several small islands that lay north of the large, colonised islands of Cuba and Hispaniola. Nassau and its nearest neighbour, New Providence, were established pirate lairs, much avoided by law-abiding, sea-going traffic.

Nassau was rocky and barren, a home to a handful of surviving scrawny goats that the visiting pirates hadn't been able to catch as yet to spit roast, and several varieties of exotic birds and parrots. It had little to commend it.

Bella climbed out of the jolly boat and waded ashore. Her legs felt strange to be on dry land. Her shoes in her hands she flexed her bare feet pleasurably in the white sand. The sun was merciless and the water like crystal.

On the beach was a shelter constructed of stakes and palm leaves. Beneath it sat the middle-aged, pot-bellied Captain Keyho. His dark brown periwig was hung on the high back of his chair. His head was close shaved. He had a tankard of ale in his hand and set it down with an uncouth thud as Bella laboured up the beach through the dry, impeding sand.

'Take a seat,' he snapped, with no patience, it seemed, before they'd even begun.

Bella sat opposite and stared at him across the table, eyeing the fruit there covetously. 'Taking me hostage was a terrible mistake. The King will have your head for this.'

'He'll have to voorking find me first,' snarled the captain. 'Men have been trying for years and haven't voorking managed it yet.'

'Well, this time you've gone too far. No one steals away a British Countess and gets away with it. Especially not when she's a Countess so highly thought of in royal circles. If you had any sense you'd forget this hare-brained scheme of a ransom and take me to Jamaica yourself. They might be more lenient with you then. Hell, you can keep my possessions, just let me go, like the decent fellow I'm certain you are deep down.'

He'd been sipping beer and watching Bella over the rim of the pewter tankard, his eyebrows dancing on his forehead. 'Bah!' he roared and banged it down on the table. The foamy head splashed all ways and Bella jumped despite herself. 'By God, you've got a voorking runaway mouth! Do yourself a voorking favour and keep it buttoned 'til I says otherwise. Ransomed I said and ransomed I intends. That royal popinjay, Charles Stuart, pays me five thousand guineas or I lets me crew have you, yes indeedy.'

Her mouth thinned. 'You wouldn't dare. If one hair on my head is harmed you'll swing, my good man.'

Keyho laughed. 'Where's the means to stop me? I don't see no voorking king's men a-coming to your rescue, Countess,' he sneered.

'Harm me in any way and I promise you they'll not be long in coming. They'd stop at nothing to find you. And when they did they'd take you back to England – to Tilbury Point or Bristol Docks, and there, if you were lucky, they'd simply hang you. Then again, if my Charles was really angry, they'd hang, draw and quarter you instead, then gibbet you,' Bella promised.

Keyho looked far from impressed or intimidated. 'If there's one thing I cannot stomach its a woman who doesn't know when to voorking shut up,' he muttered, tearing a rather unripe looking banana from a bunch on the wooden trencher on the table and forcing it into her mouth.

With a forward tossing of her head and violent expelling of air from her lungs, she launched it back at him, hitting the pirate smack in the eye.

He went livid, sputtering to the unfortunate man who seemed to have been lumbered with the task of looking after her and playing gaoler. 'Take her away! Anywhere! Just out of my sight!'

* * *

168

They remained on Nassau for a week and more, the captured brigantine and *Tortuga May* beached and careened to clean away the barnacles and help prevent the infestation of Toredo worms. The worms thrived in tropical waters and could riddle an unprotected hull, making the ship unseaworthy. Protecting the hull with a noxious coating of tar, tallow and sulphur seemed to do the trick.

While the ships were being treated, Keyho occupied his time with drafts of his ransom letter. Each time he wrote it the amount increased until, by day five, Bella wouldn't be set free for less than fifteen thousand golden guineas and a knighthood for himself!

She began to think that he was either very stupid or mad. If they ever departed and passed the demand to an England-bound vessel for transit, she expected it, by then, to be a thing very much suited to the realm of fantasy and naught else. Like as not Charles would think it a ridiculous hoax and ignore it. What then? She didn't want to think about that. Just as she didn't want to think about Hannah, Solomon, Julius, Guido and Marcus, her friends, safe now, she hoped. Safe while she was stranded on an island with a bunch of, to say the least, unpredictable pirates. Things could turn very nasty at any time. But no, she wasn't going to cry, dammit.

Better to spend her time observing Captain Keyho's reunion with his wife. It was so interesting that at times Bella could actually forget her own predicament. Occupied with the other woman, at least he was sparing Bella his company. That certainly was no bad thing.

Chastity Wise, who insisted on keeping her maiden name, saw to his creature comforts ashore.

With his crew he was a harsh, unapproachable misery; with Chastity he was a pussy-cat.

She functioned just as if she was living in a cottage overlooking Plymouth Harbour – cooking, cleaning, mending his clothes, scolding him and taking as much care of Keyho's mortal soul as she was able. It was weird indeed to watch the woman dusting about a haphazard shelter made from stakes, cane and palm leaves. Bella couldn't help but wonder whether she was stupid or mad too.

Chastity Wise ignored the other women on Nassau completely. It was as if they didn't exist at all. For her there was only Abraham Keyho – pleasing him and keeping him in line. Nothing else mattered. The fact that her husband was a pirate seemed to be of no interest to her whatsoever. Food for the table and clothes for their backs, these were the important things in life. His living was his business, man's work. From the periphery this made for great entertainment.

Chastity was a big girl, tall, heavy and severe, with her dull brown hair braided and pinned most unbecomingly at her crown. Her permanently rolled-up sleeves gave her the look of someone spoiling for a fight. Oft-times she was.

Keyho, being the centre of her simple little universe, received all her attention, pleasant and otherwise. And, because no one else existed as far as she was concerned, only Keyho suffered her temper.

The first time it had erupted, Bella, sheltering nearby and clearly able to observe, had expected Keyho to reply to the woman's diatribe in time honoured tradition by cuffing her. He'd done no such thing. He cowered visibly, backing off and trying to make himself as small a target as possible for her verbal attack and physical intimidation.

She'd advanced, much bigger than he, looming. 'What do you mean there's not enough salt in the stew, eh?' she demanded, daring him to argue.

'I, oh . . . I only thought . . . But, no, you're right, of course, my precious.' He took another spoonful and pulled an ecstatic face. 'Yes, plenty of salt really, my flower.'

Bella was left speechless, not that she had anyone to talk to. It was the first time she had smiled in days. Thereafter the light moments came thick and fast, sometimes at the rate of one per hour or so.

Captain Keyho couldn't do anything right and Chastity snarled and snapped at him continuously. If he wasn't so obnoxious Bella might even have felt sorry for him. For the life of her she couldn't understand why he put up with it. The Caribbean was full of fetching females happy to latch onto a man with money, even one as unappetising as Keyho. But Keyho seemed to be crazy about the woman and had eyes only for her. And that too was another misdemeanour.

One time she was plucking and drawing a chicken, with blood and muck up to her elbows, and Keyho was sitting at table in their open-fronted shelter that faced onto the beach, watching her adoringly. He was getting hot under the collar.

Her strong arms made easy work of the task and her vast bosom wobbled within the confines of her plain cotton, scoop-necked blouse. Keyho was mesmerised and couldn't take his eyes off her.

She looked up from the task and caught the furtive glance. She hurled the chicken giblets at him. 'What you staring at with that wicked glint in your eye?'

He shook his head in denial, his mouth looking dry.

'You were! You were staring. I seen you plain as day, Abraham Keyho. You be asking for a licking the way you be carrying on,' she threatened.

'No!' he screeched, shrilly, jarring on Bella's ears.

'Then you just be minding where you fasten your stare in future. Be warned.'

It was extraordinary. She had reduced him to a jibbering wreck.

When eventually the meal was put on the table before him Abraham Keyho had lost his appetite he was that unsettled, and then, of course, Chastity had yet another gripe to take him to task for. But she'd gone past the threatening stage. This time she reached up on the wall at the side of the table and took down a whip. It was a nifty thing. Not much longer than a riding crop, its tapering end steel-tipped. Keyho began to cry like a baby.

'Everything off,' snarled Chastity. 'Yes, everything. Don't think to keep your shirt. And hurry up. The more you delay, the more I shall punish.'

He whimpered, stripping frantically and cowering on all fours on the rush matting. The whip flicked over his buttocks, catching him like a whisper and made him squeal.

Outside Bella watched, hearing the chuckles of those pirates who passed by and lingered. Evidently this sort of thing happened all the time and was a great source of amusement to Keyho's men. Likely they also saw it as divine retribution for the miserable time they had at sea with him.

Back inside, Keyho quivered on the floor, turning this way and that – on his knees one moment, his back the next. Chastity straddled him, thrashing his belly and thighs, all around his engorged, wagging penis. Either she didn't notice it, or chose to ignore it. She thrashed and he bucked, able to see right up beneath her skirts, to a great rear and a plump, pelted mound. Such a glorious sight and the horrid pain always did the trick. His eyes rolled and he exploded in a ball of pleasure-agony, crying out in a protracted howl.

They lay belly down in a circle on the beach, listening to the waves breaking on the shore and pointing out the stars to Bella, trying to impress. Not all the pirates were so bad. This bunch were moderate; for the most part slavers who'd had enough of that disgusting profession. They had jumped ship off the infamous blackbirds – their own name for slaving vessels – and joined Keyho. Pirate and privateer vessels were full of such men. They worked cheap and demanded few benefits. Constantly told that they were the scum of the earth, they had come to believe it and oft-times acted accordingly.

One of them held out a dark green bottle. 'More ruination?'

'Don't mind if I do,' said Bella, daintily swigging at the rum. It was dark, red and exceedingly strong, and felt like fire all the way down. 'Is your captain always that way with Mistress Wise?'

Davy Billings chuckled. 'Oh, aye. Its voorking this and voorking that when he talks to the likes of us. But with his dear Chastity 'tis my lamb and my sweet. Enough t' turn a man's stomach.'

George Derbyshire took a nip and passed the liquor on. 'Aye. He's nigh on fearless with everyone except-ing her.'

'So why's he put up with it?'

'Worships her.'

'Aye, that he do.'

'And the worse she is the more he do love her.'

'Tis a fact.'

The night was so sultry Bella needed no blanket, sleeping beneath a palm at the treeline on the beach. The men lay nearby, scattered and snoring, some heavily comatosed by rum.

Davy Billings couldn't sleep and couldn't take his eyes off her. She lay on her side, her breasts lolling and a hip thrust up beneath the turqoise taffeta silk of her gown. He watched the rise and fall of her breathing and the globes of flesh almost spilling from the deep scoop of the lace-trimmed neckline. Watching was rapture and torture. He groaned and closed his eyes, but they worked open again and somehow he was spying once more, even though he didn't want to and even though it brought nothing but frustration.

He was twenty-six, a Bristol man, who, when times were hard, had forsaken a normal seaman's life to act as mate aboard a blackbirder. But he hadn't been able to stomach it long. He still got nightmares about it and the smell seemed to be forever up his nose. Three Bristol Triangles (Africa, the Caribbean, then home) had been his limit, then he'd jumped ship in Bermuda and survived from hand to mouth for several months before finally signing his mark as one of Keyho's crew. Playing gaoler to the Countess of Hawksley was the finest job he'd ever had.

He was hard in his breeches and had been for ages, it seemed. He unbuttoned himself to let the heavy, unwieldy shaft spring free. He didn't know what to do with it, so he took hold of it and thought to give himself relief.

Bella moved and threw up an arm above her head, causing her breast to rise and spill out of her gown, the soft nipple rosy in the tropical moonlight.

Billings' breath caught and his head moved, gently and leisurely, as he watched.

A while later, as he still caressed his steely length, with his eyes riveted to her, Bella moved again and turned over, her limbs thrashing restlessly. She scratched at a buttock with her hand beneath her skirt, and then sighed, lost deep in her dream world.

She had her back to him, with her skirt up, exposing most of her upper thigh and a glimpse of buttock.

He couldn't stop himself. He moved closer, lying down the length of her back, barely touching, his fingertips caressing her hip and smoothing her thigh.

She roused languidly. 'I was having a lovely dream,' she murmured. 'That you, Billings?'

'Aye,' he admitted fearfully.

She smiled unseen in the darkness. Billings was a handsome young man, wholesome too, compared to some of the others.

'I was dreaming that a stranger snuggled close to me on the beach and took me oh, so sweetly while I half slept,' purred Bella, full of enticement.

'You'd not be outraged?'

'Not if he did a real good job of pleasuring me. I dreamt I just let my top leg fall forward and the man could feel me then, my place all damp and warm and welcoming . . .'

His fingers were exploring tentatively in an instant and finding her just so – warm, sticky and tight. The same hand came up and took temporary possession of the escaped breast. He murmured.

He guided the head of his heavily swollen penis to

her spot and worked it in with difficulty. She had to raise her leg slightly to allow penetration. Then it slipped in and he groaned, feeling it slide all the way. Holding his hand at the front he cupped her mound and played on her bud. He was all inside, huge, his movements slow and deep. Bella sighed dreamily, already throbbing as he pumped on, always at fever pitch but not striving frantically to reach his goal. He had all night. He might never have such an opportunity again. He should have liked to take the Countess on her back, to penetrate her deep and show her what a fine lover he was. But fucking her in this manner was so much more discreet. To any who might casually look their way, he appeared merely to be sleeping rather closer than protocol deemed appropriate. It was only if one looked more closely that his thrusting, jerking movements could be detected and his real activity deduced.

The pirate food was pretty miserable. After a couple of days of it Bella had had enough and stormed over to Keyho's rustic shelter on the beach.

She looked little like a Countess now. Her dress was limp and messed and her hair was sticky with brine, a tangled, uncombed mane after a rinse in the sea.

Unannounced, she stepped up onto the boards of the dwelling, startling both the captain and his doxy at table. Upon the crude surface sat roasted fowl, fruit and some half-way decent looking bread. Chastity was no baker, but it looked edible. Certainly they were eating better than Bella.

'Captain.' She all but threw her plate down onto the table, drawing his attention to a mess of hard beans, unseasoned boiled rice and some unrecognisable scraps of meat. 'I simply won't put up with this any longer. This food is swill. It's muck! You do not eat it. Do not ask me to do so!'

Chastity stared, incredulous. Bella took Keyho's own plate upon which he'd placed carved slivers of breast meat and a hefty leg from the bird, she tore off a chunk of bread and added that and an apple.

They reacted slowly, completely taken by surprise. Chastity came to her feet first. 'Now just one moment,' she said, viciously, to the woman prisoner she'd had precious little to do with. 'No-one just flounces in here and – '

Bella put her off imperiously. 'Mistress Wise, I am not just anyone. I am the Countess of Hawksley. I expect certain standards.'

'This is Nassau,' spluttered Chastity, furious and yet a little uncertain of her footing as she proceeded. 'We don't put on airs and graces here.'

'That is only too plain. But I am not asking for much – just a little wholesome food.'

Chastity rallied, grabbed the dish and tried to wrest it from Bella's steely grip. 'Well you ain't having ours!'

'Tell her, will you, Captain?' said Bella, impatiently. 'I am your hostage. 'Tis you who shall answer to the King of England if I am badly treated.'

Intense, electrifying stares then passed between the three, with Keyho finally saying, with great meekness, 'Let the Countess have the chicken, my lamb.'

Her eyes blazed. Evidently she couldn't believe her ears. But Chastity gave way. She slackened off her grip upon the laden pewter plate and all but shoved it at Bella. Keyho's look for Bella was a vicious, scarlet-faced snarl. 'Take the food and voorking go.'

Bella inclined her head politely, smiled and did as bid happily. She wanted their food not their company. Smirking, she traversed the bleached beach, seeking out the ideal spot to devour her picnic. She knew only too well what kind of trouble she'd left in her wake. Well, it was no more than Keyho deserved.

'My lamb, don't scowl. Think of the money. Her ransom will make us fabulously rich. We'll be able to sail away and start a new life somewhere – Boston or New Amsterdam.'

'Its New York nowadays,' muttered Chastity. 'King Charles had it renamed in honour of his brother. You know that.'

'I forgot, precious.'

'You forget a great deal, Abraham Keyho. Like who is mistress here. Whose wishes be paramount. So she's a countess. Be that any reason for you to act like such a toady?'

'I'm only thinking of you, beloved, believe me. You catch more flies with honey than vinegar. Don't it make more sense to keep her sweet than make an enemy of her?'

'I don't see that it makes no difference at all,' shouted Chastity, clouting him about the ear. 'She's our hostage. We can do with her as we wish. We ain't obliged t'be nice. If they pays up they gets her back in one piece. If they don't I'll be glad to personally show her what I do think of hoity-toity countesses.'

'They'll pay,' said Keyho, adamantly, worried that the alternative would cause no end of problems. 'Just, well, don't do anything too unpleasant to her yet, huh? It'll take time to sort things satisfactorily, but 'twill be worth it.'

'Keep her away from me then, matey. She's your business, not mine.'

'Yes, my love,' said Keyho, taking up the knife to carve more meat from the carcass.

Chastity caught his wrist and squeezed it so tight he yelped, dropping the blade. 'Oh no, Abraham,' she told him viciously, taking petty revenge. 'You give away your dinner – you go without until supper.'

'But . . .'

'But me no buts,' she warned.

His belly growled. 'But!' he blurted desperately.

She pushed back her chair violently and reached for the whip upon the wall.

'Here we go again,' said Davy, gnawing on a meaty chicken leg that Bella had given him. He laughed derisively.

'Oh, dear,' said Bella, innocently, a twinkle in her eye. 'I seem to have caused a little family strife.'

The heated scene within the beach shelter could be heard all along the beach. Much of it could be seen too. It was compulsive stuff.

Keyho tried to reason with Chastity. He apologised, though he wasn't sure what for. Neither worked. She laid in to him with the whip. Sharp, stinging strokes. He became aroused, looking up her skirt in that artful, fearful manner of his. He was trembling with lust and fright. Chastity caught him doing so and, taking up the jug of wine on the table, flung it over him.

He yelled in alarm, his forbidden desire momentarily doused. But then she came down on him, kneeling either side of his unimpressive shoulders and thrusting her mound in his red, rabbit-startled face.

'Beg my pardon, knave. Be nicer than you've ever been before. Make me forgive you,' she demanded, as if on pain of death.

And Keyho sobbed almost gratefully, 'Yes, my precious. Yes, my lamb,' and raising his bald, wigless head he set his mouth to her heat in trepidation.

'That kind of thing makes a man stiff despite himself,' admitted Davy.

'I know what you mean,' agreed Bella, feeling moist and exceedingly amenable.

'What could be nicer, after decent grub and a drop of rum, than the loving of a good woman?'

'It's too hot and it's broad daylight,' was Bella's token argument.

'I ain't a-asking you to do anything,' said Davy, pulling her onto his lap and rifling her skirts, 'and nobody can see us here amongst these rocks so long as we stay low.'

'Yes.' She rubbed her backside against him.

He found Bella with his hands, slipping a finger through her warm dampness and losing it in her while his thumb played on her bud. She squirmed and struggled playfully. His fingers were firm inside her and stroking her, while he kissed her lightly all over her near exposed breasts. She was rubbing herself against his fingers now, highly excited. He released himself from his breeches and worked the head of his manhood between her lips, letting it loiter there, enveloped in her moistness, then he probed demandingly and it slipped sweetly into Bella, filling her to the root. Its wide base was hard against her, pushing, ever pushing. She arched and squirmed.

They played that way for some time, deeply joined

and barely moving. Then she pulled off and rolled onto her back in the sand with her skirts up and her legs wide and blatantly inviting. With her bare foot she stroked his glistening, turgid shaft.

Davy fell upon her, entering her easy wetness. Going deep, he stroked and stabbed, lost in her hot abundance. He withdrew almost completely, then plunged in, withdrawing again to tease her with the bulbous head, then withdrawing completely, to drive at her with his tongue a rigid weapon.

She gasped and bucked, half out of her head with escalating delight. Then he ravaged her with his member again, deeply, his stabbing movements quick and frenzied, his flesh afire.

She came first, wrapping her legs about him and moaning. He followed close behind, crying out hoarsely.

They slept a while until the huge sun set and turned the sky to a blazing, garish salmon colour.

Davy woke first and watched her, fascinated, feeling once again that seemingly insatiable stirring in his breeches.

She was lying on her stomach on a length of old sail canvas, her face sideways on her hands and her skirts askew, baring her buttocks. From time to time her legs opened and closed, and he would lie closer to look over her secret places within the forest of soft dark curls. He could see how she glistened still, swollen and suffused with colour from their earlier surfeit of pleasure. He inserted his index finger gently into her, watching it slide in smoothly and saw how she closed possessively about him. He smiled, withdrew the finger and sucked it.

On her plate was Bella's apple, beside it a bunch of bananas – his contribution to their picnic. Some were riper than others. He peeled one and ate slowly, watching her and smoothing her rounded white buttocks. He ran a finger from her sex to her arse to lubricate it, still eating and thoughtful, watching how that tight pucker resisted all attempts by his finger to invade it. He finished the banana.

Intrigued, he tried harder, spitting on his finger to ease the way. She moved restlessly and he desisted, waited a while and then made another attempt. At last he pushed in with Bella wriggling in her sleep but not waking. He worked the finger gently, drawing more helpful lubrication from near her sex and dipping it in.

He peeled another banana, deliberately selecting one that was long, firm and under-ripe. He held her cheeks apart and began pushing in the long, fat fruit.

Bella stirred and mumbled. She was waking.

With great reluctance he drew it out again and threw it away down the beach, watching it become hidden by a coating of sand.

She opened her eyes drowsily. 'Hello.'

He was on his back, looking up at the darkening heavens, whistling softly and innocently. 'Hello.'

It was Keyho's intention to sail for the nearby island of New Providence, there to find his messenger.

New Providence was another rocky, sun-bleached island with a small goat population and little else. The Caribbean's piratical element favoured it because of its natural harbour. With strategically placed cannon it was also relatively simple to defend. Not that New Providence came under attack very often. From time to time different nationalities sent warships there, hoping to drive out the undesirables – the British, the Spanish, and the Dutch made yearly attempts. But somehow the pirates remained and were little deterred.

Captain Keyho wanted to find himself a privateer as opposed to a pirate. The difference was subtle indeed, but immensely important. A pirate was an outlaw wherever he went and any nation's authorities wouldn't hesitate to hang him if apprehended. A privateer, however, was unofficially sanctioned by the state in his acts of piracy. Many were the British captains who sailed with Letters of Marque personally signed by their King. Basically this flamboyant document gave them carte blanche to prey on ships of any other nationality than their own.

Keyho could never sail to English waters and make the demand for ransom himself but a privateer could easily deliver it for him, at a price.

But, as with many a well laid plan, things didn't go as envisaged. He never bargained for the animosity between his Chastity and that irritating female, Bella Flowers.

Between them they were making his life a misery, a living hell. And there would be months of it ahead until such time as Bella's ransom arrived and, thankfully, he handed her over.

Keyho began to think that perhaps he had been unwise ever to give in to the tempting prospect of great wealth. Life would still be sweetly uncomplicated if he'd had her put in the jolly boats along with the other passengers off the captured merchantmen. Damn it all, yes, this was never worth it. And poor Chastity seemed to be permanently upset, vexed and vicious with him. He could only take so much.

On the day that the beached vessles were pronounced seaworthy once more, things came to a dramatic head.

'Pastor Bunyan did have the right idea. He spoke out against the sinfulness of King Charles's court and went to prison for his principles,' opined Chastity when Bella – collecting her daily ration of food from the begrudging female's table – professed herself a trifle homesick.

Bella scowled and declared. 'John Bunyan is a sanctimonious Puritan! If one must admire religious and virtuous men, then I'll take John Milton any day. At least he wrote on such things with a little humour and colour.'

'I sticks by what I says.'

'Please yourself, you bigoted hypocrite!'

'Who're you calling a hypocrite?' roared Chastity, her great arms akimbo and her stare as sharp as needles.

'If the cap fits!' Bella was antagonistic. The devil was in her and she stared right back.

'Why you – '

'What? Go one, say it. Whore? Jezebel? You'll have to do better than that. I've been called much worse than that, and by better folks than you. And what about you? What should I call you – a woman who leads her man around like a dog on a leash, a bull with a ring through his nose?'

Chastity's arm shot out but Bella ducked, throwing the contents of the plate at her. A tomato splattered down between her cleavage, leaving a trail of pips. They lunged at each other across the table, as chairs crashed to the floor and wooden trenchers and pewter-ware was sent flying. A half-carved chicken bounced across the floorboards, quickly getting coating with sand.

Bella snatched at a handful of Chastity's brown

hair and yanked viciously, punching her on the chin at the same time.

Chastity threw herself across the table, carrying the lightweight Bella with her to the floor. They rolled and cursed, and kicked and slapped.

A crowd had begun to gather on the sand around the open frontage of the dwelling. Someone called to Keyho. 'Hey, Cap'n, you'd best come see.'

Davy watched, frowning worriedly. Chastity Wise was a big, big woman. Sooner rather than later she was going to get the upper hand. He didn't want his lovely Bella taking too much of a pasting, with her flawless face turned black and blue. But what could he do? He stood with the others, feeling helpless, and trying to think, the only face not showing amusement. The only one of two faces.

Keyho came hurriedly, looking silly and bumptious. 'What's going on now?' he demanded, feeling a prickle of foreboding. It was bound to be that Flowers woman again. She had become the bane of his life.

His eyes widened and blinked repeatedly at the sight of the two women slugging it out on the floor. There was some blood, though it was difficult to say from where, and both now had torn and violently disarranged clothing. Their hair was flying about them. And, oh, the language! Keyho was shocked.

Bella fought free as the heavyweight got an arm lock around her throat and began to throttle her. She delivered Chastity a slicing blow up and at the base of her nose. The woman's eyes watered. Vision blurring and moaning sickly, she slackened her hold on the flailing, struggling Bella.

On her feet, her breasts bouncing free of her

185

bodice, Bella ran and snatched the whip. She was furious and incensed with murder in mind.

She thrashed the grunting woman as she staggered to her knees, again and again, across her back, her arms, her backside even, after first snatching up her calico skirt.

Unmindful of Keyho's presence, a number of men cheered and laughed. But he was too affected by the sight to pay them any mind and was getting himself all of a lather. He looked as though he wanted to join in and was jealous of the violent attention his Chastity was receiving.

Just then Davy Billings pushed his way through the crowd, labouring somewhat under the weight of a full pail of water. He had to put an end to this before it got frighteningly out of hand. He threw the chilly contents over the two women.

There was a united cry of alarm and outrage.

Keyho stepped in, taking a grip on himself once more and remembering that he was the captain, their leader, the man supposed to be in charge. He snatched the whip from a dripping Bella and pulled his sopping wife to her feet as he stamped his booted foot.

'That's it. I've had enough. I can't stand months of this while we wait for Lady Muck here to be ransomed. No way. No siree. I've no stomach for it. I don't want the ransom money. I'd rather be poor. God, yes. Voorking penniless!'

Keyho dragged Chastity one way while Davy prodded Bella the other. The women snarled at each other like she cats, baring their teeth, neither willing to admit defeat.

* * *

The *Tortuga May* sailed on the next high tide, heading north towards New Providence. There was a change of plan.

Bella was no longer to be held for ransom. Keyho wanted to be rid of her. He quite fancied the idea of killing her. She deserved it but it would be too quick. So he'd come up with the idea of selling her on New Providence to the highest bidder. There was bound to be a captain there with booty enough to be able to afford her. She was a rare beauty and so, doubtless, there'd be a great deal of interest. After she was sold and Keyho had sailed off with the money it would be just too bad for the unsuspecting purchaser who found himself lumbered with a virago. Poor fool, poor sap – but too late then. Keyho smirked at the thought of someone else suffering as he had done over the last several days. No man should be put through that, and God help the man who bought her, he thought, smiling and savouring the thought of being rid of her.

Mama Jo looked her over intently, making Bella blush with shame. She put up a sausage-like finger under Bella's chin and tilted her head up, smiling as she caught the intense stare of two thickly lashed, violet eyes.

Then Mama Jo looked at Keyho, raising an eyebrow. 'Why you want sell, Cap'n?' Was the man an idiot?

'She's trouble,' snarled Keyho. 'Nothing but a jinx. If I don't get rid of her, my Chastity'll end up murdering her. How much do you reckon she'll fetch?'

Mama Jo shrugged her shoulders. 'That all

depends. She's a beauty, true. But there just not the buyers at the moment.'

'I want her got rid of.'

'No problem. But don't be hasty, Cap'n. That's bad business. You leave it to me. I get best prices for suitable percentages. I'll put word around, advertise our special sale and get more buyers from other islands. We do this right and we'll make a heap of money.'

'All right. I leave it up t'you. But you be straight with me, y'hear? Don't think t'double cross Captain Keyho.'

Mama Jo looked first offended, then smiled as sincerely as a rattlesnake. 'Mama Jo is as honest as the day is long.'

'Huh!' scoffed Keyho, derisively. 'Send word when all is done.'

'I will, Cap'n.'

Off strode Keyho through the wooden stockade fence, a monumental weight lifted from his shoulders.

Mama Jo loomed over Bella, and said, in a manner that brooked no refusal, 'Follow me.'

The building to which they were heading was a substantial wooden structure. One storeyed, it had louvres at some windows, shutters at others. The low, conical roof looked much mended, as if it fared poorly from passing hurricanes.

'What line of business are you in?' asked Bella, noting casks and kegs, even great tottering piles of ballast that looked like the new wood, mahogany, from South America. It had begun to appear in England but would surely never replace oak and walnut as the cabinet-maker's staple?

'Trade. A bit of this, a bit of that. Anything the

cap'n's want to unload really. Jewellery, furniture and people.'

'I warn you,' said Bella, gravely, 'sell me and you'll be in the most awful trouble. I was mistress to the King of England. If he ever got wind of what you'd done, he'd send the Royal Navy against this place. They'd destroy you and everything on New Providence.'

Mama Jo ushered Bella inside and closed the door. Her look was indulgent. After the blazing sunshine, it was incredibly dark.

'Look, what is your name?'

'Bella Flowers, Countess of Hawksley.'

'Look, Bella,' said Mama Jo with studied condescension, making it plain, with her look of contempt, that Bella's title impressed and intimidated her not at all. 'No-one know you here. No-one shall if we're discreet. We don't need to shout your dubious pedigree to get a good price for you. You,' she said, pinching Bella's upper arm, 'are prime merchandise. Some man will pay plenty. Sit.'

A hand at her shoulder pushed Bella easily down into a chair. Chastity Wise had been big. Mama Jo was a colossus. At least the chair was soft and comfortable, doubtless a French piece intercepted on its way to one of Louis XIV's Caribbean islands, Martinique perhaps.

Mama Jo disappeared through a glass beaded curtain, across a cluttered room and through a door. Bella's eyes had now adjusted to the pleasantly cool gloom of the store's interior.

It was like Aladdin's Cave. There was stuff everywhere – expensive stuff, very grand stuff. Once it had been the prized possessions of wealthy Spanish, French, Dutch and British voyagers then, sadly, it

189

had fallen into the hands of uncouth, unappreciative pirates. They sold it quickly on in exchange for guineas or doubloons, pieces of eight, crusadoes and Louis d'or.

Bella didn't know what to make of Mama Jo. She was extraordinary. She looked Middle-Eastern, maybe Moroccan or Egyptian. She was over six feet tall, with dark, shiny skin and dark, olive eyes which were long and drawn up at the outer corners. Her jet black hair, which was dead straight and glinted blue when in the sunlight, was piled and pinned elaborately atop her head, leaving her ears free the better to display heavily ornate golden earrings. They were disc-shaped and from them hung chains of other discs. They dragged at the ears, looking incredibly heavy. Around her neck, her arms and pinned at her breasts were several more precious ounces of similar adornment.

Her dress was simple yet striking, looking to be no more than a length of cloth bound around her from breasts to ankles and secured about her waist with a golden girdle. But the stuff from which it was fashioned was delicious. It was spun in silks of turquoise, aqua, cobalt, ultramarine, violet, purple and amethyst, and all shot through with threads of gold. It made Bella catch her breath enviously, and it looked so much more comfortable than European fashions.

When Mama Jo returned she carried a silver tray laden with food – seafood, stewed peppers, tomatoes and spices, bowls of rice with herbs, spices and beans in a piquant sauce, and smaller bowls of sweet pickles and chutneys.

'You eat. Then you sleep over in the corner. Beneath the bolts of cloth, you'll find a divan.

Tomorrow will be soon enough to begin preparing you for auction. And don't think to sneak out and to escape, will you?' warned Mama Jo, making Bella flinch by pinching her nipple through the satin of her tattered dress. 'The island is full of drunken, lawless pirates. Rape to them is simple pleasure and no crime.'

Mama Jo's stockade was, on closer inspection, heavily defended. Not so surprising really considering the amount of wealth horded therein. The woman had an army of slaves at her back, guarding what was hers against any attempt at appropriation by visiting pirates. She was one of the island's few permanent residents and by far the richest.

At sun-up the next day breakfast arrived, delivered by two blackamoors. The nubile girl was called Honey Drips, the quieter, gravely serious boy, Sugar Lips.

'Where did you get such names?'

'Mama Jo, of course.'

Yes, silly question really.

'You eat,' said Sugar Lips, impatiently.

'Drink,' added Honey Drips, handing Bella a goblet of mixed tropical fruit juice to wash down the sticky pastries she was obediently munching.

'Hurry.'

'Yes. Mama Jo will be waiting.'

Bella ate more quickly, infected with their sense of urgency, but eventually ran out of steam and belched with discomfort. She was still hungry but these two took the fun out of eating.

'Enough. What now?'

'This way,' said Sugar Lips, sweeping the beaded curtain aside.

Honey Drips led the way through another door and down a short, furniture cluttered corridor. The entire building was little more than a giant warehouse. She opened a door and bid Bella enter, following close behind with her male side-kick.

Mama Jo was there and so was an older, much smaller woman, though she looked to be of the same race as the unofficial Queen of New Providence.

'Aah,' said the older woman, appreciatively, at sight of Bella.

Mama Jo smiled and nodded, saying something in their own language. They both chuckled then. Bad form that, Bella thought, and exceedingly bad manners. She raised an eyebrow in query. 'Mama Jo?'

'Goodmorning, Countess,' said Mama Jo with amusement. 'Kindly remove all your clothing so we can get down to business.'

Bella's eyebrows knit at that. She shook her head with vigorous negativity. 'I don't think so.'

'But I do,' said Mama Jo, firmly. 'Either you cooperate, or I send the boy here to fetch stronger men. They would take great delight in stripping you, no doubt. You have my word on it. Countess, nothing untoward will happen to you, not here and now.'

Warily Bella removed her taffeta gown, indignant at the ridiculing manner in which the woman kept saying 'Countess'.

'Now, up on the table, please,' said Mama Jo, patting a high level structure. It was long and narrow, the perfect size to accomodate a laid-out body. Bella shuddered.

'Why?'

'All will become clear. We'll explain as we go along. It's simpler.'

There was a soft cotton blanket for her to lie on

and a pillow for her head. Bella took a deep breath and climbed up, needing to use the wooden step provided.

'First, something for the hair,' explained Mama Jo. 'It is brittle and full of the sea. No man would want to run his fingers through it in such condition. When I lived in Alexandria I found this recipe – almond oil, jasmine and a few other ingredients. We massage it in and leave it for a while.' She set to work, sectioning Bella's seemingly ruined tresses of lustreless sable and anointing them with the greatest of care. 'Meanwhile, my assistant, Anemone, will see to your depilation.'

'My what?'

'Removal of your body hair.'

'Whatever for?' said Bella, taken aback.

'It is the done thing. You'll be nicer for it.'

'But – '

'It foreign to you, I know,' said Mama Jo, with condescending patience, 'but believe me, you'll be pleased with the result. In my country concubines would see this as a normal part of their beauty treatment. Our men like to see a woman's sex smooth and nude and find hair distasteful.'

'But in my country – '

'In many ways your country is still very backward,' said Mama Jo, cutting Bella off scathingly.

Thus silenced, Bella lay tense and docile while Anemone started on her with the tweezers. It was agony. There was no other word – agony. Each hair was individually plucked. When she rebelled and snapped her legs shut, that sweet pair Honey Drips and Sugar Lips were there to prise them open and hold onto them with malicious delight. And it seemed to take for ever.

Her finger and toe nails were filed, polished and oiled. Her body was oiled, exfoliated and smeared with bleaching paste then left to absorb the heady unguent's miraculous properties. And all the while Anemone plucked on. Once Bella tried to put her hand down between her legs and feel what was going on, but it was slapped away, the older Egyptian clacking on quite horribly so that Bella didn't doubt she was being cursed to a thousand different blood-curdling ways of dying.

'How did you end up here on New Providence?' she asked Mama Jo, her curiosity strong.

'How did you?'

'I was trying to get away from my less than satisfactory life in England. I was captured by Keyho. It's as simple as that.'

In the face of such a pocket version, Mama Jo offered a sketchy outline of her past.

'I killed my master one night as he slept and fled his house with his wealth sewn into my clothing to take off with a corsair who was enamoured with me. Anemone came too, fearing that she might be blamed in some way for the death if she was left behind, for my master was a vile man and so too were most of his family. The corsair sailed us out of the Mediterranean and into the Atlantic, as promised. We remained a while on one of the Cape Verde Islands, then sailed for the Caribbean. I got rid of my corsair eventually. I think he knew it was wise to let me go my own way, considering what befell my master. I had no qualms about killing. Me, Anemone, we settled here. We're happy in our way and no man will be our master ever again.'

Bella was impressed.

With a relieved exclamation Anemone stepped back, finished.

'You are done. Now, up you get. Next you must be rinsed,' said Mama Jo, leading the way to another room. It was naught but a small, windowless cubicle with a drainage channel.

Bella looked down at herself. She felt like a plucked chicken ready for the spit and the mixture of substances coating her body was so heavily scented that she felt a little faint and rocked on her heels.

'Stand there. Keep still.'

Standing on two ledges either side, directing movable bamboo water shutes, were perched Honey and Sugar. Down came the flow, slowly measured, pouring steadily over Bella, who gasped and sputtered, letting fly with a few choice epithets for the pair. While, with a soft bristled, long-handled brush, Anemone quickly scrubbed her down, staying dry and professionally composed herself.

The flow of water stopped after a while and Bella flicked sopping hair from her eyes, wiping her face with a swipe of her palms. 'Thank God it's all over. Let me tell you, I've had quite enough for one day. It's an experience I shall never forget.'

Mama Jo chuckled. 'We not quite finished yet, Countess. This way if you please.'

Bella felt so thoroughly seen to that she didn't have the strength even to argue and trudged off obediently. Apparantly she wasn't to be spitted and roasted, but steamed instead.

The room was small and windowless – indeed Bella suddenly realised that she hadn't seen the sun all that day – and, after she was commanded to lie upon a wooden couch in the middle of the room, water was sprinkled around on the oddly slatted floor and great floods of steam began to rise.

'What in Heaven's name!' Bella began to get up again in alarm but Mama Jo restrained her around the shoulders.

'It's all right. Lie still. The steam will cleanse you, sweat out all the impurities and purge your flesh. It is an ancient and tested practice from Turkistan. It will do you no harm, I promise.'

Bella frowned dubiously, but lay back again, finding the Egyptian, in general, a trustworthy woman.

The steamy heat was draining and seemed to sap at her energy and will. Soon she was drowsy, then she fell off to sleep.

She awoke on her back, staring up at the thatched roofing, and totally disorientated.

'Feel better?' She could see Mama Jo through a break in the steam. 'I'm going to put some oil on your mound, between your lips.'

'Why?' Bella felt too languid to move, even though she knew that her legs had lolled open at the knees, completely exposing her sex.

'So that I might insert a stretcher.'

'Why? What?' Bella raised her head then and looked at the woman positioned between her legs.

Mama Jo had a tray of wooden shapes, all polished to a lustre – long, fat, fatter and fattest – penis-like shapes only exaggeratedly large.

'You're not going to – '

Mama Jo caught her knees to keep them down and open. 'Now just lie still. Be good. It won't hurt, you are no virgin.'

'No. So I don't need stretching, now do I?' she argued.

'A little, yes. Especially the other hole. Some men like that one but don't like struggling to get in.'

'It's a struggle because it's wrong!'

'What a prude you are,' laughed Mama Jo loftily. Ignoring Bella's indignant protests she selected the first false phallus. 'In my country when an important man with a harem buys a new concubine he doesn't waste time breaking her in himself. His harem masters – eunuchs – do it for him, with instruments like these. They smooth the female opening with sweet, natural oil, coat the instrument and then, see, put the head to the mouth and gently insert. There now. Not so bad?'

Bella opened her mouth. But what could she say? It was the indignity more than anything. It was her body and she didn't like losing control over it.

Honey Drips entered, carrying a tiny silver goblet.

'It is a cordial,' said the Egyptian. 'Sip while I work. It will relax you.'

Why not? It was very pleasant and it took her mind off what was going on between her legs too, or at least made it more acceptable.

The wood was pulled out, a fresh one oiled and slid in. Bella relaxed and even began to feel a curious kind of pleasure in it all.

The next one looked big, its nobbly surface intriguing. She held her breath while it was pushed in, rippling at her entrance and causing delicious sensations.

She must have murmured because Mama Jo smiled. 'You like it?' She wiggled it playfully inside Bella.

Teasingly she took it out and pushed it in again, watching the Countess's tight abdomen tighten even more with pleasure and her nipples harden like distended buttons. Bella was all pink in the heat and glossy with sweat.

She left it in, moving it every now and again to keep Bella in a heightened state of lust, and took up a slim tapering probe which she introduced to her other, tightly puckered opening. It was so thin at the tip that it was in almost before Bella realised it, then Mama Jo pushed it right in, up to the widened base that stopped it from disappearing completely up her arse. She moved the other one rythmically, pleasuring Bella's bud as she did so.

Bella let a hand stray down to her mound, now that Anemone was no longer present to slap her, and shook her head at its nude smoothness. 'It feels so strange. How does it look?'

'You may see, if you like. Honey Drips, bring the mirror for the Countess.'

Honey hurried obediently to carry out the order.

Bella stared at herself, with the two instruments invading and stretching the pink, exposed folds. 'Men like that?'

Mama Jo nodded. 'Nothing in their way. They will want to tongue you from end to end. From here,' she circled Bella's arse 'to here.' She ran her thumb up past the full vagina, to the proud little bud, then bent and put her tongue to it, circling it and pulling at it with her teeth.

'God's nightgown, Mama Jo!' squealed Bella, and went off like a rocket, throb upon throb.

Some time later she tottered from the steam room, suffering from an excess of heat and pleasure.

'In here,' said Mama Jo, holding open a door.

Bella entered another windowless room, tiled this time in the eastern fashion, and accomodating a sizeable sunken bath.

'The final phase,' assured Mama Jo. 'We bathe you, perfume and oil you, wash your hair and comb it dry. Then you can go to sleep.'

Bella's eyes rolled blissfully at the thought. How could doing nothing be so exhausting?

When they'd finished she was taken back to the room with the divan. Mama Jo instructed Sugar Lips to bring the full length Venetian mirror. Bella stood before it with her mouth open. Well, yes, she knew it was her, but, goodness gracious! She looked wonderful.

She was pale and smooth and seemed to glow pearl-white in the light from the many candles in the room. Her mound shimmered, its contours catching the light beautifully, much as her breasts did. Her hair hung like a veil of the darkest silk, thick, shiny and very slightly wavy, nearly to her waist.

'There,' said Mama Jo, 'what man could resist?'

Bella couldn't help but smile smugly with satisfaction. What man indeed? But then she remembered why all this had been done. Likely she'd be sold off to some loathsome, rich old lecher of a pirate. He'd probably stink, be permanently drunk and have nothing very special in his breeches. Yes, that would be just her luck. She could have had Guido. She'd end up with an oversexed version of Captain Keyho!

Life was a bastard. Her smile faltered.

'We shall repeat today's procedures twice weekly until such time as the auction is arranged,' Mama Jo informed her before retiring.

Chapter Nine

She was very much a bird in a gilded cage. They pampered her unashamedly and gave her anything she wanted that was within their power. But she didn't ask for much. Mostly she became morose and withdrawn, thinking about her future or, as she saw it, her lack of one. She'd had her years of wealth, success and happiness and one could not expect life to be perfect indefinitely.

Days passed alarmingly quickly for Bella who saw each one as another step towards unhappiness. Ships sailed in, brought – so Sugar Lips and Honey Drips informed her – by the promise of a truly memorable sale by auction. Mama Jo was being deliberately evasive concerning the nature of the lot on offer. Potential buyers were told only that she was a female slave of unsurpassable beauty. Rumours started and then abounded. Some said she was from the harem of the Bey of Tangiers, a sultry, black-eyed beauty so skilled in the arts of love she could melt a man's heart at twenty paces. Others had heard that she had been seized on the Baltic, was half Russian and half Norwegian and was called Hingi. God alone knew where such rumours got started, laughed Sugar Lips, giving Honey Drips a comradely dig in the ribs and exchanging a conspiratorial snigger.

Where indeed! Bella thought wryly, impressed by the skilled way in which events were being manipulated.

The auction was only four days away. Bella was now so apprehensive that she'd gone off her food, causing Mama Jo to fret and go to great lengths to tempt her with the choicest tidbits.

Increasingly the stockade became a hive of activity. The sale platform was being constructed out in the yard while the room behind the beaded curtain was treated to a thorough sort out and clean up. Bella watched these preparations, at first mystified by the latter.

The room behind the curtain was transformed. The divan on which Bella slept was moved against its back wall and the walls were hung with captured oils of Spanish grandees and infantas. A Turkey rug graced the boards. Cordially Bella was invited to use that room from then on. At night two candelabra were lit, their soft pools of light falling purposefully on the gold damask divan and the lovely creature reclining there.

At the quietest hour of night the door opened and into the Egyptian's domain crept her invited guests. The French pirate, Jean-Philippe Lebeq, came the first time Bella was put on show. He was reputedly one of the richest sea rovers in the Caribbean. The others had invitations for subsequent nights.

Tall, slim and dressed most splendidly dandified in sky-blue satins and a profusion of dripping Belgium lace, he made Honey Drips hot between her legs. If this man bought Bella it wouldn't be so bad, the girl reasoned hopefully. His face was regular and typically Gallic. He had dark skin, shoulder length hair and smouldering eyes but, unfortunately, he'd been in a bad swordfight once on Barbados and had a nasty scar that sliced down through one eye and cheek, disfiguring him badly. A person could grow used to it though and forget that the crooked eye surrounded by unevenly healed, puckered skin could no longer see. It was staring but sightless. In all other respects Jean-Phillipe Lebeq was a personable man. He had no bad habits and no vices save the obvious piratical one. He would make Bella a decent enough master.

Before entering her strong-room Mama Jo had warned him to silence, explaining that this night was just for looking. It was a taster so that he might have time to think before the auction. He had been a valued customer in the past and thus he was getting a rare privilege not afforded to many.

'M'lady will not go cheap. I let you see so you can be prepared. It would be a shame if you were outbid on the day. Now keep quiet and follow me.'

He crept in behind her, full of expectancy, but still unprepared for the sight that greeted him. Invisible in the dark, he stood looking thrugh a glass-beaded curtain, his senses suddenly acutely alive.

On a divan bathed in candlelight slept the most exquisite creature imaginable. She was not naked but she might as well have been, for the diaphanous robe that draped her was of gossamer-fine rose-coloured silk shot through with threads of gold. Her nipples prodded at the filmy material and her legs were slightly ajar, giving a tantalising glimpse of her secrets.

Mama Jo took him by the shoulder and pushed him back the way he'd come.

'Divine, no?' she grinned, once outside in the torchlit yard.

Lebeq took a shuddering breath. 'Magnifique!'

'Better start scraping your cash together, Monsieur.'

Eduardo Bambosa was a pig of a man, an uncouth dog, shit on the shoe of mankind. He'd heard most of the names levelled at him, though never, of course, first hand; no-one would be foolish enough to say such things to his face. And he quite revelled in his unsavoury reputation.

He was Spanish or Portugese (there was some argument over this – both nationalities vehemently denied ownership), and had been sailing the Caribbean for many years, preying on anything that floated and indulging in every excess.

He ate too much and killed too much. He swore, raped, double-crossed and carried out just about any despicable act imaginable to make an extra doubloon or two. He had a thousand enemies and no friends. He was filthy rich and, if he took a liking to Bella – and Mama Jo thought that Bella might be just his type – it would be difficult for any other man to outbid him at the auction. The fact that Bella would likely be dead within the month if sold to him was neither here nor there as far as the procuress was concerned. She only bought and sold; she couldn't be a moral guardian as well, she reasoned. His money was good. That was all that mattered.

He'd been partaking of the rum before his appointment with Mama Jo, and he reeked of it, for he was a messy drinker and several measures had apparently spilled down his already food-encrusted shirt-front. He stumbled after her in the dark, knocking into the furniture and cursing.

She stopped him, warning in a hiss. 'Silence or we go no further. She must not be woken.'

'My pardon,' he slurred and burped. 'Carry on.'

At sight of Bella sleeping in the nearly-nude he began to make animal noises of appreciation. Grunting and growling he pressed forward with sub-intelligent persistence. Mama Jo was hard pressed to restrain him.

'I'll give you five thousand doubloons for her now. Forget the auction.'

Mama Jo shook her head and led him away forcefully. It wasn't easy and became a real struggle. Much more and she'd have to call for assistance, but she didn't really want to do that and mayhap wake Bella. It was best if that woman didn't know of the machinations that were going on behind the scenes on her behalf.

'Come away, Bambosa. No, you can't have her. Not yet. I can't possibly disappoint the others. The auction is advertised and I have my reputation to think of.'

'I want her,' insisted the drunkard, grasping his member through his soiled breeches. 'I want her now.'

'Well y'can't,' snarled the Egyptian, screwing up her face in distaste at his unsavoury mannerisms. 'You'll have t'be patient.'

'You're a hard bitch.'

'I'm a business woman and I must be seen to be fair. Now, goodnight,' she bid, putting her foot to the small of his back and ejecting him out into the yard, then quickly barring the door against a possible re-entry. She gave a shiver of disgust.

'Scumbag!'

'I'm not interested in purchasing a woman,' said Kit Tremayne, following Mama Jo through the darkness of the store. They were business acquaintences of old. Indeed, Mama Jo had quite a soft spot for him.

'Then why did you answer my invitation?'

'Curious, I suppose. I heard she was English.'

'You heard a-right. There are rumours to the contrary. But, yes, she is, and a countess no less.'

'Then what the hell's she doing here?'

'Got herself captured by Abraham Keyho en route to Jamaica. He had some crazy notion of ransoming her, but she proved so troublesome that he handed her over to me for sale instead. He wanted to be shot of her.

His blond eyebrows lifted thoughtfully, taking that in and digesting it. He asked, 'A countess, you say. Do you have a name?'

'Arabella Flowers, Countess of Hawksley.'

'Good God! Do you know who she is, or was?'

'Apparently, according to Keyho, she was the King's mistress for a spell,' said Mama Jo, quite unimpressed. 'I only buy and sell. I'm not much interested in their past history.'

'Lead on,' urged Tremayne. 'I've never seen the celebrated Arabella Flowers and I am intrigued.'

'You've changed your tune,' said the shape in the darkness ahead of him, wryly.

She stopped. 'There,' she whispered, indicating.

He could look easily over her shoulder. 'My God!' He breathed.

He was enchanted and he was perplexed. He'd never seen her before and yet – something troubled him. He shook his head in consternation, his eyebrows knitting. 'Damned if there ain't something familiar about her.'

'You like her?'

'I like her very much,' he admitted without reservation.

'You'll think about buying?'

'As a gentleman and a fellow countryman of hers, it's my duty.'

Mama Jo chuckled softly as she led him back outside. Such gallantry. Such reserve. Such handsomeness. If only she'd been sold to a master such as he in Alexandria, she'd never have become a murderess. If only she were ten years younger and five stone lighter. She sighed raggedly. Ah, what the hell!

Kit Tremayne lay on his back on the bed in the sleeping alcove of the great cabin aboard his ship, the brigantine *Wyvern*.

Rebecca fussed over him. She always came aboard when he was on New Providence. She was a whore of uncertain nationality; some said Cuban. Sometimes she looked more African than Spanish, and sometimes the opposite. Often it depended on how she wore her tightly-curling brown-black hair.

She'd never been invited aboard, she just seemed to have attached herself to him and Kit, being a healthy male who could appreciate a pretty woman, wasn't so foolish as to reject her obvious advances. He spent a lot of time at sea and a little light relief was much appreciated. But there were times when her singular devotion irritated him. She could be too much, too adoring, too solicitous and too stifling.

'Wine?'

'No thanks.'

'A little supper then?'

'I'm not hungry.'

His mind was full of pictures of Arabella Flowers, his thoughts all a-jumble. What a gorgeous creature! She was divine and unforgettable, but it was more than that. What was it?

'Not hungry for food, but perhaps for love?' Rebecca knelt by the bed and smoothed her palm down his torso, across the hollow of his belly and on to the snug-fitting breeches over his dormant phallus. He grumbled and pushed her hand away.

'Not tonight, Becky. I'm too tired. I've got things on my mind.'

He didn't even bother to look at her.

Her eyes blazed. He'd never turned her down flat before. She was humiliated and she felt murderous. She slapped him, determined to get something other than indifference.

He jumped off the bed, captured her arms and marched her to the door. 'Pickles!' he shouted to the night-watch, who appeared pronto in the moonlit companionway, 'Get rid of her. She's barred henceforth.' He slammed his door and went back to the bed.

Arabella Flowers. He sat upright, exclaimed, and then laughed uproariously. Bristol. Now he remembered. Well, he'd never really forgotten. She'd had the mask there. It was surprising what a skimpy piece of red satin could conceal. He'd never thought to see her again, despite leaving his hopeful note at The Mermaid Inn as a means of introduction. He'd tried and almost succeeded in putting her from his mind. And now here she was, on New Providence of all places and about to be sold into slavery!

How in God's name was he going to raise enough money?

Today was the day. And what a very long day it might prove for Bella. She was the last lot up for auction and mightn't even step up onto the platform until sunset.

Her eyelids flickered open reluctantly as the strong smell of coffee roused her. She squinted through her thick lashes at the tiny cup and saucer and the steam-belching pot on the low table beside her divan. Faintly she could hear the sound of rhythmical mur-murings and, peering out beyond the beaded curtain, she could see Honey Drips and Sugar Lips, seated and joined together, as they faced each other on an Indian rug with their arms and legs entwined. They were like two very supple Buddhas.

'What time is it?'

Honey Drips looked at the tall, walnut clock cap-tured off a British merchantman. It wasn't terribly accurate out here in the tropics, but it gave them a rough and exceedingly stylish guide to the time.

'About eleven.'

'Eleven!' Bella sat up urgently and poured coffee. This was likely to be the most monumental day of her life and she'd slept through half of it already! That wasn't normal. She wasn't normal. No sane person would have been able to sleep at all. This time tomorrow she'd be heaven only knew where with some man, some stranger, and she'd be his property, to do with what-so-ever he damned well liked!

God damn and blast and bugger it all! This couldn't be happening. She was a king's favourite and a wealthy, influential woman. But not here, she reminded herself, not on New Providence. Here she was nobody, with no-one to listen or care for her plight. Here there was no law to save her and no influential friends or lover to call upon. She was on her own and she was lost.

Sugar Lips cried out with his eyelids flickering as he moved his girl upon his shaft. He grasped at her hips and squeezed his length between her dusky thighs, causing the most delicious friction.

'Oh, shut up!' snapped Bella, gulping back the coffee with anger and dread, and grimacing as it burned a trail all the way down. Usually their endless sexual cavorting bothered her not at all. She surreptitiously watched as a means of passing the time somewhat more interestingly than watching the swinging of the clock pendulum.

Sugar Lips poked out his tongue and pulled a face, then, knowing that Bella was glaring his way, he stuck his tongue in Honey's ear and wiggled it. Honey Drips arched with delight, showing where he possessed her, his length shoving back and forth, while her nipples, hard and distended, rubbed against his lean, hairless torso. He gleamed dark like treacle toffee. He had a lovely body.

Suddenly Bella wanted to cry. She wasn't likely to get a pirate who looked anything like him. No. – she'd get someone like Keyho, she just knew it. Fate had a way of doing things like that to her. She'd be the love-slave of some pot-bellied old lecher. The dam burst and her tears flooded.

'I wish I was dead,' she sobbed.

Honey cooed sympathetically. 'Don't cry. Please.' She began struggling free of her lover, disentangling her limbs. He was mortified and held on, trying to mount her from behind as Honey crawled, leaden-limbed, through the twinkling facets of the swaying curtain, holding out a handkerchief. 'Don't cry. You'll ruin your lovely face and then Mama Jo will get mad.'

'Devil take Mama Jo and you all. I want to go home,' wailed Bella.

At around two of the clock Mama Jo entered Bella's room. She carried a copper-coloured robe of the finest silk draped carefully over her arms. Behind her was Anemone, in her hands a tray of perfumes and cosmetics. They were personally taking charge of readying Bella for the sale. Outside the seats were filling, the poster at the stockade gate proclaiming:

Today
AN EVENT OF GREAT EXCEPTION
For Sale By Auction
All money to be paid at time of purchase
Many Examples of the Finest European
Furniture
&
LADY ARABELLA of the ENGLISH NOBILITY
Brightest Jewel of the Caribbean

Mama Jo's trusted auctioneer, the Hispanic art and furniture expert, Jose Rodriguez, was in charge of things. He had set and knew the reserve of each piece by heart. There were many fine lots: Louis XIV chairs, English silver, even an elegant sweep of oak staircase built specially for a plantation house in the Bahamas.

'I don't want to do this,' muttered a belligerent Bella, having to be dragged up from the divan and stripped of her lounging robe. She certainly wasn't going to cooperate.

'You have no alternative,' said Mama Jo, taking up a sopping sponge and dousing her roughly, over her breasts, belly, puss and thighs, then around the back and over her buttocks and under her arms.

Anemone was ready with the towel to pat her dry in a no-nonsense manner. The rinse had left a lingering smell of jasmine and sandalwood. These were added to as the older woman dabbed neat perfumed oil on strategic parts of Bella's anatomy – her nape and behind her ears, her breasts and naval, on her mound, her wrists, ankles and her inner thighs. For the lips of her sex there was almond oil and for her nipples a russet paste that was left for several minutes and then cleansed away, leaving the tips dyed darkly like two visual magnets that were certain to draw a man's appreciative eye.

Mama Jo brushed her hair with savage thoroughness, so that no knot remained and it fell, gleaming and crackling with life. She rouged Bella's lips and smudged brown shadow into the sockets of her eyes, carefully lining the lids with a fine sable grease stick. Then she stood back and smiled with satisfaction.

'You can't make me,' snarled Bella, even as she allowed Anemone to put her arm through the sleeve of the fresh gown.

'No, I can't. If you don't do as you are bid I shall kill you. That is all,' Mama Jo told her flatly.

A chill ran down Bella's spine then up again. It was no idle threat, she knew.

She stood ready, swathed in copper gossamer silk, the gown cinched around her waist with a heavy golden girdle. It was Mama Jo's and several large links had had to be removed to make it fit properly. On her feet were strappy golden sandals.

'There is a place you can wait and observe until it

is your time,' Mama Jo said, turning at the door. 'Anemone will show you. Good luck.'

Bella scowled, thinking that it would be rather inappropriate to say thank you under the circumstances.

Seated by the louvred window where the side of the auction block was wholly visible, Bella watched, feeling sick with nerves. She'd never felt this bad before going on stage at Drury Lane, she thought wryly, shaking her head at the spit-roasted spicy chicken that Anemone offered on a tray. No, she couldn't have eaten a thing.

Lots appeared and were carried up onto the platform by members of Mama Jo's army of native helpers. They were everywhere: seeing that things ran smoothly behind the scenes; patrolling, because there were some choice items on offer and it wouldn't do for anyone to try to steal rather than buy, and pirates were not the most honest of men; serving the more select of the buyers – who had seats reserved for them at the front of the audience – with tempting dishes and a good class of wine; roasting a goat and spitted chickens over fires away from the main event and manning a rum and ale tent. Certainly Mama Jo's auction was the big event of the year on New Providence.

Bella noted that one or two of the front row seats were still empty. She could only pray that there was better to come than sat there already.

They were either disappointing or downright disgusting. She tried not to, but her gaze kept going back to one particular man who seemed to occupy his time picking his nose, spilling his wine down his front and belching. She could hear him plainly, even as far removed as she was. She'd find a way of killing herself rather than let a man like that touch her, she decided. Compared to him even Captain Keyho was appealing!

The furniture was running out with only a dozen lots remaining. A finely carved Spanish coffer from Toledo; an eighty piece silver-gilt canteen of cutlery (someone's wife must have been heartbroken when that didn't turn up on the ship as expected); a Dutch marquetry cabinet and so on.

Bella's stomach started to churn.

Another gentleman arrived to take his place in the front row. Now he was more like it. Her hopes lifted just a little. Tall, dark, black haired and rather foppish in dress and manner, he didn't look like your typical slavering sadist or wife murdering monster. He actually looked quite handsome, until he turned fully towards Bella and she could see the other half of his face sadly disfigured. She could get used to it, she told herself. Please God, let him have lots of money and let him like me. Please!

Mama Jo came to collect her. Taking a firm grip upon Bella's puny bicep she led her up the wooden steps at the back of the auction block. She remained hidden from view behind a tarpaulin sheet until it was her turn to go on and the Egyptian released her, her fingers leaving a series of red marks upon Bella's arm.

'You cannot prevent this thing from happening,' she told the pale little Countess, 'so bow to the inevitable with dignity.'

'How can you do this? You were a slave once yourself,' said Bella, scathingly.

Mama Jo smiled sweetly. 'But I am a business woman now.'

The last item of furniture was a Genoese-made

lady's dressing table of padouk wood, inlaid with thousands of ivory flowers. Its price steadily rose to a handsome hundred and forty pounds.

'Do I hear one hundred and fifty? Your last chance, gentlemen.' Rodriguez paused and scanned one last time, thorough in his work. 'Sold then to Monsieur d'Olivant for one hundred and forty!'

Bella didn't hear the rest. Everything was becoming foggy. She thought she might faint. Mama Jo handed her a tiny cup full of rum. Bella knocked it back in one go.

'And now, gentlemen, for the prime article of the day. A once in a lifetime opportunity to purchase your very own blue blood!'

Its a lie, Bella wanted to shout. I haven't got one single drop of aristocratic blood in my veins. But she had no voice, and felt disembodied.

'A beauty. A rare beauty indeed.'

Two blackamoors parted the tarpaulin and Mama Jo prodded Bella forward with her sharpest fingernail. In a trance Bella took four exceedingly slow steps and was at the front of the platform.

All noise and conversation had ceased. Everyone was looking at her, examining her from head to toe and taking in every luscious curve. They ogled her breasts, her denuded, vulnerably exposed puss, her curving buttocks and her slim legs which were just visible under the silk. Someone whistled. Someone else swore softly. There was a general murmur of appreciation. Even Rodriguez, the auctioneer, who hadn't set eyes upon her until that moment so well had she been guarded by Mama Jo, couldn't help but pause, startled.

He cleared his throat. 'I shall start the bidding at one thousand guineas,' he declared loudly.

Eduardo Bambosa, eating chicken and spraying everyone in close proximity with specks thereof as he spoke, demanded, 'Let's not waste time. Two thousand.'

It was an astronomical sum. Jean-Philippe Lebeq raised an eyebrow at him as if pleading caution and shouted, 'Two thousand one hundred!'

'Bah! Three thousand!' spluttered Bambosa, making Lebeq grimace and flick with his handkerchief as the front of his immaculate oyster satin frockcoat was liberally flecked with essence of fowl.

Bella was horrified. Her worst nightmare was coming true. She was going to be bought by a pig. No, no, correction. She'd rather be bought by a pig.

'God's nightgown,' she ground out between her clenched teeth, her eyes rolling. She went a ghastly colour and could feel sweat breaking out on her forehead.

'I want to see more,' demanded the uncouth Bambosa. 'Have her strip.'

Rodriguez was reluctant. 'You can already glimpse her charms, Sir. Perhaps we should consider the lady's feelings.'

'You'd do better to consider mine. I'm the one with all the money. She must be flawed.'

'She is perfect. And she is a lady,' declared Rodriguez, protectively. 'I will not ask such a thing of her.'

'Y'can keep her then,' spat Bambosa, sitting back in his chair and folding his arms.

Mama Jo came up behind her auctioneer and whispered in his ear. 'Strip her.'

'But!'

'Do it, man. The customer's always right.'

Bella heard them plain enough for such quibbling cut through the fog that surrounded her. As Rodriguez approached, looking apologetic yet purposeful, she gave him an understanding half smile.

'It's all right. I'll undress.' Dignity, she thought. Yes, dignity. No-one was going to strip her, she'd disrobe. There was a great difference. One way would achieve only her humiliation, the other would show them all her contempt.

She clicked open the front fastening on her golden girdle, handed it to the attending auctioneer, then unwrapped the copper silk that had so lightly shrouded her, letting the slippery garment slide off her shoulders. She caught it like a veil between her hands. She trailed it behind herself, turning slowly this way and that. There was a hush.

She was pale, slim, unblemished and perfect. For several seconds she held the assembly in thrall, completely spellbound. Then the fool, Bambosa, shouted absurdly, 'She's got a mole. There. By her knee! Told you so!'

Jean-Philippe Lebeq looked down at the gross joke of a man and curled his Gallic lip contemptuously. 'Imbecile!'

Bambosa swiped him across one cheek, then the other with the chicken leg. 'Popinjay Frog!'

Lebeq, seething, slapped him in return. 'I demand satisfaction, sir.'

'Name the place, flower, I'll be there.'

'Gentlemen, please,' pleaded Rodriguez.

'Let the lady have her clothes back.'

It was a different voice, smooth as velvet but also as strong as steel. From out of the descending darkness near the stockade gates, stepped Kit Tremayne.

He came up the aisle into the torchlight, his long legs taking lengthy strides. He looked beautiful in scarlet leather breeches and jerkin. The metal studded clothing fitted him like a second skin. On his head was a large, plumed black hat, and his hands and legs were encased in supple black leather. He removed the gauntlets leisurely, frowning disapprovingly at Bambosa and Lebeq but then ignoring them.

Rodriguez meanwhile had handed Bella back her gown. She slipped thankfully into it and fastened shut the tight girdle about her waist with a relieved snap. Never had she felt so vulnerable and so alone. But now . . .

She stared at the new arrival, as intrigued by his appearance as the next person, and wondering how long he had been there in the shadows, waiting. Even in her present plight she couldn't help but register how devastatingly handsome he was. He looked like an angel with his platinum-white hair and silver-grey eyes, but she guessed he could be the very devil. She forgot all about the affected Frenchman and prayed that the newcomer had enough money to back up his initial show of gallantry in calling for her clothes.

Rodriguez inclined his head to the gentleman. 'Captain Tremayne! I am happy to see you, Sir. Now, if you will all take your seats once more, the auction will recommence. The bidding was at . . .'

'Three thousand,' reminded Bambosa.

Bella watched Kit Tremayne. But he seemed more interested in inspecting his fingernails and positioning his dress sword so that the bejewelled pommel didn't prod painfully at his thigh. He reminded her of someone she'd known once. Perhaps Buckingham? No, not really. They had similar hair but that was about all they had in common. Buckingham was a manipulator of kings and a social schemer. Mister Tremayne looked more straightforward and more honest. This was absurd really, considering he was a pirate! But looks could deceive. If he wished to buy her and succeeded, Bella would be enternally grateful. Then again, he couldn't be a very pleasant human being if he could do such a thing, now could he? So who was perfect? If he bought her, she thought she might be able to find it in her heart to forgive him!

'Three thousand one hundred,' offered Lebeq.

'Four thousand,' said Bambosa, belly-laughing at the Frenchman's mounting agitation.

'Four thousand one hundred.'

'Five thousand.'

The crowd buzzed. After the first two bids most of those present had given up any wild hope of acquiring the lady themselves. It seemed a two horse race. They kept looking at Tremayne, but he was concerned only with his fingernails, the sky where the stars were coming out or a neutral spot on stage somewhere beneath Rodriguez' kneecaps. Nothing and no-one was being allowed to catch his eye.

Rodriguez didn't have much to do at the moment save to try and keep order. The Frenchman and Spaniard were battling it out between themselves. At last Lebeq, concluding that Bambosa wasn't prepared to waste time bidding in hundreds, gave in and followed suit.

'Six thousand.'

'Seven.'

An agonised pause. 'Eight.'

'Nine.'

Lebeq looked on the brink of frustrated tears. 'Ten!'

'Eleven,' Bambosa cried, laughing dementedly. He had so much money, he'd have paid almost anything. Making Lebeq suffer so greatly was worth it even if the English lady wasn't, he'd decided.

Lebeq sank his head in his hands and shook it. Those very close could hear him sobbing and see his shoulders shaking.

Rodriguez took a deep breath. This was extraordinary.

'Eleven thousand guineas I am bid. Do I hear twelve?'

Bella held her breath until she thought her lungs would burst, her eyes were riveted on Tremayne as she tried to will him by telepathy to bid for her. She'd repay him somehow. He'd have her undying devotion.

'Twelve,' said Kit simply, still not looking up.

She exhaled, rocking on her heels.

'Thirteen!' shouted Bambosa, glaring around Lebeq to the Englishman.

Tremayne was a long time in answering. 'Fourteen, plus my ship, the *Wyvern*.'

He looked up then. His jaw was clenched and he was grave, even someone as vague as Bella could be on occasion, had no doubt as to the sacrifice he was making on her behalf. Her heart went out to him. She had a lump in her throat and a terrible feeling in her guts that it wouldn't be enough.

Bambosa got to his feet, sneering and triumphant. 'Seventeen thousand pounds!'

Captain Tremayne looked apologetic and shook his head. She was lost.

Bambosa roared with jeering laughter. He looked as if he'd've liked to give the Englishman a gloating slap on the back but, prudently, he refrained.

Bella had gone stiff and took a step backwards.

'Seventeen thousand pounds I am bid. Do I hear

any advance? Seventeen thousand guineas? No? She goes then, sirs, for seventeen thousand pounds. Once, twice . . .'

Frowning, his head shaking in disagreement, Tremayne came up out of his seat. 'No, sorry. Can't just sit here and see her sold to a gross fart like him.' He drew his sword and skewered Bambosa on the spot.

It was done in the blinking of an eye. Everyone gasped. Bambosa was still laughing nastily as the blade went in, but he cried then, clutching at the cold steel of the rapier blade protruding from his chest. His eyes popped incredulously and blood trickled from his mouth. 'Is this English fair play?'

'English good manners, you pot of piss!' ground out Kit, pulling out the blade and wagging it at the crowd in general. 'I don't want to do the same to anyone else but if I'm forced – '

He reached up to the stage, took Bella's hand and swung her down, catching her and setting her on her feet. Then he stood protectively in front of her.

Bambosa sank to the floor with his quivering fat belly uppermost.

Lebeq put up his hands placatingly, smiling friendly-like. He laughed nervously. 'You'll get no argument from me, my friend.'

'I thank you.'

Mama Jo was running to the front of the stage, shouting for her slaves to help and almost pushing Rodriguez at the sword-wielding privateer. 'Stop him! Don't just stand there!'

'I am unarmed,' pointed out Rodriguez, somewhat relieved at being spared the necessity. And her slaves had all been rendered harmless by Tremayne's crew.

He'd realised all along – once it came to his notice that Bambosa was on New Providence for the auction

– that he wasn't likely to have enough to buy the Countess. He'd had to make a contingency plan. Thank God he had. Though, whatever happened, Kit thought that he'd likely have killed Bambosa anyhow.

Sword slashing the air about him to ward off any attempt at apprehending them, the Captain took Bella by the hand and ran with her, down the aisle and out of the stockade. His crew swarmed close behind him. They could hear Mama Jo's voice far behind, cursing them to hell and eternal damnation.

They ran and ran. Bella's lungs pained her terribly, burning and feeling like they'd explode, but she'd rather have expired, her body giving out, than flag behind and get caught.

He'd saved her. Yes! Oh, yes! She was in the jolly boat, being pushed out through the surf. Men piled in around her in the moonlight, rowing, laughing and thinking it all a great lark. She gasped, her breath rasping, laughed crazily and, when she wiped the hair out of her eyes, she realised she was crying as well.

'Keep your heads down!' called Tremayne from the second boat. And before any could wonder why there was musket fire from the shore. Bella ducked. It hit the water, skimming all around them but no-one was hit and, by the time Mama Jo and her boys had reloaded and could fire again, the boats were out of range. Tremayne's crew stood up and waved, jeering, then took to the oars once more.

Bella looked across to the other boat, to the Captain and smiled when she caught his eye, the look purposefully full of gratitude and adoration. He was her hero. Not many men would have acted so recklessly and so wonderfully.

He smiled back, removed his hat with a flourish and bowed his head respectfully.

He opened the door to the great cabin at the stern of the ship and ushered Bella in. Candles were lit, and the oaken table set by the diamond-leaded windows that ran the full width of the ship, was laden with fresh fruit, cold meats and silver plate. An eight pronged candelabra stood centre table, its glowing bees-wax candles scenting the room.

'Relax and eat. I shan't be too long,' bid Tremayne, stepping back into the companionway and closing the door.

Bella had opened her mouth to reply but closed it again.

For several moments she just stood in the midst of the darkly panelled room, the wood glowing mellowly and her bare toes wriggling in the deep pile of the Turkey rug beneath her feet. She still couldn't believe it. Bambosa was dead and she was saved. She half laughed and half sobbed. It was staggering.

Finally the appetising fruit looked too tempting to resist any longer and she moved. She guzzled a whole bunch of grapes and quickly polished off a banana, then belching loudly, giggled because there was no one to witness her temporary lapse of manners.

There was wine too. She poured some from the silver jug and drank from a silver cup. It was all very civilised.

She took a look around, glancing quickly over framed maps on the walls and lingering longer on the substantial bed in the alcove. It had neither posts nor tester but was grand for all that, its headboard of ebony carved with wyverns, griffins, zephyrs and all other manner of heraldic beasties. Its bolsters, cushions and coverlet were all furnished in coral and gold brocade. It was lovely.

Bella ran her hands over the rich, tactile material, tracing an index finger along single golden threads. She sat on the edge of the bed, then lay down completely, watching how the moonlight on the waves beyond the window made strange patterns on the cabin ceiling.

What would become of her? She had nothing but the ridiculously insubstantial dress upon her back. Not even her shoes, for they had been lost during her flight from the stockade. She wasn't worried.

She could hear the Captain up above her on the quarter-deck giving orders. They had weighed anchor and were under sail.

She awoke. He was lying beside her, quite naked. His lean, long body and pale hair that brushed his shoulders, were strangely silvered in the moonlight from the window. He was sniffing deeply, inhaling her perfumes.

He smiled easily at finding her awake. 'Must give Mama Jo her due: she has prepared you quite delightfully.' His silver eyes, ringed around with a darker grey, swept over her, lingering on her soft pink mound. 'A nice Eastern touch,' he mused.

'Not for long,' Bella told him. 'It makes me feel too vulnerable, too exposed.'

He nodded. 'You're probably right. I think I liked you better with a pelt.'

She raised herself on an elbow, raising an eyebrow. 'What d'you mean? We've not met before.' And yet, even as she said it, Bella remembered her earlier feeling of familiarity as she'd contemplated him.

'Have we not?' he teased, his hand gliding down over the curve of her hip, and running with palm flat over the rise of her womanliness and on down over her inner thighs, so that Bella tingled despite her perturbed attempts to sort out the puzzle.

'No.' But she didn't sound sure.

He laughed. 'I think you need something to jog your memory.' And he quit the bed, catching a startled Bella beneath the knees and shoulders and swinging her up into his arms.

She laughed, trusting him implicitly for some unfathomable reason. 'What're you doing?' Why was he removing her *from* the bed? It didn't make any sense. She was willing, very willing. He had a delicious body and a handsome phallus reared from between his legs. It looked huge and cumbersome. She giggled. It was a wonder he could walk properly! She wanted him without reserve, being so highly charged with sexual tension after her days of pampering and the endless loveplay of Honey Drips and Sugar Lips that leant itself to voyeurism.

He laid Bella on her back on the table, reached for the grapes and peaches and bit greedily so that the juice flowed. Holding a grape between gleaming teeth he proceeded to transfer it to Bella's mouth. She chewed, choking on the juice as she laughed and gasped with delight.

She'd remembered. 'Bristol!'

He gave a burst of laughter. 'Ah-ha! The lady's memory returns. Yes, Bristol.'

'The sea captain.'

'The very same.'

'Who went off without a word,' she chided, before another grape was pushed between her lips, silencing her.

'I wrote you a note of introduction and left it with Meg Pudney.'

'Never got it,' she said, slurping on the juice.

'Doesn't matter now. Fate was kind. Countess, may I introduce myself?'

She inclined her head with mock formality. All very absurd cosidering the position they were in. 'Please do, sir.'

'Captain Christopher Tremayne, privateer. Known to all as Kit. At your service.'

'I am very pleased to meet you again, Kit. Now, please, can we get back to the bed? Or have you got a special liking for dining tables?' said Bella, looking uncomfortable.

'Tabletops and chairs, you may recall,' he joked, 'and I'm partial to rugs, up against wainscoting . . .'

'Just bed tonight, Kit? And hurry. I'm burning.'

'I'll put out the fire.'

'But not too quickly. Let's enjoy the flames a while.'

She hit the feather-filled mattress and bounced, as Tremayne lay between her legs, spreading them.

'Forget the honeyed claptrap. I've but one thing on my mind, and haven't been able to think of aught else since I spied it. It's not going to last long and so I've to make the most of it while I can.'

She feigned wide-eyed innocence.

He ran his strong hands up from her knees, shifting aside the delicate transparency of gossamer. His fingers claimed her, opening her, all pink, dark, warm and dew-kissed, as salty as the sea. He put his face to her, circled her thighs with his hands and closed her legs about the sides of his head. Straight off Bella was gasping and moaning, her fingers snaring in his hair as his tongue licked her folds, rigidly probing. She squealed, her legs clamping tightly and making him chuckle. She came, wave upon wave lapping then receding. She fell back, panting, floppy and seemingly devoid of bone.

He parted the material of her bodice, tweeked the darkened nipples, then cupped her breasts, prodding at her relaxed womanhood as he did so with his considerable penis. He inched it in, but went no deeper, letting the wide head play just within Bella's entrance, where she was most sensitive. She writhed and moaned with steadily mounting volume all over again.

She laughed up at him, 'Clever devil!' and watched his generous thing at play, teasing and beguiling her, until she was willing and ready for anything.

Then he left off his breast fondling, put his hands either side of her midriff and kissed her, hard and deep, plunging his shaft into her as he did so, to the very limits. She cried out against his mouth with pleasure, snaked her arms about his back and captured him close, riding against him then, arching, straining, and squeezing him deep within her. He spiralled crazily out of control, plunging deeper and harder, grinding against her as she scratched and clutched. She grasped at his shoulders in spasms as they reached the pinnacle together and came crashing back to earth, panting, groaning and exhausted.

He brought the candelabra closer to the bed, lighting Bella within its pale pool as her nude, pale body slipped upon the unravelled bolts of oyster and coral silks – a prize from a Spanish galleon.

She drowsed, languid from lovemaking, the sultry night bestowing a sapping kind of indolence. She was at ease and seemingly would have allowed him any liberty.

He rummaged his coffers of stolen booty, threw out more lengths of precious cloth, and then came back to the bed with a jewel casket. It was sizable and looked heavy. He set it down on the vacant half of the bed where earlier he'd slept, and lifted the hinged barrel lid. Bella watched with dreamy curiosity.

One by one he brought out different pieces, single gems, whole necklaces, earrings, golden bangles, buckles, chains, gem-encrusted bracelets, hair combs and coronets. From Bella came an endless stream of appreciative murmurs.

He stuck a ruby in her naval. It glowed darkly, like the proverbial droplet of blood. Around her neck he draped half a dozen golden necklaces. The different gem colours and settings dazzled the eye. He secured bracelets around her wrists and ankles, kissing the soles of her feet as he did so and smoothing her calves with his palms until she felt the mounting thrill of desire again.

She smiled, devouring him visually. He was like a hero out of a story book. Dashing, brave and generous, a defender and adorer of womankind. Too good to be true. She thought, I've lost everything and I don't care one little bit.

He circled her breasts with golden chains. 'Everything seems to have been made just for you.'

'I think I love you.' She hardly realised she was saying it. It just slipped out.

He raised an eyebrow, seeming to find that mildly amusing. 'Do you now?'

'Yes, I think perhaps I do,' she said, feeling uncomfortable.

'Interesting.'

She had the nasty feeling he was laughing at her and began to feel just a little indignant. Perhaps she'd been a bit impetuous. After all she'd known the man for less than twenty-four hours all told. Maybe it was lust, like the others. But no, she was certain.

'Forget I said it,' she said, blushing.

'How could I?'

There was a knock at the cabin door.

'Yes?' called Tremayne, impatiently.

'Need t'see y'Cap'n,' called Horn, the mate, through the stout door.

'Come in.' Kit left the secluded bed alcove and went and stood on the Turkey rug, wearing naught but his breeches. A sizable bulkhead hid Bella from the view of any who might enter.

Horn took a long time entering, seeming reluctant. He poked his head around the door. 'Delicate matter, Cap'n,' he whispered.

'Whatever's up?' demanded Kit, exasperated by the interruption.

'Well,' Horn said as he entered, holding tightly on to the girl Rebecca, 'this piece has stowed herself aboard. Cook just found her in the provision store.'

Tremayne frowned and stuck his thumbs in his belt. 'What the hell are you doing here?'

'I'm your woman. I've had enough of always being left behind. I decided to sail with you this time,' she explained defiantly, staring back at him boldly.

Bella had knelt up in the bed and was watching behind the great wooden bulkhead of the ship. Very quickly she concluded that she'd made an utter fool of herself. How could she have expected a man like Tremayne to love her? How could he when he had

228

someone like this young, slim and fetching Rebecca creature throwing herself at him? Bella was getting old, and had been so even when Charles II had taken her as his mistress. Her looks were fading. It was true and she knew it. Only two days ago Anemone had gone through her mane of sable hair and pulled out no less than six white hairs! It was the beginning of the end. At last she'd found the man she loved, but he'd obviously prefer the younger, nubile Rebecca. What man wouldn't? They all had their brains in their breeches and let their dicks rule their heads.

Tremayne spun the girl around by the shoulders and marched her out again.

'Who's that woman?' Rebecca insisted on knowing as she was shoved ahead of Tremayne along the passage. She'd caught a glimpse of Bella.

'None of your damned business.'

'What'll we do with her, Cap'n?' wondered a worried Horn. Women were nothing but trouble in Horn's view. That's why he tried to stay permanently at sea; the less he saw of his wife and her mother the better.

'Chuck her over the side for all I care. Just keep her away from my cabin,' ordered Tremayne.

'Aye aye, sir.'

'You cannot mean it!' cried Rebecca, incredulous and red with temper. 'Where'd you find another woman who can give you love like mine?'

'Believe it or not, m'dear,' said Tremayne, icily, 'its not as impossible as you might think.'

He jerked his head and Horn took over, knowing that he was lumbered. He resented the fact mightily too, but knew there was nothing for it. She tried to snatch her arm out of his gaoler's grasp but he took a firmer grip and held on the tighter.

She was his responsibility, it would seem, and he decided there was nothing for it but to confine her to his cabin. At least it had a lock on the door and he'd know exactly where she was all the time. He pushed her inside and slammed the door, searching through his pockets for his tinder-box so he could light a candle.

Rebecca searched frantically too, and found the single brass candlestick before he could. She swiped Horn around the side of the head with it.

He swayed and staggered, but didn't go down, swearing most colourfully and snatching at her. Once imprisoned, he took up rope from his box of bits under the bunk and tied her hands behind her back, shoving her face down on the bed. Then he removed his belt, cursing all the while.

'Defy me, will you? Test my will?'

He lit the candle and set it down on the locker beside his tiny bunk, snatching up Rebecca's skirts and exposing her rounded backside. She shrieked and squirmed, showing a tight arse and darkly hidden cranny.

'You'll learn obedience or you'll go over the side, like he said. I'll not take any messing, not from a chit of a girl like you. No siree.'

The leather belt slapped across the fleshy globes, leaving a livid mark and making Rebecca rear and cry out. He struck twice more, then he laid aside the length of leather, untied her wrists and turned her over.

'Got the message?'

There were tears in her eyes. She nodded slightly.

He dropped his breeches, sat on the edge of the

bunk and pulled her around to straddle him, catching her buttocks and levering her down onto his rigid shaft. She was wet and warm, and didn't resist. He pumped hard, holding her tight and working her body upon his, torturing his sheathed flesh.

Bella felt too naked suddenly, and much too vulnerable. She'd looked at her silly excuse of a garment from Mama Jo's establishment and dismissed it contemptuously. No, that simply wouldn't do.

She headed for Tremayne's clothes chest, throwing open the lid and getting down on her knees to have a good rummage. She found velvet breeches in damson and midnight blue stripes, a voluminous shirt, greatly ruffled with lace at the throat and wrists, a cummerbund of black satin and black stockings. She'd managed to scramble into everything save the stockings when Tremayne returned. She threw them down and snatched up his sword instead from near the bed.

He stopped, cocked an eyebrow, frowned, then laughed scornfully.

She pointed the rapier at him and tried to look mean. The bloody thing weighed too much and began to wobble in her grasp, starting up an excruciating ache in her wrist.

Tremayne seated himself in a chair from under the dining table, drawing one foot up onto the seat in a casual manner and smirking.

'What's so damned funny?' snarled Bella.

'You, m'dear. What's all this in aid of? Have you turned pirate too and intend taking over the *Wyvern*?'

'Don't be stupid! I'm merely protecting myself. I have no intention of joining your harem. I like a man to be my own.'

'Why don't you put that thing down? You might hurt yourself and you look so uncomfortable.'

'Don't concern yourself with my welfare. I'm fine.'

'Really?'

'Yes.'

He was out of his seat as if sprung, catching her wrist and squeezing it so sharply that Bella dropped the rapier with a yelp of pain, jumping gingerly as the blade cluttered on the boards at her feet.

His eyes blazed. 'Never try anything like that again!'

He kissed her brutally hard, bending Bella over backwards until she went clean off balance, snatching at her clothes and wrestling her to the floor. He all but ripped off his oversized – on her – breeches and took her on the Turkey rug without preamble or endearment. He fucked her silently, almost savagely, his teeth clashing with hers, his lips bruising, his flesh piercing her, filling her, and mastering her. It was glorious. She clung to him, cradling his thrusting thighs with her own and crying out again and again as she clutched at him. She reached the heights of pleasure, he racing and coming close behind.

They lay there a long time after the panting had quietened. Eventually she began to pull up her breeches and secure the cummerbund.

'What was all that about?' asked Tremayne.

'Your woman,' Bella told him.

'I have no woman. Or I didn't until I brought you on board.'

'I don't believe you,' said Bella in a tone that told him she was open to persuasion.

'Suit yourself,' he said, shrugging.

* * *

They anchored briefly in one of Nassau's southern bays. Tremayne kept pressing Bella for information concerning Keyho: whereabouts he'd been encamped, how many men were at his command, his intentions for the captured British merchantman and the booty still aboard.

Bella could only shrug vaguely, wondering at his interest. All she could tell him was that Keyho had maybe two hundred men under him. He would tell her nothing.

Since she'd held him at swordpoint and he'd overpowered her, imposing his will, Tremayne had left her well alone. It was as if, wordlessly, he was letting her know that if she didn't want him to touch her, he didn't want to touch her anyhow, her hardening of attitude bothering him not at all.

One thing was certain from their reconnoitering of Nassau's coastline – Keyho was gone, and this time he'd even taken Chastity with him.

Two days out of Nassau, heading south-west towards the Leeward Islands, they sighted another ship. She was British – a merchantman – though her lower deck had been partially converted to take cannon instead of cargo. Evidently her master was determined that she shouldn't fall prey to pirates and was happy to sacrifice some of the profits for the sake of a safe arrival virtually guaranteed.

Tremayne watched her through his spyglass with Bella at his side. The ship ran up flags, wanting to make contact with the *Wyvern*. Kit obliged, finding nothing suspicious in his perusal of the craft.

'Why're we meeting with her?' asked Bella, looking charming in breeches and frilly shirt. Her hair was brushed free of all contrived ringlets and curls and lay in a thick braid down her back.

'Her captain wants words.'

'Bit unusual, isn't it?'

'Yes. But not unheard of.'

'Mightn't they be pirates in disguise?'

He laughed, unworried. 'Not in a tub like that. Granted, she's got a dozen cannon, but she's not suited, nor even rigged, for warfare. I think we're safe.'

Bella went below to answer a call of nature, emptying the chamber pot out through the grand rear window of the great cabin. Coming back through the companionway she opened the door to Horn's cabin and glared in at the confined Rebecca, who likewise, glared back. Neither would lower herself to speak. They just made plain their undying hatred with a series of hostile expressions, ranging from snarl to icy stare and every permutation in-between.

Back on deck Bella could see the people on the deck of the other ship quite clearly now. They were maybe only a hundred or so feet apart. She wondered if they'd lower a jolly boat, but no, they seemed happy just to shout.

The captain removed his hat and waved it, bellowing at the top of his voice as the vessels drifted closer, aided by some excellent rudder work from the men at the wheels.

'Captain Tremayne, good day to you, Sir!'

Kit nodded. 'Captain, how might I assist you?'

'I have been informed, sir, that you attended an auction on New Providence recently. That you ran off, under rather bizarre circumstances, with the prize lot of the day.'

'And why would that be of any interest to you?' Kit wanted to know.

'I have a man on board who is most anxious to

learn of the Countess of Hawksley's whereabouts and general health. These past weeks he's been scouring the Caribbean for her.'

'Really?'

'Yes,' shouted the captain against the whistle of wind and a sudden, shrill seagull squawk. He turned and beckoned someone forward to the quarter-deck rail.

Bella gasped and stepped instinctively behind Kit, hissing at Master Horn who stood nearby, 'Your hat, sir, if you'd be so kind.'

Horn's eyebrows knit bemusedly, but he removed the battered article and handed it over. Bella crammed it hard on her head, pulling the front brim low so that only her mouth was still visible to any onlooker.

She tugged at Kit's jerkin, whispering urgently, 'I'm not here. Tell them I'm dead.' She was glad to see that her suitor had survived but didn't care to become reacquainted.

Kit half turned, raised an eyebrow suspiciously, and spoke out the side of his mouth. 'And why should I want to do that?'

'I'll explain later,' she pleaded, 'just do it.'

Tremayne turned back to the other ship, struck by the handsomeness of the man who now stood beside the captain. He was tall, swarthy, rapier-slim and stylishly attired in black with a ruff of silver lace at his throat. Kit looked from the man to Bella, then back again speculatively. Just what was going on? Instinctively, he didn't care for the man.

'Sir, what was your business with the lady?'

'We had an arrangement and were to be married,' said Julius Pelegrini, looking Captain Tremayne over very thoroughly in his usual superior manner.

'Well, I'm sorry to have to tell you,' Kit bellowed, 'that the Lady Arabella was shot during our bid to rescue her from the island. We were fired upon as we fled in the boats. It was most unfortunate. I'm terribly sorry. We buried her at sea with full Christian service, you'll be comforted to hear, I'm sure.'

'Dead?' Pelegrini was very upset, stunned to an odd quietness, poor fellow.

'Sorry.'

He seemed to stagger and took a step back behind the ship's captain, shaking his head. He needed to retire, dismayed by the news.

The sight affected Bella too. She got a lump in her throat and was touched to think news of her demise could upset anyone so greatly.

'Thank you, Captain,' yelled their captain. 'We'll detain you no further.'

Each vessel put on sail and maneouvred away from the other. Kit Tremayne took Bella by the arm and led her purposefully below. 'Explanation time, I think.' The door shut and they were private. 'So, who was that gentleman?'

'His name was Julius Pelegrini. An Italian gentleman living on Jamaica. We were aboard ship together, headed for the islands when Keyho attacked. He had proposed – but I had not accepted – that we were to be married. I never had time to give him an answer.'

'Until today. Telling someone you're dead counts as a definite no I think. Why? he's a handsome fellow, monied by the sound of it. Why stay with me when you could go with him?'

Bella shrugged but didn't care to be drawn. 'Why indeed?'

'Because you love me.'

'Rubbish, Tremayne, that was said in the afterglow of passion. People often say ridiculous, silly things at times like that. It doesn't mean anything.'

'No?'

'No. And why are you making such a debate of this? It just seemed kinder not to become reacquainted with the man and to let him think me dead. Why're you getting all fired up?'

'I'm not,' he denied, hotly.

'You are. Jealous?'

'Ha!'

She smirked and looked very smug.

He caught her by the upper arms and snatched her close, kissing her deeply, his teeth clashing with hers, his tongue ravaging and plundering, and causing hot arousal between her legs.

She struggled free and gasped. 'Take me by force and what'll that prove?'

'I've never had to force a woman in my life. Never.' And he found her mouth again, coaxing her lips open and robbing her of breath, until Bella was wobbly at the knees.

Bastard! She hated people who always thought they were right and oft-times were.

She fumbled with his belt and breeches, tearing at the buttons in exasperation. It was easier for him. He had only to untie her cummerbund, and her baggy breeches simply fell down.

He dropped to his knees taking Bella with him. Nudging her knees he found her warmth with the head of his awesome stiffness and pushed it into her. He clenched her buttocks and thrust, as she grabbed him close, her hands roving adoringly, lustily. The kiss never faltered throughout. They cried out, the noise muffled and their breathing difficult, then clung to each other as the moment came and went, fusing them and draining them, leaving them shuddering with aftershocks.

A while later he went back up on deck, pooh-poohing still her accusation that he was jealous.

'Jealous! Nonsense!'

She smiled, almost certain of him now. Rebecca truly didn't mean anything to him. Thank God Julius hadn't discovered her. How unpleasantly different things might have been if he had. Tremayne would have fought him and one of them might have died – Kit probably, considering that Pelegrini had been a fencing master back in Italy. It didn't bear thinking about.

Chapter Ten

Women were at a premium aboard ships in the Caribbean. To some men, deprived of feminine company, even Chastity Wise began to look kind of attractive after a while!

She did her washing on deck every day, rinsing chemises and petticoats in pails of salt water and hanging them over the lower reaches of rigging to dry. She washed on her hands and knees, bent over the pail, with her ample breasts wobbling and hanging pendulous within the scooped neckline of her Spanish blouse, and her skirts hitched up for the sake of practicality and fastened into her buckled leather belt.

This meant that she showed off a great deal of meaty leg – surprisingly shapely ankles, rounded calves, and sizable, white thighs. It was the occasional flash of thigh as she worked away, oblivious to the lewd thoughts she evoked in many a head, that enflamed more than one member of the motley pirate crew working topside.

Keyho passed, muttering to himself at seeing his ship turned into a laundry and his woman's underwear dangling and flapping everywhere for everyone to see.

'What's that you say, Abraham?'

'Nothing, my lamb, nothing. Just thinking aloud about the weather,' he lied, smiling obsequiously.

She narrowed her eyes and rubbed her undies with greater vigour, her breasts juddering.

Up in the rigging men paused, mesmerised, yearning for those great big breasts and those dauntingly strong-looking thighs. Nut crackers, they called them.

'When do we eat?'

'When I get around t'cooking,' she said crossly.

'Fair enough, my sweet. Think I'll go below and check my charts.'

Chastity mumbled dismissively, not in the least interested in Keyho's present preoccupation with finding Captain Tremayne and thus, Bella Flowers. She had Christian duties enough to occupy her: cleanliness, Godliness and keeping her man's belly full. These were her priorities. Frankly, she just wished that he'd forget about that amoral witch. The brazen piece was nothing but a jinx.

Her washing had become quite violent, as she fancied Keyho's breeches to be the embodiment of the Countess. She went to the side, tied the pail to a rope and dangled it over, filling it from the rushing sea and then struggling to haul it back up. She had arms like a horse-fair wrestler but even so she staggered and went purple in the face.

Some fellow ran to help at the precise moment that she toppled, half-spilling the full pail, with her legs flying up in the air. He grabbed her, to help, only to fall with her or, rather upon her. Chastity squealed and struggled.

He couldn't control himself and grabbed a breast, latching on to it like a ravenous pup. She couldn't make up her mind whether to be outraged or not, but decided not to be hasty. She admired a man with spirit.

More bodies descended from the rigging, going under hand down ropes and ladders, dropping all around. Male bodies. Rampant bodies, their breeches straining to contain erect members. She was overwhelmed by the delight of it all and actually giggled.

That was all the encouragement they needed. She was surrounded. Breeches were unbelted and unbuttoned, and penises were put on display. Long, longer, slim, fat, grimy, veined, bent, her eyes darted about them all and she opened her legs.

Someone lifted her skirts with trembling fingers, still hardly daring to believe that the Chastity they all knew could behave in such a wanton fashion. She must have hit her head when she fell. At any moment they expected her to scream and bellow, and to cow them like she did poor old Keyho. But no. She was as meek as a lamb (very appropriate when one considered Keyho's white and woolly term of endearment), and more accomodating than the most enthusiastic dockland whore.

She lay back and gave herself over entirely to their undivided attention. How novel to be in the complete power of others after all these years of wiping the floor with Keyho. It caused an excitement in Chastity that she had never known before.

They had descended almost like vultures. There wasn't an inch of her body left unattended. Like worker ants they swarmed everywhere, super efficient and too numerous to count.

They raked her hair, they kissed her face, her limbs, her rotund torso, they pulled her great breasts free from her loose blouse, several hands wanting to touch and to stroke, to cup and to caress, and to knead her with rough urgency.

They went down on their knees, looking at her big juicy womanhood which was willingly opened, a pink tip protruding from russet lips furred with brown curls. Tentatively someone inserted his pinky finger and wiggled. Someone else dived at her puss head first, courting Chastity with his tongue, slobbering over her and inhaling her heady scent.

A burly seaman rinsed his length in the pail of cold water, giving it a superficial scrub, then nudged it between her full lips. He was brave indeed considering just how vicious that mouth could sometimes be. But no. She was a changed woman. She wanted him, them – all of them. She was laughing and enjoying it all greatly.

They were mad. This was crazy. They might well hang for this, but the devil was in them and they didn't care. Afterwards she'd like as not betray them to Keyho and they'd be flogged, keelhauled or strung up from their own rigging. But that was afterwards. This was now. And now it seemed worth the risk. Weren't they fearless pirates after all?

The penis filled her mouth and worked against her lips. She made sucking noises, as if she was eating a tasty sausage, and her eyes sparkled. Someone pushed between her legs, filling her and taking her hurriedly in excited, short stabs. Someone followed quickly afterwards, not so hurried. His blade was slimmer and longer, and he found his passage easy after the lubricating of the first.

This was lovely. This was joy. How long had it been since she'd had a man properly? Had let one love her, not just dominated and humiliated one to order, like Keyho? Too long.

She clenched her inner muscles around the shaft that pleasured her and heard the man call out in transports of delight as he jammed at her urgently and came wildly and noisily.

His place was taken by the next. Someone wriggled beneath her delicious bulk, cradling her, and introduced a finger into her arse. He teased her while the man above thrust to the thick based limits of his phallus, his balls dancing lightly and sweetly upon her tender flesh. The thing in her mouth went off and she had to gulp frantically to cope.

When the man withdrew, leaving her throbbing and ecstatic, Chastity struggled wearily onto her knees, languid from a surfeit. 'Enough,' she murmured, her voice containing none of its usual harshness.

Nobody took any notice. She was grabbed from behind, her buttocks splayed and another rigid shaft slipped into her wetness. She sighed and groaned with pleasure, throwing back her head and arching her throat as someone caught her breasts and cupped them lovingly. She came again, screaming. She tried to crawl off as the man pulled out, sated, but someone else was already catching at her ankle, trying to lay claim to her.

'No more, for pity's sake,' she laughed, quiet and exhausted. 'Another time.'

She was staggering to her feet and rearranging her

clothing when Keyho emerged from his cabin beneath the quarter-deck.

His eyebrows disappeared into his hairline at the sight of a dozen and more of his men caught with their trousers down. For once he lost his cool in front of Chastity. 'What's voorking going on here?'

She was sharp and quick, much too much so for him. 'Dirty bodies breed dirty minds,' she declared, dipping a scrubbing brush in the pail of cold, salty water and proceeding to scrub down the belly of the seaman nearest her.

The poor grimacing fellow stood there fearfully and had himself cleaned raw. Not surprisingly his manhood quickly shrank as Chastity told him, in her more usual voice, to put the nasty thing away.

Keyho watched, frowning, one eyebrow cocked. He didn't know what to make of it. He didn't think it altogether right and proper that she should take the personal hygiene of the crew upon herself as well as her other domestic duties, but wasn't brave enough to venture a question of doubt.

'Very commendable,' he mumbled. 'But mayhap they should scrub themselves, my lamb, while you oversee that it is done properly.'

'You may be right. Perhaps they can be trusted to do it properly now that I've showed them the right way,' agreed his wife, dropping the bristle brush into the pail. 'Carry on, men. I'll go start the cooking.'

Keyho gave a crashing sigh, so glad to have handled the situation without making the dear woman angry for once.

The tub was modest and her knees stuck up in the air. Her breasts were floating just upon the waterline, bobbing with her nipples jutting clear.

244

It was divine. Real, soft water from the ship's water barrel, not brine from the sea. Bella luxuriated, half lost beneath a load of bubbles.

'Now there's a picture to gladden the heart.'

Her head swivelled and her eyes narrowed on Kit Tremayne in the doorway. 'How long have you been there? Can't a body have any privacy?'

'Perhaps M'lady would prefer another cabin?' he asked cooly.

Her lips thinned.

'Shall I do your back?'

It wouldn't have mattered if Bella had said no. He was kneeling behind her already, taking up an expensive tablet of heavily scented soap and building a lather within his palms. He worked on her shoulders and neck, smoothing her shoulder-blades and rubbing with his palms.

It was very pleasant indeed. Bella closed her eyes. His hands ran down her arms, then up again on the delicate inner flesh, gliding over her hard-tipped breasts, circling and cupping them.

'Why're you smiling?'

She shrugged evasively. 'I didn't know I was.'

'Oh, yes. Do you like this?' His hands dipped beneath the water, sweeping her belly and her sex lips, touching so fleetingly that Bella wasn't certain whether the move had been deliberate or not. She murmured a response.

'Come on. Stand up.'

Her eyes opened. 'Why?'

He was standing before her then, holding out a giant bath sheet. She was more than a little reluctant. The water felt so good and he had such a gentle touch. But she did as she was told, thinking that if she played along she might begin to fathom the man

245

and even get him to bare his soul. She wanted him to make her believe that he loved her as much as she loved him. All he needed was some encouragement.

She stepped from the tub, allowed herself to be wrapped in the sheet and carried to the bed. He laid her down. Her heart was beating quickly now with mounting excitement. But he didn't unwrap Bella, like a present, all pink and warm and willing.

He stripped, getting into the tub and making short work of washing himself from sunbleached hair to rather large feet on the ends of longs legs, then stood up again, hefting up a pail and rinsing himself with the contents.

All the while Bella had been watching him, having freed her trapped arms and made herself comfortable. She reclined on her side, her weight on one elbow and her chin in her hand.

He was nicely tall and lean with not a surplus ounce of fat on him. His arms and legs were golden-flecked with hair and sinewy. Between his legs his dormant shaft nestled, thick and knobby, like a beast slumbering.

He squeezed the surplus water from his hair, shook his head, flicking the mane back off his face, and padded, dripping, to the door. There he stood and yelled up the companionway 'Tub!' At once the men were back, hefting away the used water and keeping their eyes on the tub and pails and not risking a glance around for Bella in a state of undress.

For a long time after they'd gone there was silence in the cabin. Tremayne went and stood, still beautifully naked, to look out of the great window and watch the *Wyvern's* foaming wake. Bella watched him speculatively; she didn't feel uncomfortable.

246

At last he half turned, looked at her stonily. 'What was Pelegrini to you?'

It took some effort not to smile. 'What was Rebecca to you?'

He frowned. 'I asked first.'

'Nothing.'

'Likewise.'

There was another silence. 'I hope you love me as much as I love you,' he said.

Bella smiled tenderly, her heart leaping. 'More so.'

'You couldn't possibly,' he declared emphatically, playfully, adding 'I adored you the first time I laid eyes upon you.'

'Likewise.'

'But I saw you before you e'er saw me.'

'Nonsense.'

''Tis true.'

''Twas Bristol – '

'Nay. There was a time before. In London. Before fame and fortune had ever touched you, Bella Flowers.'

Her eyebrows had knit. 'London? When?'

'Let me tell you a story. One night on the corner of Chancery Lane, when I was returning to my ship after visiting a friend, I came across a young woman being accosted by drunken ruffians. One gentleman was being particularly tiresome. I dealt with him and told the young lady to run off home. 'Twas stupid of me, of course, because she did just that and then I had no idea where she'd gone or how I might contact her again.'

She spluttered, 'You! It was you who killed Jasper Sweetly? Heavens above!'

'Small world, isn't it? It all came back to me after we were reacquainted on New Providence.'

Bella was sat staring and open-mouthed. 'God's nightgown!' Then she laughed scoffingly. 'But how could you love me even then? It was dark, for heaven's sake. You'd have hardly been able to see me.'

'But I did,' said Kit, laughing. 'Fleetingly, 'tis true. But there was the briefest moment when your face caught in the weak light from a lantern and I was, let us say, greatly affected.'

She smiled at him wonderingly and slipped from the bed, trailing the sheet behind her like Salome with the seventh veil.

He stood rigid and unyielding, determined to stay strong. His jaw was clenched tight and jutting, but there was a twitch at the side of his mouth. He was finding it more difficult than she – the one time actress – not to laugh.

'Don't you trust me?' she said, kneeling before him. She ran her hands, then her tongue up his strong thighs, licking around his genitalia, and watching them reorganise, plump up and grow.

'No,' he croaked.

She teased the end of him, took him into her mouth and sucked, then abandoned to run her wet tongue down his leg, to the knee, then up the other. He trembled slightly. He drew in his breath but remained still, his hands behind his back out of the way. How trusting!

She grinned and chuckled, licking the length of him once more and then, straightening up, she rubbed her body the length of his, squashing her breasts against his chest. She came up to his nipples which she could just circle with her tongue if she stood on tiptoe. She stroked him, kissed him and glanced her body lovingly over his.

248

She fetched a chair from the dining table and set it before him. Standing on it, she kissed his face, his forehead, his ears, his neck, his mouth; kissing him the way he kissed her, both hard and demanding. She took his breath away though he stayed a living statue.

She lowered herself down over him, taking his turgid length and guiding it to her spot. He slipped in and up, went deep then deeper still when Bella kicked the chair away, wrapping her legs around him as he staggered and fastened her mouth to his.

He was forced to act. He cupped her buttocks and supported her then, while Bella worked on him, arching and raising her body upon his to bring them both to a whirlwind climax.

'I love you,' he said.

'I love you too. For now,' she added, not wanting him to get too sure of himself.

'Oh aye, for now,' he echoed, pushing Bella onto her back and pinning her there, his silver eyes sparkling with mirth.

He was hard again. He pressed against her inner thigh and caressed her warm flesh, his chest tickled by her upthrusting nipples, then he entered Bella again. He took her slowly and thoroughly, rolling with her, moving his legs, sometimes between her spread limbs, sometimes one moving outside, so that she felt tighter and an exquisite friction was caused. Always, when she looked too dreamy or too lulled, he came back to his favourite position with his weight on his hands and body raised to give great impetus on his thrusts.

He slowed, gently toying, just moving in circles until he felt on the point of exploding. Desisting, he came down close and lay the length of Bella, buried in her. They seemed somehow fused, their hips, bellies, chests and breaths all as one as they moved, slowly, murmuring and wrapping their arms around each other. His shaft flexed and she tightened her muscles in response, drawing at him and exciting Kit torturingly.

He came up onto his hands once more and began to thrust in earnest, gritting his teeth and stroking deep, he slammed against her mound and made her bud riot with sensation. Bella caught at his hips and dug in her fingertips to bring him possessively close. Moving closer with each thrust, their bodies welding in the final seconds before the floodgates opened and ecstasy burst forth, making them cry out, over and over, then growing fainter and weaker.

Chastity knelt on the hard floor of her cabin, reading the Good Book and trying to find some reasonable excuse for her lapse into wantoness. She couldn't abide the thought that she had fallen into temptation and succumbed like that lewd creature Bella Flowers. But there was no excusing what had happened. No. She was a wicked woman. No-one had forced her and she'd liked it. Yes, she had, there was no point in trying to deny it. She'd liked it and she couldn't help but wish it might happen again. How sinful were such thoughts! She hated herself. No, she didn't. She knew what she should do, though.

She opened the door and yelled for Keyho. He hurried in, looking worried and sheepish, and wondering what he'd done wrong now. He blinked in consternation at her naked form standing amidst a pile of hastily doffed clothes. 'Yes, precious?'

'Mount me, Abraham.'

'Now?' He looked aghast. He didn't care for his

sex this way at all. He liked to be scared and humiliated and needed the thrill of fear to excite him. It was a very long time since he'd had straight sex. He doubted he was able, especially when it was demanded cold like that. If he'd had a rum or two he might have been able to manage it better, being more relaxed and warmed up.

'Yes, now,' she demanded, jumping on the bed so that all her ampleness wobbled. The structure groaned dangerously and dust motes rose up in the air.

He felt his manhood shrink rather than grow and his hands trembled as he pulled off his boots and holey stockings.

'Hurry,' she insisted, with no warmth in her voice. 'Come along.'

He climbed between her legs obediently and lowered himself onto Chastity almost fearfully. She got fed up with his fumblings, slapped his hand away and grabbed him. He gave a startled yelp.

She wiggled him in, then, putting her hands to his buttocks, she slapped him once, hard, to get his petrified body into action.

With a gasp of fright he was off, prodding and pumping, but keeping his eyes closed so that she shouldn't intimidate him too much. This kind of fright wasn't exciting at all and didn't add anything to the act for him. No, this was just terrifying, this awful, fearful certainty that he couldn't possibly please her. And, once the seed of doubt was planted, he felt himself soften and dwindle, lost in her juicy depths.

'Oh dear,' he lamented, his voice lowering to a fearful whisper, 'oh, deary, deary dear.'

He battled on desperately and valiantly for several

more ineffectual thrusts before feeling himself slip from her completely.

Chastity threw him off, hit him two stunning blows about the ears and then furiously set about putting Keyho over her knee and spanking him.

'Useless! Worthless!' With each word of reproach her palm rained down, leaving a large red patch where it made stinging contact.

Keyho hollered and writhed, with tears in his eyes, his penis now growing huge and rubbing against her vast white thigh.

'Don't! I beg you!' he whimpered, his voice broken with emotion and his body jerking as another blow struck.

'Ugly! Pathetic!'

He came, spurting messily all over the bedcovers. She growled with frustration and flung him from her like a rag doll.

She'd gone around several of the crew, whispering low and conspiratorially, 'Come to my cabin after the midday meal. It'll be worth your while and you've nothing to fear.'

Fear they did. But they had a pretty good idea what Chastity Wise had in mind and their lust was stronger than natural caution. They did as bid. For many it was the first time they had ever been in the master cabin on Keyho's ship. There were a dozen of them and when the last man was in Chastity turned the black iron key in the stout lock.

She smiled and produced four bottles of rum and a dozen pewter snifters. Expectantly and lasciviously, each held out his cup, and took his nip. They watched the woman, the way she moved, how differently she looked somehow.

She was still Chastity but she had done something. Nothing too drastic, but noticeable. Her clothes were clean and the bodice was snug fitting, tailored so that her breasts were forced high and together creating an awesome area of cleavage. Her hair was different too. It was combed for a start and looked kind of sleek in its fiddly, unattractive style. An improvement at any rate. But what was so very, very striking was her lack of harshness. The flinty look was gone from her eyes to be replaced by a wicked glint.

All the while she served them drinks she smiled. 'Doubtless you're wondering why you're here.'

Some nodded and some didn't but they had a pretty good idea.

'Life at sea be dour t'say the least.'

'Oh aye, indeed,' said one of the men politely.

'After our little bit of fun on deck the other day, I got t'thinking about what I've been a-missing and about good old fashioned, wholesome sex. I was troubled, men, by what we'd done.'

The twelve hung their heads and looked guilty, swallowing their rum suddenly with difficulty and feeling uncomfortable.

'But I consulted the Good Book and after much soul searching and agonising I suddenly realised that God is a-wanting me to do a service to you honest working seamen. He's made me see that my life with the Captain has been wicked and unnatural. The Almighty tells us to go forward and multiply. My husband will not do his duty but I must do mine.'

Some of them were a bit slow and looked at Chastity blankly. Others got the gist but couldn't believe their ears or their luck.

'I be a woman, Mother Earth. Put fruit on my branches, men.'

They exchanged wry glances and knocked back another measure of rum. The woman was mad. However they weren't about to deny her, or themselves. Keyho had been set aside. Their time was at hand. His power was on the wane, for none had ever doubted that Chastity Wise was the man's real strength.

They began jostling each other, an elbow here, a shove there, each wanting to be first as they struggled with their breeches.

'Let us sing,' insisted Chastity, hitching up her skirts above her knees and perching herself on the edge of the battered top of the cabin table. 'A nice hymn to lift our spirits.'

'Oh aye.' They chuckled amongst themselves, nudging and obligingly trying to agree on one particular hymn. They refilled their glasses and lifted their voices enthusiastically, crowding around their accomodating, singing hostess.

She sang, eyes full of what, perhaps, was divine brightness, and unlaced her bodice so that her breasts were more accessible. Several hands at once tried to slide a hand down betwixt flesh and stiffly boned clothing.

'Sing! Sing!' She rallied them when their voices petered out, their minds on other things. 'Sing praises unto the Almighty.'

They boomed out the chorus, lying her back on the table, as the first man stood between her awesome thighs and spread them. He ran his hands up the tender inner flesh, stroking a finger through the lips of her womanliness.

Her bud sprang forth, pink and strong, like a little tongue. One man's head bent and his mouth claimed it and drew it out further, pulling on it so that they might all see it. The others watched avidly, as they played with her breasts, her shapely ankles and strong arms, singing all the while.

She was a lusty woman. Big and not fragile. Just right for a good time. They had no fear of breaking her or being bruised upon her bones. And she was so willing. They felt they could have tried anything and she wouldn't have minded. After Keyho it was evident that Chastity just wanted a man – or men – who had normal needs and some small perception of her own.

'Procreation, my man,' she said to the pirate playing with her bud, 'Let's not waste time.'

'Right y'are, mistress,' said the man, taking his penis and shuffling just a little closer with his breeches around his ankles. He put the globular head to her, all engorged and angry looking, and opened her folds around it. He could feel her drawing in around him, sucking him in almost. He held open the milky white thighs and pushed into her.

She sighed long and deep. 'Ah, what a lovely cock. What a beauty. Oh, men, let me tell you, that feel doth defy description.'

'Feels good t'me too,' said the man deep in her, pulling out then plunging in again.

Chastity looked around at the singing, avid, happy band and smiled radiantly. 'So many lovely cocks. I want you all. All. This is a good and natural thing we do. And we must do it often. The Almighty tell's us so.' That statement was greeted with hearty approval.

The first man finished and another took his place and, when he'd reached his point of crisis – the hymn he was singing becoming an ecstatic howling – Chastity was coaxed onto her belly and taken from behind.

She came then, shuddering and twitching around the fat shaft that thrust into her with such determination to find her spot. Half sliding, half falling to the floor, languid with pleasure, she stayed on her hands and knees with her backside exposed.

The man had managed to stay in her and she moved back with her haunches to meet each thrust, greedy and delighted as their sweaty flesh slapped. They collapsed in a groaning heap, their breathing ragged and their bodies seemingly liquified. Neither moved for a while.

Another man approached and kicked his comrade off. He turned a floppy Chastity over and drew up her legs, so that her knees touched her breasts, squashing them, and her flaring sex was exposed in all its glistening, ravaged loveliness. He plunged his hard member into her, making her cry out, sinking deep and pushing and grinding against her. He slipped in the wetness of the man who had gone before. He didn't last long.

'Rum!' she cried, licking her lips as she lay upon the floor with her skirts awry and her legs wide in an exhausted state of abandon. 'And sing, sing! Come on. Another hymn. Something rousing. Something to make the sap rise.'

They laughed uproariously. She was mad and wonderful too.

Rum was brought and the bringer lay down beside her, waited for her to knock it back, then pulled her astride him. She slid down over him, his large phallus plunging in and slipping up her easily, to the hilt where her bone rubbed him torturously. Her mound seeming to engulf and surround him. He grinned blissfully, reaching up and cupping her great hanging breasts, the big handfuls of wobbly loveliness spilling out of his grasp, the nipples teased between his fingers.

She worked upon him and made him gasp and cry out. Pretty soon her enflamed bud was rioting again, exploding with sensation and Chastity threw back her head, exposing her throat and gurgling.

There was a hard rapping of knuckles upon the door and a violent and ineffectual turning of the handle.

The men exchanged glances, still singing as required but looking a little apprehensive at this turn of events. What happened now?

Keyho's voice shouted furiously, 'Chastity, are you in there? Who's with you? I can hear voices, singing. Chastity, can you hear me?'

She climbed off the man on the floor, pulled and tied the laces of her bodice and smoothed the dishevelled hair back off her face. The men took their cue from her, buttoning up their breeches and standing in orderly fashion as they lifted their voices enthusiastically in the hymn.

She turned the key and flung the door open. 'What do you want, Abraham?'

He stood on the threshold, her bulk in his way, making it only too plain that his presence wasn't required.

He tried to look around her and could see some members of his crew a-singing. Damned if that didn't beat all. Still, he knew only too well how intimidating she could be. It seemed she wanted to turn them all into choirboys.

'I just wondered what was going on in my cabin,' he said defensively.

'We're having a prayer meeting. Someone has to look after the spiritual well-being of the men aboard

257

this ship, Abraham. You have been very lax in this regard. Perhaps y'would care t'join us in the hymn singing?'

He backed off, shaking his head and full of bluster. 'Regretably I'm very busy on deck. You won't keep the men from their duties too much longer will you, my lamb?'

'Only as long as it takes,' she told him, uncompromisingly, closing the door in his face and locking it again.

The next day there was silence and a locked door. Abraham Keyho knocked again. One of his men opened it and acknowledged him with a nod. 'Cap'n.'

Keyho scowled and pushed past him. He didn't know what he expected to see. But he didn't expect to see what he did. In his bones he felt sure something was going on, something to which he was not a party. And yet here he was apparently being proven wrong again.

Chastity was on her knees with her bible open in her hands. His men – a dozen or so – were kneeling facing her, repeating in a quiet mumble the prayers she recited a line at a time.

She looked up and raised her eyebrows askance. 'Abraham? Come to join us?'

Still frowning, he shook his head, turned on his heel and hastily retreated. She'd always been religiously inclined but, he had to admit, this new zeal was making him uncomfortable.

The key turned in the lock and the kneeling figures fell about laughing. Chastity tossed aside the Good Book and rolled onto her back with her legs in the air.

One of the men poured a measure of rum into her laughing mouth, kissed the wet lips, threw up her skirts and pushed himself into her. Wedged tight, they rolled with her legs folding around him. Someone's fingers probed where the two were joined, feeling the girth piercing her and how she tightened and relaxed about him. Someone else came and stood behind her, rubbing his swollen flesh against her body, and cupping and squeezing her breasts rhythmically. She began to breath raggedly, to tense and arch, squeezing the shaft that thrust up into her and crying out loudly when her passion reached its zenith.

The man behind her pulled Chastity off and pushed her against the wall. Nudging her legs he worked his way up into her wetness. Quickly he took her, thrusting and pumping with every inch crammed into her as her buttocks thudded softly against the wainscoting. She clung to him with her arms around his neck, gurgling in delight.

Bella watched Kit at the table in their cabin, plotting his courses, studying his charts and measuring with compasses across the old, tattered parchment. He conversed with Horn, agreeing on one point and arguing another, so at ease in his role. He'd been born to rove the seas.

Playing with jewellery in the bed alcove, Bella tried idly to decide what accessories she'd wear that day. Oh, decisions decisions. Should it be the rubies or the topaz? Necklace and earrings, or would that be too much? Bracelets perhaps? She fixed two on, matching manacles of heavy gold studded with amethysts. Were there earrings to match? She began to search, looking up occasionally to see if Tremayne was still playing at captain and admiring the neatness of his buttocks.

His suede breeches which alternated damson and black depending on which way the hide was rubbed, encased his long legs admirably, snuggling around his neat arse. She loved his arse.

Horn left with a rolled chart under his arm and a smile and a wink for Bella on his way to the door. He seemed happier in his work these days despite his constant grumble that women were nothing but trouble. Bella surmised that it had a great deal to do with the fact that Rebecca was incarcerated in his cabin.

Kit rolled up the remaining charts and stacked them in the corner barrel, glancing her way and smiling.

'We seem to be doing a great deal of course changing,' she observed.

'Quite normal for shipping,' he told her.

'Where're we headed?'

'Nowhere in particular.'

This conversation was going nowhere.

'I like the bracelets,' he said, pulling Bella close and smoothing his palms up her arms. 'They look a lot like slave irons. Quite appropriate really?'

She tossed her head.

'You are mine, aren't you, Countess?'

'As you are mine,' she said smoothly.

'I stole you away from Mama Jo, and claimed you for myself.'

'And there was I thinking you'd liberated me, sir. What a foolish, naive creature I am.'

They smiled charmingly at each other, enjoying the banter.

'What's to become of me, Sir? Shall you use me

endlessly, exhausting me, then sell me on when you tire?'

'Who knows?' he wondered, grinning wickedly. 'Meantime I should like to have chains attached to your golden bracelets to secure you to my bed. You should lie there, naked and ready, waiting for me and eager for my attentions any time of the day or night. Your beautiful pale body on my coral coverlets, soft, warm and tamed.'

'Dream on!' She laughed. 'It takes more than chains to bind a woman to a man, Captain Tremayne. If there is love, chains are no longer necessary.'

'But what if the woman is used to the finer things in life? Won't she become discontent?'

'Perhaps the finer things meant very little in the first place,' she suggested wisely.

He thought on it.

'What this particular woman craves more than anything, dearest Captain, are breeches that fit properly. These are a disaster – tight here and baggy there.'

'I rather like them, especially the way them come off so easily. But if its new ones you're after . . .' He laughed and took her by the hand.

From beneath the wine locker he dragged forth a large, metal-studded trunk and flipped open the hinged lid.

'Livery,' he explained. 'Every size and in just the colour for m'lady – violet.' He threw items at her. Breeches, cravats, waistcoats, frock-coats, lacy-fronted shirts and white silk stockings. 'Dutch. Destined for the house-servants of some wealthy patroon in the colonies. Unfortunately for them – but very fortunate for you – I intercepted them en route. Shall you be able to fashion a wardrobe?'

'Yes. Doubtless. I'm certain of it. Oh, Kit, they're perfect, and might have been stolen to order,' said Bella, holding a waistcoat up against herself and parading before his sadly cracked full-length mirror – another prize from another ship.

She found what she thought looked an ideal pair of breeches, stripping off her own double quick. Tremayne caught only a fleeting, highly tantalising glimpse of her loveliness before she was covered again.

Next she found a shirt. It was frothy with Bruges lace and was certainly never meant to be worn whilst doing heavy domestic chores. Maybe it had been destined for the head footman or the patroon's valet. Bella pulled it on eagerly, crying out in frustration when it became only too obvious that it wouldn't fit.

Tremayne sat on the corner of the dining table, a foot planted on the arm of the chair beneath. He couldn't hide his amusement. What a picture she made as she tried to force the white lawn material across an ample expanse of breast where it simply couldn't reach.

She growled furiously through her clenched teeth while he laughed, his eyes on her bouncing breasts, where her nipples were straining through the tautly pulled fabric.

'Looks like you'll have to pick something larger and plainer, my sweet.'

She agreed, pouting.

He left his perch and came up behind Bella. Her delightful, half-exposed body was enflaming him. His hands grasped and caressed her all ways, greedy and possessive, rough and demanding. He kissed her nape and her lips, hungry and insistent, then at

262

her ears, her throat and her shoulders where he pushed aside the rejected frilled shirt.

His kisses, as always, sent thrills through Bella. She arched back against him, close and eager, her breathing turning ragged. He turned her in his arms, kissing her exposed throat and her jutting breasts, then bending her backwards and blazing a trail of kisses down to the waistband of her fetching new satin breeches. In the twinkling of an eye he had them undone, and likewise his own, and was pressing his body to hers, moulding Bella, deviously persuasive. She melted, her knees were weak and she trembled when he worked his generous girth into her damp warmth and pushed home. She groaned, her haunches quivering, and clung to him, fused, at her happiest always with him at such moments.

This was pleasure before it spiralled out of control and grew hot and animal. This was lazy deep loving. However, even to think of it was to set into motion the next phase, the urgent, demanding, forceful striving towards climax. Such things were difficult to resist and Bella would admit to being of poor willpower.

She liked to be fucked. She liked to give herself over to the man and his imagination, and to let him have his way. How would he please her? She could never be sure. That was one of the delights. Sometimes wondrous experiences started out of nowhere.

He had her on the floor now with the Turkey carpet as soft as velvet on her back. His hands beneath Bella's buttocks, he lifted and offered her to his engorged sex, stroking so demandingly and so deeply into her that she cried out softly at every thrust, her head lolling and her eyes glazed.

He gloried in the look of her, in her response to him, and buried himself the deeper. He could feel her crossed wrists in their golden manacles at the back of his head, her body willingly bound to his.

She cried out loud and long, then clung to him tightly, milking his shaft with her internal muscles as his moment arrived, and watching his pained expression and his gritted teeth. He growled his delight and clung to her like a man drowning, his manhood twitching inside of her with its essence flowing.

Who was the slave and who the master? Or was each enslaved by the other?

The sun was setting. It was Bella's favourite time of day in the Caribbean. Tremayne knew it and had taken to going on deck with her at that time of night if the weather was good. The rest of his well trained crew always made themselves scarce at such times. When he was with his lady he didn't take too kindly to being interrupted to answer nautical questions.

This evening he was demonstrating how to steer the *Wyvern* and had Bella standing before him, turning the handles on the great oak wheel in her heavily bejewelled, dainty hands. She wore her stylish violet boy's garb, bracelets and earrings, and an emerald brooch that dripped three enormous baroque pearls. She cut an undeniable dash.

Steering she was, after a fashion, while her lover was taking her from behind. He had her breeches pulled down to expose her rounded, pale arse, and had slipped his turgid flesh into her warm depths. More than one seaman below remarked wryly on the erratic passage of the ship in the following minutes.

She moaned and groaned, pressing herself into

him, enticing and enflaming him, and herself, so that they didn't last long. They came, their passions molten but trying not too cry out too loudly and give themselves away. He wiped her with his cravat and tied it back around his neck so he could enjoy the lingering smell of her, and then thoughtfully rebuttoned her breeches.

Close against her back, his face bent and half in her hair, he turned the wheel gently with his hands upon hers. They were both grinning, smug and contented.

'Is that a ship over there?'

'Where?'

'That way.' She pointed to the right.

Kit peered hard through the descending gloom his brows knitting. 'Could be.' He fetched his spyglass and perused the dark silhouette of the vessel with a growing look of grim satisfaction. He knew the big-busted figurehead. 'Yes!' he exclaimed gleefully, slapping his thigh. '*Tortuga May*.'

'Keyho's ship.'

'Just so.'

'You've been searching for him all along, haven't you? We haven't been sailing around aimlessly at all.'

'Correct, Countess. How bright of you.'

'What're you going after Keyho for?'

'Your belongings. I don't like the idea of him holding on to them. I figured, too,' he said, smiling devilishly, 'that you might look more favourably on this humble captain if he could reunite you with your worldly wealth.'

'More favourably? How could that be possible?' Bella wanted to know, thinking it nonsense. 'You've already rescued me from Eduardo Bambosa. I am for ever in your debt, sir.'

'It is not enough. Not for me. You are Arabella Flowers. A great lady. I cannot begin to feel worthy or adequate.'

She shook her head incredulously. 'Stop talking like an idiot, man. My father was a shopkeeper. You have given me love and life. Who could be more worthy?'

He smiled winningly, so that Bella began to have the suspicion that he was looking for an excuse – any excuse – to have a fight. 'But if I gave you back your goods?'

'If you got me back my belongings wouldn't the gulf between us grow all the wider, Kit? I don't want any of that stuff. It belonged to the old me, can't you understand? I love being with you, on this ship, wearing boy's clothing. I don't want more or less.'

He considered, but Keyho was too close and too tempting. He'd been searching for him for days and couldn't just let him go, not when he had him in his grasp. He became rigid and determined. He was, to Bella's mind, worryingly pigheaded.

'I'm the captain and I want Keyho,' he told her.

She opened her mouth but didn't get a chance to speak.

'Start arguing and you can go below.'

She held the wheel steady, silent and frowning while Tremayne roused his crew from their supper. 'All hands on deck. Ship sighted. Prepare for action.'

She put up her hand.

'Yes?'

'I was just wondering. Where's the other ship, the merchantman, the one that had my belongings on board? Both were gone when we reconnoitred Nassau. But there's only one now.'

He nodded with his eyebrows almost meeting as he took to wondering also. 'Well spotted, Flowers. We'll make an able seaman of you yet.'

He called to a man already going like a monkey up through the rigging, 'Scour the seas. We're looking for the companion ship to *Tortuga May*.'

They couldn't find her. Keyho's ship was on her own.

'Kind of quiet, ain't she, Cap'n?' observed Horn, taking Bella's place at the wheel, while Tremayne watched the other vessel through his spyglass.

'Indeed,' he agreed. 'There is no movement on her decks at all. There's light, though, from the great cabin window.'

'Think they're up to something?'

'Who can say? Best to be prepared. Be ready to take evasive action if she fires.'

Another hand ran up from below. 'Cannon all primed, Cap'n.'

'Good work. Stand by.'

They sailed nearer, wary and watchful, the ship's company quiet and tense. But no one on the other ship spotted them. No alarm was raised.

'Could be they're all drunk, Cap'n.'

Tremayne was thoughtful. 'Not even the most lax of captains would fail to post a night-watch. Something's wrong.'

'Don't like it,' whispered someone to his neighbour as he checked for his cutlass and dagger for the umpteenth time.

Bella watched silently, standing to the back of the quarter-deck. She figured that if she was quiet she

267

wouldn't be noticed. And she didn't want to miss a thing.

'Its a trap,' said someone else.

The ships were very close now, the navigator turning the great wheel with practised precision, bringing them broadside on. If *Tortuga May* were to fire her cannons now she'd sink the *Wyvern* like a stone before Tremayne's gunners had a chance to return fire.

Everyone held their breath. The ships touched, lurched slightly and groaned. Tremayne's men clamboured aboard, securing her with grappling hooks and drawing their cutlasses.

They swarmed over the deck, bursting into the fo'c'sle where any off duty crew should have been. No-one. They searched in consternation, coming back to report to Temayne.

'Nobody, Cap'n. She's abandoned.'

'Check below, just in case,' he cautioned, heading for the quarter-deck cabins. Empty. Empty. The boards creaked behind him. He spun around, his cutlass pointing at Bella.

She squealed.

He snarled. 'What the hell are you doing here? You should be on the *Wyvern*.'

'You never told me,' she argued.

He rolled his eyes in exasperation. 'Stay back and watch our rear.'

More cabins. Empty. Empty. Then the great cabin. He kicked open the door. At first glance it looked empty too. Kit dashed in, ready to fight anyone hiding behind the door but there was nobody there. There was, however, an odd noise coming from the bed.

Cautiously he stepped over, his cutlass brandished and ready for action. Bella crept behind him.

On the bed, his clothes all awry and stained with

red wine, lay Captain Keyho. Any more the worse for drink and he'd be unconscious.

His bleary eyes focused, sort of, on Kit, but he didn't bother to reach for the dagger tucked in his wide leather belt. He didn't even move.

However, at sight of Bella he groaned in some distress.

'Witch! Voorking bitch! Bane of my life. Come back t'torment me some more? Well, I don't care. Y'couldn't make Keyho any more miserable than he already be.'

'Where's your crew, Captain?'

'Gone. All voorking gone.'

'Gone where?'

'Off with my woman, my lamb, my Chastity. Witch! Whore! She seduced my whole damned crew, stole my ship and all my booty; left me in an empty tub with not even enough rum t'mercifully bring me oblivion. Gone, all voorking gone.'

'Well, well,' said Kit, lost for words.

Bella had to bite her lip. It would have been cruel indeed to have laughed.

He took her by the arm and led her out again. There was no point in remaining. They met their crew on deck.

'Empty, Cap'n. Not a thing of value left on board. Any idea what happened?'

'Seems that Mistress Wise instigated a spot of mutiny and went off with his crew, his ship and his booty.'

Someone whistled, impressed. Several chuckled.

'What do we do now, Cap'n?'

'Get back aboard the *Wyvern*. Keyho's got a problem but I'm certain he'll sort it when he sobers up. I for one have no intention of assisting him.'

They freed themselves from the *Tortuga May* and maneouvred clear, setting their sails and leaving the drifting vessel behind.

Bella stood with Tremayne at the bow. Ahead of them the last red rays of sunset were fading, the inky blue of night taking over.

'Where're we headed now?'

'Where d'you fancy?'

'Anywhere together.'

'After Chastity and her gang?'

Bella shook her head. 'Let her have my things. She's welcome.'

'To the colonies, then? To buy a little cottage and become respectable,' offered Kit, though obviously not over keen.

Bella hugged his arm as she stood by his side, the breeze drawing out her dark hair behind her in a streamer. 'Eventually yes, when we're old. But not yet, not for a long tme. This is what I want.'

'Glad t'hear it. Now I shan't have t'get a set of manacles made after all.'

NO LADY
Saskia Hope

30-year-old Kate dumps her boyfriend, walks out of her job and sets off in search of sexual adventure. Set against the rugged terrain of the Pyrenees, the love-making is as rough as the landscape.

ISBN 0 352 32857 6

WEB OF DESIRE
Sophie Danson

High-flying executive Marcie is gradually drawn away from the normality of her married life. Strange messages begin to appear on her computer, summoning her to sinister and fetishistic sexual liaisons.

ISBN 0 352 32856 8

BLUE HOTEL
Cherri Pickford

Hotelier Ramon can't understand why best-selling author Floy Pennington has come to stay at his quiet hotel. Her exhibitionist tendencies are driving him crazy, as are her increasingly wanton encounters with the hotel's other guests.

ISBN 0 352 32858 4

CASSANDRA'S CONFLICT
Fredrica Alleyn

Behind the respectable facade of a house in present-day Hampstead lies a world of decadent indulgence and darkly bizarre eroticism. A sternly attractive Baron and his beautiful but cruel wife are playing games with the young Cassandra.

ISBN 0 352 32859 2

THE CAPTIVE FLESH
Cleo Cordell

Marietta and Claudine, French aristocrats saved from pirates, learn that their invitation to stay at the opulent Algerian mansion of their rescuer, Kasim, requires something in return; their complete surrender to the ecstasy of pleasure in pain.

ISBN 0 352 32872 X

PLEASURE HUNT
Sophie Danson

Sexual adventurer Olympia Deschamps is determined to become a member of the Légion D'Amour – the most exclusive society of French libertines.

ISBN 0 352 32880 0

BLACK ORCHID
Roxanne Carr

The Black Orchid is a women's health club which provides a specialised service for its high-powered clients; women who don't have the time to spend building complex relationships, but who enjoy the pleasures of the flesh.

ISBN 0 352 32888 6

ODALISQUE
Fleur Reynolds

A tale of family intrigue and depravity set against the glittering backdrop of the designer set. This facade of respectability conceals a reality of bitter rivalry and unnatural love.

ISBN 0 352 32887 8

OUTLAW LOVER
Saskia Hope

Fee Cambridge lives in an upper level deluxe pleasuredome of technologically advanced comfort. Bored with her predictable husband and pampered lifestyle, Fee ventures into the wild side of town, finding an outlaw who becomes her lover.

ISBN 0 352 32909 2

THE SENSES BEJEWELLED
Cleo Cordell

Willing captives Marietta and Claudine are settling into life at Kasim's harem. But 18th century Algeria can be a hostile place. When the women are kidnapped by Kasim's sworn enemy, they face indignities that will test the boundaries of erotic experience. This is the sequel to *The Captive Flesh*.

ISBN 0 352 32904 1

GEMINI HEAT
Portia Da Costa

As the metropolis sizzles in freak early summer temperatures, twin sisters Deana and Delia find themselves cooking up a heatwave of their own. Jackson de Guile, master of power dynamics and wealthy connoisseur of fine things, draws them both into a web of luxuriously decadent debauchery.

ISBN 0 352 32912 2

VIRTUOSO
Katrina Vincenzi

Mika and Serena, darlings of classical music's jet-set, inhabit a world of secluded passion. The reason? Since Mika's tragic accident which put a stop to his meteoric rise to fame as a solo violinist, he cannot face the world, and together they lead a decadent, reclusive existence.

ISBN 0 352 32907 6

MOON OF DESIRE
Sophie Danson

When Soraya Chilton is posted to the ancient and mysterious city of Ragzburg on a mission for the Foreign Office, strange things begin to happen to her. Wild, sexual urges overwhelm her at the coming of each full moon.

ISBN 0 352 32911 4

FIONA'S FATE
Fredrica Alleyn

When Fiona Sheldon is kidnapped by the infamous Trimarchi brothers, along with her friend Bethany, she finds herself acting in ways her husband Duncan would be shocked by. Alessandro Trimarchi makes full use of this opportunity to discover the true extent of Fiona's suppressed, but powerful, sexuality.

ISBN 0 352 32913 0

HANDMAIDEN OF PALMYRA
Fleur Reynolds

3rd century Palmyra: a lush oasis in the Syrian desert. The beautiful and fiercely independent Samoya takes her place in the temple of Antioch as an apprentice priestess. Decadent bachelor Prince Alif has other plans for her and sends his scheming sister to bring her to his Bacchanalian wedding feast.

ISBN 0 352 32919 X

OUTLAW FANTASY
Saskia Hope

On the outer reaches of the 21st century metropolis the Amazenes are on the prowl; fierce warrior women who have some unfinished business with Fee Cambridge's pirate lover. This is the sequel to *Outlaw Lover*.

ISBN 0 352 32920 3

THE SILKEN CAGE
Sophie Danson

When University lecturer Maria Treharne inherits her aunt's mansion in Cornwall, she finds herself the subject of strange and unexpected attention. Using the craft of goddess worship and sexual magnetism, Maria finds allies and foes in this savage and beautiful landscape.

ISBN 0 352 32928 9

RIVER OF SECRETS
Saskia Hope & Georgia Angelis

Intrepid female reporter Sydney Johnson takes over someone else's assignment up the Amazon river. Sydney soon realises this mission to find a lost Inca city has a hidden agenda. Everyone is behaving so strangely, so sexually, and the tropical humidity is reaching fever pitch.

ISBN 0 352 32925 4

VELVET CLAWS
Cleo Cordell

It's the 19th century; a time of exploration and discovery and young, spirited Gwendoline Farnshawe is determined not to be left behind in the parlour when the handsome and celebrated anthropologist, Jonathan Kimberton, is planning his latest expedition to Africa.

ISBN 0 352 32926 2

THE GIFT OF SHAME
Sarah Hope-Walker

Helen is a woman with extreme fantasies. When she meets Jeffrey – a cultured wealthy stranger – at a party, they soon become partners in obsession. Now nothing is impossible for her, no fantasy beyond his imagination or their mutual exploration.

ISBN 0 352 32935 1

SUMMER OF ENLIGHTENMENT
Cheryl Mildenhall

Karin's new-found freedom is getting her into all sorts of trouble. The enigmatic Nicolai has been showing interest in her since their chance meeting in a cafe. But he's the husband of a valued friend and is trying to embroil her in the sexual tension he thrives on.

ISBN 0 352 32937 8

A BOUQUET OF BLACK ORCHIDS
Roxanne Carr

The exclusive Black Orchid health spa has provided Maggie with a new social life and a new career, where giving and receiving pleasure of the most sophisticated nature takes top priority. But her loyalty to the club is being tested by the presence of Tourell; a powerful man who makes her an offer she finds difficult to refuse.

ISBN 0 352 32939 4

JULIET RISING
Cleo Cordell

At Madame Nicol's exclusive but strict 18th-century academy for young ladies, the bright and wilful Juliet is learning the art of courting the affections of young noblemen.

ISBN 0 352 32938 6

DEBORAH'S DISCOVERY
Fredrica Alleyn

Deborah Woods is trying to change her life. Having just ended her long-term relationship and handed in her notice at work, she is ready for a little adventure. Meeting American oil magnate John Pavin III throws her world into even more confusion as he invites her to stay at his luxurious renovated castle in Scotland. But what looked like being a romantic holiday soon turns into a test of sexual bravery.

ISBN 0 352 32945 9

THE TUTOR
Portia Da Costa

Like minded libertines reap the rewards of their desire in this story of the sexual initiation of a beautiful young man. Rosalind Howard takes a post as personal librarian to a husband and wife, both unashamed sensualists keen to engage her into their decadent scenarios.

ISBN 0 352 32946 7

THE HOUSE IN NEW ORLEANS
Fleur Reynolds

When she inherits her family home in the fashionable Garden district of New Orleans, Ottilie Duvier discovers it has been leased to the notorious Helmut von Straffen; a debauched German Count famous for his decadent Mardi Gras parties. Determined to oust him from the property, she soon realises that not all dangerous animals live in the swamp!

ISBN 0 352 32951 3

ELENA'S CONQUEST
Lisette Allen

It's summer – 1070AD – and the gentle Elena is gathering herbs in the garden of the convent where she leads a peaceful, but uneventful, life. When Norman soldiers besiege the convent, they take Elena captive and present her to the dark and masterful Lord Aimery to satisfy his savage desire for Saxon women.

ISBN 0 352 32950 5

CASSANDRA'S CHATEAU
Fredrica Alleyn

Cassandra has been living with the dominant and perverse Baron von Ritter for eighteen months when their already bizarre relationship takes an unexpected turn. The arrival of a naive female visitor at the chateau provides the Baron with a new opportunity to indulge his fancy for playing darkly erotic games with strangers.

ISBN 0 352 32955 6

WICKED WORK
Pamela Kyle

At twenty-eight, Suzie Carlton is at the height of her journalistic career. She has status, money and power. What she doesn't have is a masterful partner who will allow her to realise the true extent of her fantasies. How will she reconcile the demands of her job with her sexual needs?

ISBN 0 352 32958 0

DREAM LOVER
Katrina Vincenzi

Icily controlled Gemma is a dedicated film vampire producer, immersed in her latest production – a darkly Gothic vampire movie. But after a visit to Brittany, where she encounters a mystery lover, a disquieting feeling continues to haunt her. Compelled to discover the identity of the man who ravished her, she becomes entangled in a mystifying erotic odyssey.

ISBN 0 352 32956 4

PATH OF THE TIGER
Cleo Cordell

India, in the early days of the Raj. Amy Spencer is looking for an excuse to rebel against the stuffy mores of the British army wives. Luckily, a new friend introduces her to places where other women dare not venture – where Tantric mysteries and the Kama Sutra come alive. Soon she becomes besotted by Ravinder, the exquisitely handsome son of the Maharaja, and finds the pathway to absolute pleasure.

ISBN 0 352 32959 9

BELLA'S BLADE
Georgia Angelis

Bella is a fearless, good-looking young woman with an eye for handsome highwaymen and a taste for finery. It's the seventeenth century and Charles II's Merrie England is in full swing. Finding herself to be the object of royal affections, Bella has to choose between a living life of predictable luxury at court or following her desire to sail the high seas – where a certain dashing young captain is waiting for her.

ISBN 0 352 32965 3

THE DEVIL AND THE DEEP BLUE SEA
Cheryl Mildenhall

A secluded country house in Norfolk is the setting for this contemporary story of one woman's summer of sexual exploration. Renting a holiday home with her girlfriends, the recently graduated Hillary is pleased to discover that the owner of the country estate is the most fanciable man in the locale. But soon she meets Haldane, the beautifully proportioned Norwegian sailor. Attracted by the allure of two very different men, Hillary is faced with a difficult decision.

ISBN 0 352 32966 1

WE NEED YOUR HELP . . .
to plan the future of women's erotic fiction –

– and no stamp required!

Yours are the only opinions that matter.

Black Lace is the first series of books devoted to erotic fiction by women for women.

We intend to keep providing the best-written, sexiest books you can buy. And we'd appreciate your help and valued opinion of the books so far. Tell us what you want to read.

THE BLACK LACE QUESTIONNAIRE

SECTION ONE: ABOUT YOU

1.1　Sex *(we presume you are female, but so as not to discriminate)*
　　Are you?
　　　　Male　　　　　　　☐
　　　　Female　　　　　　☐

1.2　Age
　　　　under 21　　☐　　21–30　　☐
　　　　31–40　　　☐　　41–50　　☐
　　　　51–60　　　☐　　over 60　☐

1.3　At what age did you leave full-time education?
　　　　still in education　☐　　16 or younger　☐
　　　　17–19　　　　　　☐　　20 or older　　☐

1.4　Occupation _____

1.5 Annual household income

under £10,000	☐	£10–£20,000	☐
£20–£30,000	☐	£30–£40,000	☐
over £40,000	☐		

1.6 We are perfectly happy for you to remain anonymous; but if you would like to receive information on other publications available, please insert your name and address

_____

_____

_____

_____

SECTION TWO: ABOUT BUYING BLACK LACE BOOKS

2.1 How did you acquire this copy of *Bella's Blade*?

I bought it myself ☐   My partner bought it ☐

I borrowed/found it ☐

2.2 How did you find out about Black Lace books?

I saw them in a shop ☐

I saw them advertised in a magazine ☐

I saw the London Underground posters ☐

I read about them in _____

Other _____

2.3 Please tick the following statements you agree with:

I would be less embarrassed about buying Black Lace books if the cover pictures were less explicit ☐

I think that in general the pictures on Black Lace books are about right ☐

I think Black Lace cover pictures should be as explicit as possible ☐

2.4 Would you read a Black Lace book in a public place – on a train for instance?

Yes ☐   No ☐

SECTION THREE: ABOUT THIS BLACK LACE BOOK

3.1 Do you think the sex content in this book is:
     Too much   □   About right   □
     Not enough   □

3.2 Do you think the writing style in this book is:
     Too unreal/escapist   □   About right   □
     Too down to earth   □

3.3 Do you think the story in this book is:
     Too complicated   □   About right   □
     Too boring/simple   □

3.4 Do you think the cover of this book is:
     Too explicit   □   About right   □
     Not explicit enough   □

Here's a space for any other comments:

SECTION FOUR: ABOUT OTHER BLACK LACE BOOKS

4.1 How many Black Lace books have you read?   □

4.2 If more than one, which one did you prefer?

4.3 Why?

SECTION FIVE: ABOUT YOUR IDEAL EROTIC NOVEL

We want to publish the books you want to read – so this is your chance to tell us exactly what your ideal erotic novel would be like.

5.1 Using a scale of 1 to 5 (1 = no interest at all, 5 = your ideal), please rate the following possible settings for an erotic novel:

Medieval/barbarian/sword 'n' sorcery ☐
Renaissance/Elizabethan/Restoration ☐
Victorian/Edwardian ☐
1920s & 1930s – the Jazz Age ☐
Present day ☐
Future/Science Fiction ☐

5.2 Using the same scale of 1 to 5, please rate the following themes you may find in an erotic novel:

Submissive male/dominant female ☐
Submissive female/dominant male ☐
Lesbianism ☐
Bondage/fetishism ☐
Romantic love ☐
Experimental sex e.g. anal/watersports/sex toys ☐
Gay male sex ☐
Group sex ☐

Using the same scale of 1 to 5, please rate the following styles in which an erotic novel could be written:

Realistic, down to earth, set in real life ☐
Escapist fantasy, but just about believable ☐
Completely unreal, impressionistic, dreamlike ☐

5.3 Would you prefer your ideal erotic novel to be written from the viewpoint of the main male characters or the main female characters?

Male ☐ Female ☐
Both ☐

5.4 What would your ideal Black Lace heroine be like? Tick as many as you like:

Dominant	☐	Glamorous	☐
Extroverted	☐	Contemporary	☐
Independent	☐	Bisexual	☐
Adventurous	☐	Naive	☐
Intellectual	☐	Introverted	☐
Professional	☐	Kinky	☐
Submissive	☐	Anything else?	☐
Ordinary	☐		
		_____	

5.5 What would your ideal male lead character be like? Again, tick as many as you like:

Rugged	☐		
Athletic	☐	Caring	☑
Sophisticated	☐	Cruel	☐
Retiring	☐	Debonair	☐
Outdoor-type	☐	Naive	☐
Executive-type	☐	Intellectual	☐
Ordinary	☐	Professional	☐
Kinky	☐	Romantic	☐
Hunky	☐		
Sexually dominant	☐	Anything else?	☐
Sexually submissive	☐		
		_____	

5.6 Is there one particular setting or subject matter that your ideal erotic novel would contain?

_____

SECTION SIX: LAST WORDS

6.1 What do you like best about Black Lace books?

_____

6.2 What do you most dislike about Black Lace books?

_____

6.3 In what way, if any, would you like to change Black Lace covers?

_____